An Extrao

A Gnome's Odyssey

for
Talia and
Theodore

best wishes

P. R. Elli

Also by P.R. Ellis

In the bleak Long Winter
in Existence is Elsewhen

An Extraordinary Tale

A Gnome's Odyssey

P.R. Ellis

Elsewhen Press

An Extraordinary Tale
First published in Great Britain by Elsewhen Press, 2023
An imprint of Alnpete Limited

Elsewhen Press, PO Box 757, Dartford, Kent DA2 7TQ
www.elsewhen.press

British Library Cataloguing in Publication Data.
A catalogue record for this book is available from the British Library.
ISBN 978-1-915304-25-4 Print edition
ISBN 978-1-915304-35-3 eBook edition

Designed and formatted by Elsewhen Press

This book is a work of fiction. All names, characters, places,
governments, research establishments and events are either a product
of the author's fertile imagination or are used fictitiously. Any
resemblance to actual events, institutions, states, places or people
(living, dead, or hoo-man) is purely coincidental.

Daimler is a trademark of Jaguar Land Rover Limited. Use of
trademarks has not been authorised, sponsored, or otherwise
approved by the trademark owners.

Contents

To Lou

Part 1

The pursuit begins

Chapter 1

A meeting on a train

The woman who sat in the corner of the railway carriage with her eyes shut was attracting a good deal of attention. A band of armoured, outlaw mice scrabbled at the catch of her capacious handbag with their steel-tipped claws. The skeleton sitting beside her swatted at the creatures with its brittle, white fingers with no obvious result.

I leaned against the entrance to the compartment, swaying with the carriage as the train rattled along the rails. From her long-limbed body and pale pink complexion the woman was one of the mages, and she clearly had something in her bag the mice desired. I knew from previous encounters with the creatures that it could only be the precious and magical metal, electrum. The woman obviously had a valuable stash in her bag. With red hair that matched the fur collar of her tweed jacket and the hem of her skirt, she looked a class above the usual incompetent conjurors and miserable magicians that made up her diminishing race, but mice could smell electrum in the next county. They would have been driven into a frenzy by its proximity. Simply telling them to stop would never persuade a fighting mouse to give up its quarry.

I had to act.

I raised the brow of my pointed hat, releasing my flight of dragonflies. They swarmed the mice, emitting tiny gouts of flame. Some of the outlaws defended themselves valiantly, thrusting their short swords at the fluttering insects. Others continued to scratch at the bag while getting a roasting from the dragonflies' fire. Nevertheless, I could see that my dragonflies could not defeat the mice alone. I stepped forward, brushed a couple of the rodents from the bag and booted them away from the witch. That did the trick. The remaining mice paused and looked up at me.

"Gnome!" one sneered in its squeaky voice. Then they scampered off into the upholstery and were gone. I whistled and the dragonflies returned to roost on my bald head. I replaced my hat.

The mage stirred and rubbed her eyes. "Are we there yet? What is the time?"

The skeleton spoke in a dry, hoarse voice, "Not yet, Madam. It is half past midnight."

"Then why did you awaken me." Her eyes opened and she looked up at me standing in front of her. "Why are you standing there?" she added with a tone of disinterest.

"This gnome drove away some mice that were attempting to rob you," the skeleton explained.

The woman gave the fleshless creature a disdainful look. "What were you doing, Bones? Just sitting idly?"

I addressed the witch. "They were too numerous for your fragile companion, ma'am."

"Oh, you speak as well as provide protection?" she said, looking me up and down.

"They seemed intent on gaining access to your possessions," I said pointing to the cloth bag on her lap. It showed little evidence of the mouse raid.

She gave it a cursory glance. "I suppose they would, but no mouse, even one equipped with an electrum blade, could succeed in penetrating it." She seemed unconcerned about the attack on her person. However, the skeleton felt a need to respond.

"The mice were determined, Madam. They could have caused you some injury if this person had not intervened."

She sniffed. "In that case, it seems I must thank you for that intervention." She gave me one of the least sincere smiles I've seen.

"It is my job," I replied, offering an excuse and cover for my presence, "although my usual task is to simply check tickets, not provide protection."

"Ah, a gnome with a job and public spirit. How rare." She seemed not to realise the insults implicit in her words nor notice my lack of a ticket inspector's uniform. Perhaps my face did reveal my emotion because she immediately went on. "I'm sorry, that sounded rude. Please join me for some refreshment." She raised a gloved hand to indicate the vacant seat opposite her. "Bones, find that bottle of ambrosian gin."

The skeleton clattered to its feet and reached down a small valise from the luggage rack. It withdrew a glowing bottle of the liquor and two small glasses. The woman held the glasses while the skeleton poured the luminescent liquid. She held one glass out to me.

"I really shouldn't while on duty," I said, knowing that I would be beguiled simply by the scent of the fiery liquid assailing my nostrils.

"A gnome refusing the offer of ambrosia," the woman grinned, "Surely not. Take it and sit a moment so I can thank you for your assistance."

It was impossible to resist. I took the glass and sat down. "What about you, Sir?" I said to the skeleton.

"How do you expect me to drink?'" Bones replied, "I don't have any guts. Enjoy."

I took a sip. The sweet, oily fluid slipped down my throat and filled me with warmth and contentment. I closed my eyes. It had been a busy evening. Surely I deserved a few moments rest.

I awoke to find the compartment empty. Well, not quite. An armoured mouse with slightly singed fur stared at me from the couch opposite.

"A fine example of a gnome you are," he squeaked.

I yawned and sat up straight. Ignoring his comment, I asked, "Where are they, the witch and the skeleton?"

"Gone," the mouse replied, "with the electrum, of course."

I realised that the carriage wasn't rocking from side to side; wasn't moving at all. "The train's stopped," I said.

The mouse clapped its front paws together. "Well, we have a *genius* of a gnome here. Of course, the train has stopped. How do you think our passengers got off?"

I peered into the dark beyond the window. It was a clear night, with a moon. I saw a platform.

"How long since they left?" I asked.

"I thought you'd never ask," the mouse said. "A few minutes. The ambrosian gin didn't knock you out for long."

"It must have been charmed," I said, "Ambrosia doesn't usually have that effect." That was a small untruth. When I have it – which isn't often – sleepiness does tend to fall on me.

"But you can't resist it can you? She knew she had you when she offered you the glass."

"Yes, we *may* have that slight weakness." I hauled myself to my feet, still feeling as if I should be asleep. "I must go after them." I reached for the handle of the door.

"You're not just interested in checking their tickets are you," the mouse said.

"No," I said, "that was a disguise, a ruse to put them at their ease."

"Like attacking us with your dragonflies was."

"You were trying to get at the electrum," I protested while pushing the carriage door open.

"And you're not?"

I paused. "I'll have you know that I have been engaged by the Queen of the Fairies to recover electrum stolen from the Palace."

The mouse laughed. It was a high-pitched squeaking. "She must have been desperate to ask a gnome."

"A gnome with dragonflies," I said.

"Ah yes," the mouse said nodding a grudging agreement, "But don't you think you could do with some real assistance?"

"Such as?"

"The first platoon of the Grand Order of Renegade Mice." The mouse whistled. A dozen other armoured mice appeared from the upholstery, brandishing their swords.

"I don't need your help," I said.

"Do you know where they've gone? Do you have transport to follow them?"

"Er, no and maybe, maybe not," I replied.

"Then you need me, Major Montgomery Mouse and my fellows."

I considered their offer. I weighed it up, looked at the pros and cons of working with a bunch of ruthless rodents. I replied almost instantly.

"I accept."

The mice leapt from the couch in trajectories that saw them land on my arms, my shoulders and the pockets of my velvet jacket.

"Let's go then," said the leader clinging to my lapel with all four feet.

I pushed the carriage door open and stepped down onto the platform. It was deserted but illuminated by a line of lamps. I looked towards the end of the station. A silver carriage drawn by two unicorns was lurching into motion. The ghostly driver cracked a whip and the carriage raced off into the night.

"They've got away," I said, again regretting the weakness for ambrosian gin.

"Just for now." Major Mouse said, now standing on my shoulder alongside my right ear. He let out another piercing whistle. There was no response for at least three moments, then there was a gust of air and a great commotion of flapping. A huge pigeon descended from the dark sky and settled on the platform in front of me.

"Here is our transport," the Major said to me, then addressed the pigeon. "Do you think you can manage one medium-sized gnome?"

The pigeon turned its head to one side and looked at me with one eye. "It'll cost you," it cooed, "that will be two bags of best mixed seed, not one."

"Don't worry," Major Mouse said, "You can have as many bags as you want when we get our hands on that electrum."

The pigeon nodded its head and crouched down. The mice poured from my jacket onto the pigeon's broad back.

"Come on," squeaked the Major. "Get on. We have to catch that carriage before it reaches the Parting."

I scrambled onto the pigeon's neck with as much urgency as I could muster. Once my legs were astride its neck its wings beat against the air making a noise like an elephant rampaging through the jungle.

There was little to see as we climbed into the night sky but the silver glow of the carriage speeding along the track. Ahead, in the distance, was the black fog of the Parting.

"Follow that carriage!" cried Major Mouse in his squeaky voice. The pigeon swooped towards it. I held onto my hat to prevent my dragonflies from being blown away, while gripping the great bird's neck feathers.

While the unicorns drew the carriage at breakneck speed, the pigeon was faster despite – or, perhaps, because of – being encumbered by my weight. We dived toward the carriage, gaining on it.

"Will we land on the roof?" I cried.

"Of course, not," the mouse squeaked in my ear, "The pigeon doesn't want to be carried into the Parting. You must leap on to the carriage when we draw close."

I thought of protesting, but I could see no alternative way of getting aboard. The pigeon flapped its wings furiously, approaching closer and closer.

"Now!" screeched Major Mouse. I released my grasp of the pigeon's neck and reached down to grab the edge of the carriage roof. My legs slipped from the bird and my knees hit the wood with a painful thud. I was spreadeagled on the roof of the carriage as it careered along the track. Mice emerged from my pockets, forming a rodent chain over the side until the bottom mouse was able to bounce up and down on the door handle.

The door slammed open and the dangling mice flew inside. My heart almost stopped as I eased myself over the roof and scrambled down to join them.

The skeleton sat on the seat, alone.

I drew a breath and cried out, "Where is she?"

"Who?" the skeleton asked.

"The woman, your mistress. You know who I mean."

"Ah, not here." I'd swear that the skeleton looked smug, except it had no flesh on its face for making expressions.

"Where's the electrum?" I asked.

The skeleton shrugged, "I do not know what you mean."

"It must be in her bag. Where is it?"

"Her bag? With her I presume."

Major Mouse had climbed back onto my shoulder. He squeaked in my ear. "The Parting is not far away. I don't know about you, but I have no wish to enter it."

Neither did I.

"Stop the carriage," I said.

"Why?" asked Bones.

"We don't want to be swallowed by the Parting."

"Ah, well that is where we differ. I am quite happy to travel into the darkness from which nothing returns. An end to existence is an attractive prospect."

"There's no time to argue," Major Mouse squeaked. "We have to disembark now."

"Alright," I said, "But he's coming too."

I reached through the skeleton, beneath his ribs. My fingers closed around his spine. Then I launched myself through the carriage door.

Neither Bones nor I bounced. Luckily for us, the ground at the side of the track was somewhat boggy. We landed with a languid splash. Well, I did. There were a number of splashes as bits of Bones parted and made their own landings, and there were a dozen plips and plops as the mice reached ground level too.

I sat up in the mud to see the unicorns, whipped by the ghost, draw the silver carriage into the Parting. The black fog closed behind, and all sight of them was lost.

I found I was still gripping Bones' torso. I hauled myself to my feet and stepped onto the harder ground of the track. A trio of mice rolled Bones' skull to my feet. I picked it up and slotted it back over the spine.

"Thank you," Bones said. "As you have prevented my departure from this world, I would appreciate it if you could retrieve my limbs."

Other pieces of his anatomy were scattered around, gleaming in the moonlight. I picked up his right leg and pushed the hip joint into its socket. I did the same with the left leg. Meanwhile the mice retrieved the arms. I put those back into place and released the skeleton. He tottered on his bony feet.

"Well, that was embarrassing," he said, "I do dislike coming apart. And I seem to have mislaid a digit." Bones held up his right hand, missing its little finger.

"I'm not bothered about you," I said. "Where is she, the witch?"

The skeleton pulled himself upright. "I've already told you. Not with me."

I was in a good mind to separate his bones again, but I felt a tugging on the bottom of my trousers. It was Major Mouse. I stooped to scoop him up.

"It's obvious isn't it," the mouse said.

"What is?" I replied.

"This lark with the carriage heading for the Parting was another ruse. She was never on the carriage. She probably stayed on the train."

I stared across the plain. We'd come some way from the railway line and there was no sign of the lights of the station.

"We must catch the train and find her," I said, "Call the pigeon."

"I thought that's what you'd say. I already have."

As the mouse spoke there was the familiar noisy performance of the pigeon's landing.

"Room for another one?" Major Mouse said. "There's not a lot of weight on him."

The pigeon examined the skeleton with one wide round eye. "Get on, I expect I can manage," it cooed.

"I'm not getting on that creature," Bones said.

I glowered at the skeleton. "You're coming with us in one piece or many. Which do you prefer?"

The skeleton clambered onto the pigeon. "One dismemberment in a day is enough," he said. I climbed on behind him with the mice in my pockets.

"To the train," I shouted. With an excessive flapping of wings, we rose into the air once again.

Chapter 2

The city of the elves

As we flew, I reflected on the night's activities.

Things hadn't quite gone as I had planned.

A bit of lucky eavesdropping had allowed me to trace the Fairy Queen's electrum to the train, but I hadn't known the thief was the woman till I saw the mice in their frenzy. She had proven more resourceful than I expected. How was I to know that she would carry a bottle of ambrosian gin, solely for the purpose of tempting an innocent gnome and putting him to sleep? How was I to know that a motley band of fearsome mice would be after the electrum too, even if that seemed to be turning in my favour. And how was I to know that the witch would use the skeleton as her decoy?

What I did know was that the Fairy Queen desired the return of her electrum, and if it wasn't me who returned it then her notoriously bad-tempered guards would be after me as well. We had to find the sorceress again and, this time, extract the electrum from her.

How to do this, however, remained a mystery to me.

The pigeon followed the railway line. We soared straight over the Danann mountains while the railway track meandered its way up to the pass and down again. Nevertheless, there was no sign of the train. It had raced on ahead of us.

Despite the cold air blasting into my face, I decided I must know more about Bones the skeleton. His height suggested that like the witch he too must have been a mage while he lived.

"Have you been in the woman's service long," I shouted at him.

"All my life and beyond," he replied, the wind whistling through his eye sockets.

"You mean..."

"I was indentured to Madam Carmine, or rather, her forebears, as a child, to serve them all my days. They took care of me. Like many of my race I lacked any great skill in sorcery, so they worked me hard on menial tasks. I looked forward to death when I would be free, but I had forgotten the eternity clause."

"Eternity clause?" I had heard the term but had no idea of its meaning.

"Yes, it said I was bound to my employers and them to me forever."

"Forever, meaning, er, forever."

"Yes. I died and was buried but I only enjoyed a brief period of peaceful decomposition before Madam had me dug up, my bones cleaned and set me to work again. A different type of employment of course – I no longer have the muscles for heavy labour, nor a name, hence I am referred to as Bones."

"I see. So, you accompanied your mistress to Fairyland..."

"Let me stop you there, gnome. Madam Carmine has set a charm forbidding me from recounting her dealings in Fairyland, and she wields the most powerful magic in all the lands."

Foiled again. How would I ever find out how the woman came to possess the Fairy Queen's electrum?

After hours of flight, I was heartily tired of being the pigeon's passenger. My hands ached from gripping both the skeleton and the pigeon's feathers, and I could no longer feel other parts of my anatomy because of the cold air rushing past us. Dawn had appeared on the horizon ahead of us when I felt the scrape of tiny claws against my cheek.

"Look. There," Major Mouse squeaked in my ear. He was pointing to the ground. Ahead of us, the spires of Elfholm were poking out of what appeared to be a morning mist, except that I knew it was nothing so harmless as water vapour. It was the smoke from the elvish workshops and manufactories that hung in the air close to the ground morning, noon and night.

Elfholm was laid out rather like a jigsaw completed by a jigsaw cheat, one who squeezed the pieces together without a concern for the design. Streets ended in dead ends; alleyways doubled back on themselves; buildings were crunched together competing for space. Then of course it had, in all probability, changed since my last visit, as if the jigsaw had been tipped up and the pieces fitted together again in new, wrong positions. Elvish lords striving to outdo each other with the tallest towers and most active manufactories, all pumping out their noxious fumes.

At the outskirts of the metropolis, just visible at the edge of the smog, was the railway station. The train was there, its engine adding to the emissions.

The pigeon tucked in its wings, and we plummeted in a tight spiral downwards. I gripped the bird's neck and Bones even more tightly, wondering if the bird had tired and was going to dash us against the ground. At the last moment it flapped its wings energetically and we descended to a gentle if untidy landing on the platform beside the train.

I dismounted; my legs reluctant to take my weight. My back complained as I stretched the hours of immobility out of it. Bones too straightened out his joints, clicking tarsals and carpels into place. The mice meanwhile scampered along the platform, leaping onto the carriages to squeeze through partly open windows. They were not gone long before returning to me and scrambling up my trouser legs and jacket.

Major Mouse sat on my shoulder. "All the passengers have left. She's gone."

"We must look for her in Elfholm," I said, "Surely one such as her will stand out amongst the elves."

"Elfholm is a big place. It may take some time to trace her," the mouse said, "And she may not need long to dispose of the electrum."

"Hmm," I said. I was lost for ideas.

"There is a quicker way," the Major said.

"There is?"

"Yes. Him." The mouse pointed a steel tipped claw at Bones. "Isn't he bound to the woman by contract? He should be able to make his way to her."

"What an excellent idea," I replied. "Bones, did you hear that. Do you know where your Mistress is?"

The skeleton shook its head. "No. I am unable to state her location, but the mouse is correct. I am drawn towards her."

"Let's go then."

"But that will lead you to her."

"That's the idea." I lifted up the brim of my hat. The dragonflies' wings buzzed. "If you don't start moving, Bones, I'll set my dragonflies on you. I wonder what they will do when they get inside your skull."

The skeleton shrank away from me raising its hands in an ineffectual defence. "No, not that. I can't bear it when insects get inside my head. The noise is maddening."

"Get moving, then," I urged.

Bones set off along the platform. I followed a step or two behind. In heartbeats we were in the city, grey and yellow and brown smoke swirling around us. We passed foundries beating metals into complex shapes, the cacophony of the hammers accompanied by belching clouds of sulphurous fumes. Glimpses through filthy windows revealed bubbling vats processing hides and fibres of all descriptions, the effusions adding to the toxic atmosphere of the city, while a noxious slime seeped from doorways and into streets crowded with elves. There were factories taking in materials of all sorts, metals, textiles, wood, stone and turning out products for all classes and types of customer. Each and every process it seemed involved excessive noise and emissions.

In every workshop and factory were the elves – working elves that is; short thin creatures with gangly arms and legs and pointed ears, clothed in tattered bits of cloth, backs bent from the loads they were carrying and the tasks they were engaged in.

Elsewhere, I had been told that I could be mistaken for an elf but for my grey beard. Yes, we were of similar height, but I carried rather more flesh around my girth and my conical hat proudly stood up, while those of the elves hung limply over their shoulders or backs. I would not have looked kindly on being taken for an elf, though here there was little chance that I would be.

Of course, the lords in their towers provide a different picture, but that is another part of our story.

Bones lurched onwards through the understorey of the city, his bones and joints rattling. Our passage was observed but was rarely of interest. Occasionally an elf gave us a glance before bowing their head to their task. I supposed it was not unusual for strangers to visit to make purchases. The mice, however, stayed out of sight because of the enmity that existed between their kind and elves of all levels. I pursued Bones, hoping that some time soon he might slow down. The heat from all the works of Elfholm was exhausting.

At last, in a narrow, cobbled alley, Bones paused. There were no elves around us here. Little light penetrated the tall spires and the orange-tinted air. We were outside a workshop, smaller than most although it stank just as much. The door was open and a bluish-white glow emerged.

I recognised that light. It was the glow of electrum.

Chapter 3

We meet an elven lord

The workshop was probably the most cramped and untidy in all of Elfholm. There was barely room for Bones and I to enter. Around the perimeter of the tiny space were strewn barrels, bottles, jars, boxes, cans and a variety of other containers I could not name. All empty. Only the worktable in the centre of the room was clean and bare but for the nugget of electrum. It was tiny, hardly the size of my thumb, yet its blue-white glow filled the room and spilled out into the smoke-filled alley.

There was just one elf in the room. His back was bent, his hair grey and wispy and he was dressed in a filthy and torn tunic. He stood at the table staring at us with a frozen expression of terror. That was probably because the mice had emerged from my pockets and cuffs and had rushed across the table to surround the morsel of electrum. They had their swords raised, daring the elf to oppose them.

"Do not touch the electrum," I commanded. Despite the small size its value was probably greater than all the gold in Elfholm.

"But it is electrum," Major Mouse appealed. His sword trembled as he contemplated the object of his desire.

"It is not that which we seek," I said. "No doubt it has been charmed so any hand other than the smith's will bring a force of guards upon us." I did wonder at the lack of even a token guard, but did not want to consider the implications of that apparent lapse in the elf lord's security when the mage had been here before us. Instead, I said, "This is obviously the property of the elven lord in whose workshop we stand." Indeed, the Fairy Queen's stolen horde was considerably larger. The mice paused in their advance but took up defensive stances to prevent the elf from removing the glowing metal.

I addressed the visibly shaking elf. "Is that true, elf?"

He looked at me with contempt mixed with fear. "Yes, gnome, it is the property of Lord Pelladill."

"A mage came here recently. Do you have the electrum that she carried?"

The elf froze as if transfixed. No sound came from his mouth.

I turned to Bones, who was having trouble standing erect in the low-ceilinged workshop. "She has been here has she not?"

Bones shrugged his shoulder bones. "My bond has brought us here, but I do not know where Madam is at this moment."

"She must have come to trade the fairy electrum. What have you done with it?" I demanded of the elf.

He shook once then curled up into a ball and rolled across the floor. I bent to examine him. He was unbreathing, cast into a state close to death. There was nothing I could do for him. I straightened up.

"She must have cursed him to stop him from speaking to us."

"That is her normal practice," Bones said but offered no other information. I felt some sorrow for the poor elf. His obviously difficult life, made more precarious, because he came into the presence of the sorceress.

"There is no more electrum here," Major Mouse said sniffing the air. "Only this miserable but enticing fragment."

"Then she must still have it," I said.

"May I make a suggestion?" Major Mouse said. I nodded agreement. "She had a large quantity to get rid of. The only person who could deal with that amount would be the elven lord himself."

"That is true," I said, "What do you think, Bones?"

"The rodent is correct. I feel that my mistress is or has been somewhere above us."

"That's it then," I said as I crossed the workshop. "We

must ascend to the lord's dwelling above the clouds. I pushed the door at the back of the workshop open and stepped into a circular space. There was no ceiling above and the walls rose up into the tower.

Bones and the mice joined me.

"It is a stairwell with no stairs," Bones said.

"That's correct," I replied, "You would not expect an elf with status and a fortune to climb steps all the way to their penthouse, would you?"

The skeleton nodded. "That thought had not occurred to me, but this is my first visit to Elfholm. How do we then ascend?"

"Climb on board, mice," I said and grasped hold of the skeleton's thin wrist. The mice scrambled up my trouser legs. Once they were settled about my dress, I added, "A stairwell without stairs is a well. Imagine falling into it." I stepped forward into the centre of the empty column.

A dry cry issued from Bones' throat as we fell upwards. A high-pitched squeaking emerged from my pockets. I too, let out a scream of delight.

There really is no other experience like an elven elevator.

We tumbled and rolled but our fall was over in moments. I found myself lying on my back on the parapet at the top of the tower. The conical ceiling rose to a point somewhere above. I got to my feet and brushed myself down. Over the edge I could just see the ground floor far below.

The skeleton, fitting some bones back into place, said, "I can't imagine that the elvish aristocracy travel in the same manner."

"I believe that the well-off elves who live up here ascend and descend in a more elegant fashion," I agreed, "but I haven't mastered it. That was my first, er, solo experience."

"Perhaps you will give us a little more warning of unfamiliar... *experiences* in future," Bones said straightening out his joints with a series of clicks.

"I'll try to remember," I said, "Now where is your mistress?"

Bones pointed to a wide pair of gilded double doors. "She passed through there."

I stepped forward and pushed on the doors. They swung silently open and revealed a spacious almost circular room with windows offering a view of the towers of Elfholm on every side. The pillowy clouds far below hid the sordid ground level of the city. The morning sun reflected off all the shiny surfaces and objects in the room, shiny because they were made of precious metals or encrusted with valuable gems. In the middle of the room stood an elf. He was the shortest adult elf I had ever met, the top of his head hardly coming up to my chin. He made up for his unimposing presence with fine clothes. The usual elvish tunic was green satin adorned with gold thread in complex patterns over which he wore a cloak formed from hundreds of butterfly wings stitched together. On his feet he wore silk slippers which came to the longest points I have ever seen. They were rolled into a tight spiral.

"Well, I have visitors, I see," he said with an unexpected jollity. "A skeleton and a gnome. What a strange pair."

I was about to reply when the mice erupted from my jacket and trousers and advanced across the marble floor, swords at the ready. A flicker of fear crossed the elf's face but when the mice stopped and took up a defensive formation, he regained his apparent cheerfulness.

I addressed the elf. "You are Lord Pelladill, the owner of the electrum establishment down below?"

"That is true," he replied, "Do you have business with me?"

"It's the business you may have done with a certain red-haired lady, that interests me," I said.

Pelladill smiled. "Ah, you mean the sorceress."

I thought of her more as a witch, but sorceress would do. "That is true. Did she make you an offer of a quantity of electrum? A considerable quantity in fact."

The elf lord did not reply immediately but crossed the room to sit on a well-padded and ornate easy chair. He indicated a similarly decorated and embroidered sofa.

"Please sit while we continue our discussion. I will call for refreshment." He clicked a finger and from hidden doors in the walls beside the liftshaft, a parade of elvish servants emerged with trays bearing jugs and goblets.

I sat on the sofa. Bones took a glance at the elf-sized furnishings and decided to remain standing beside me. I signalled to the mice to stand down. They retreated under my seat. I took a goblet from the tray offered to me and found it contained mead, a favourite of elves, sweet and syrupy with an alcoholic kick. Bones declined but Lord Pelladill took one and swallowed the contents in one go. He placed the goblet on an occasional table.

"To your question," he said. "The lady you mentioned did make me an offer."

"And?"

"I refused it."

"Why?"

"The quantity of electrum she had in her possession was, as you said, considerable. If I were to introduce it to the markets of Elfholm, the finances of the city would be ruined."

"How?" My questions were apparently stuck in a monosyllabic form.

"That amount of electrum would have destabilised the value of the metal, reducing it to the value of gold. Electrum holders, of which I am the most important, would find our fortunes reduced in value. Not a good result of a business deal."

"So?"

"I told her to go elsewhere with her electrum."

"Not hers, the Fairy Queen's."

"Ah, yes. That was another reason. While we are not exactly on good terms with the fairies, my fellow Lords of Elfholm would not thank me for bringing a fairy siege upon us."

"They would be forced to defend the city?"

"The chance of my fellow lords cooperating sufficiently to resist an invasion of fairies is very small. We hardly ever agree to act together on anything."

While I am no financial wizard, I could understand the elf lord's unwillingness to bring both financial ruin and the wrath of the fairies on himself and his fellows. That left the problem of where she had gone next with the electrum.

"How did she respond to your refusal?"

Lord Pelladill produced a thin smile. "Not with good grace, gnome. She tried to charm me but I have strong defences up here. No fairy, mage – or gnome – can overcome me in my own home."

"Unlike in your workshop, down below," I noted.

"Oh? Has something occurred?

"Your electrumsmith froze and became mute when we asked for the lady's whereabouts."

Pelladill shrugged. "They're always dying or becoming useless. I can find another."

"Really? Are smiths with the skills to shape and mould electrum so common?"

The elf lord declined to answer.

"So, what did she do?" I asked.

"She left."

"How?"

The elf pointed to the window through which the Sun's rays shone. "That way."

"Did she indicate where she might take the electrum next?"

Pelladill shook his head. "Where could she take it? Everyone wants electrum but none can afford it and no-one wants to experience the effects of a sudden glut of the stuff."

"If she did not have you lined up as a purchaser, why did she steal it in the first place?" I was quite at a loss.

The elf spread his hands. "Not my concern. Presumably, it is one that exercises your gnomish brain."

"The Fairy Queen is very determined to have her electrum returned."

"I am sure she is. But with no purchaser, the sorceress may decide to use its properties for her own purposes."

"She will need to find a smith that will carry out her wishes."

"That is true, and she will not find such a character among us elves. All the electrumsmiths in Elfholm are indentured to the lords."

I downed the last drops of mead in my goblet and placed it on the table with its fellows. I stood up.

"Well, if you do not know the mage's whereabouts, we must follow her trail further. I must thank you for your hospitality and for answering our questions, especially as you cannot know what we might do with such information."

Lord Pelladill gave me a smile which seemed to contain more malice than goodwill. "I care not what value you attach to my words, gnome."

"Why speak so freely, then lord elf?" I said mystified by his response.

"Because they bring you no benefit but bought me a little time." His smile grew even broader.

My suspicions aroused, I grabbed Bones' wrist and tapped Major Mouse with the tip of my shoe. The mice took the hint and took hold of my trouser cuffs.

"Time for what?" I asked, hearing my voice tremble somewhat.

Lord Pelladill, rose to his feet and clapped his hands.

The doors opened and a wave of armed elves flooded into the room. They carried short pikes and advanced towards me with the points lowered in a very threatening manner.

"Time to leave," I cried and ran for the window that the sorceress had departed by. I dragged Bones along, and skeleton, mice and I exited the tower with our only destination the ground.

As we tumbled, somehow, I kept my grasp of Bones. The mice, with their steel-tipped claws, retained a grip on the cloth of my trousers. For a moment I felt the warmth and light of the morning Sun around us.

Everything turned dark. I landed with a thump onto a firm but yielding surface. That we were no longer falling was my first perception then, as I groped in the darkness to orient myself, I realised that the material of our landing was not grass but a coarse fur and though soft and springy had a strong sturdy base. It felt warm. Bones was still by my side, his wrist clamped in my hand. I was sitting and reluctant to get to my feet because, although our fall had been arrested, our support was in motion. In the absence of light, blacker than a cellar, my eyes told me nothing of our new situation.

Still keeping a hold on my trouser leg, Major Mouse squeaked. "Where are we? What has happened to us?"

"A good question," Bones said, "I anticipated being dashed into a million fragments, but it seems we have landed on some creature that is airborne."

Before I could reply, a deep, booming voice came from the darkness above my head. The words came slowly.

"What is this flotsam that I have collected?"

"Who are you?" I called.

"I am the Knight," the voice replied.

It was indeed as dark as night, but I did not understand what he meant. "But it is morning. The Sun not halfway to its zenith. How can it be night?"

"It is night wherever I, the Knight of the Night, roam."

I was confused. Bones extricated his wrist from my hand. "I think he means he is a member of the class of chivalry, and we are on his charger. Together they are the cause of the darkness."

"Ah," I said, "Thank you, Bones. I think I understand. If only we could see."

Just then one of the mice struck a spark. I heard the metallic click as steel hit the flint. The spark ignited a tiny candle. Though the light was dim and small and barely penetrated the darkness around us, being the only source of light, its glow enabled me to see something of our surroundings.

We were sitting astride the broad back of a mighty horse. To the front, its mane rose to a dark and distant head while on both sides, great wings with feathers as black as jet extended into the night. I twisted around to view the rider who sat behind and above us. I could see little. The pommel of a great saddle rose like a wall obscuring my view but above was a huge figure in black armour which was only visible because it glinted in the feeble candlelight.

I gulped with awe at our situation and wondered whether this armoured knight was our saviour or another threat to our wellbeing.

I summoned my voice. "Thank you, good sir, for saving us from a deadly fall. Yet, I wonder at your timely arrival since it was day when we stepped from the elf lord's tower. It seems to have been a strange chance that brought you to our rescue."

"Not a chance," The slow, booming voice said from above. "I sensed activity in the capital of the elves and decided to investigate. Our trajectories appear to have coincided."

"Um, what was this activity that attracted you?"

"The exposure of a large quantity of electrum."

The subject of my pursuit, the sorceress, must have shown Lord Pelladill the fairy electrum she carried in her bag.

"Why does electrum interest you, Sir Night?" I asked in my most innocent tone.

"Its luminescent quality causes me anxiety. My task is to extinguish all sources of light so that darkness covers the world. I must seek any hoard of electrum that is revealed."

"All sources of light?" I asked. "What about the Sun?"

"He and I have an arrangement. He drives his chariot across the sky each day following the agreed route. He leaves half the day to me."

"I can see that is a good agreement," I said, "It would be troubling if daylight were to last for days on end. How would beings sleep?"

"Exactly," the knight replied. "We have maintained our division of the day for millennia."

"But not today. You have interrupted the Sun's passage."

The knight seemed to pause before replying and then

his voice was a little less authoritative. "It was an emergency. It's not unknown for there to be an eclipse. The other understands that I had to investigate the electrum."

Bones tugged on my sleeve. I heard his grating whisper in my ear.

"You are annoying him with your questions. Take care that he does not cast us off his mount."

"Um, yes," I replied quietly, then I raised my voice. "I too wish to return the electrum to its place of safekeeping with the Fairy Queen. Perhaps, sir, you and I can cooperate."

"Me, cooperate with a gnome?" boomed the voice.

"Well, perhaps we can assist you," I said. "You seek the sorceress who carries the electrum."

"I do."

"She stepped from the window a short while before us. You were a little late in your arrival."

"I was at the other end of the world."

"Of course, you were, but we have been following her for a while now and Bones here can guide us to her."

"Hmm. The hoard has been hidden from my view again and I do not know its location."

"She's closed her bag," I said. I leaned towards Bones. "Can you still feel her path?"

I heard Bones' neck bones grate as he nodded. "Yes. She flies northwards."

"Flies?"

"I know not how. She carries no broom in her bag and had no means of flight when we fled the Fairy Kingdom last night."

"Hmm, well, if we follow and catch her, we will find out how she travels." Again, I raised my voice. "Knight. We can direct you to the bearer of the electrum. If you allow us to travel with you, the skeleton will point the way."

The booming voice replied. "That does indeed appear to be a solution to the problem. You may accompany me. First however extinguish that insufferable light"

26

Bones stretched out his right arm, hand and fingers, each white bone glistening in the dim, guttering light of the mouse's candle. The wick hissed as the mouse put it out with its paws. The wings of the horse rose and fell in slow, immense flaps. I had to grip the coarse fur on the horse's back, the skeleton and the mice too, as the horse increased its speed. We soared blind through the night, no source of light to show us the way, only the current of air rushing past us showed we were moving.

Chapter 4

We encounter watchers in our flight

We flew *in* the darkest of nights. Not through. We were at the core of the night, the source of the shroud of darkness that must envelop half the continent. What must all the peoples beneath the untimely night be thinking, I wondered. Their day plunged into the black of night without reason.

It was impossible to see where we were headed. The only sense of movement I had was the air blasting my face and tugging at my jacket and trousers where the mice hung on. I kept one hand on the brim of my hat to stop it and the dragonflies from being swept away. I felt Bones at my side with his arm still raised, still resolutely pointing our direction.

Northwards. Why north? I did not understand. There were many lands further south reaching to the ocean, the rarely sailed and un-charted ocean, which marked the edge of the world. To the east there were many days of travel until one reached the wasteland at the end of the continent where the Sun rose, and similarly to the west where it set. All of these provided ample hiding places for the sorceress and the electrum. There really was little to the north except for the Parting, the dark rolling cloud from which nothing emerged and from which nothing returned. Why was she headed in that direction carrying the fairy hoard?

We had not been in flight for long, though my freezing limbs thought otherwise, when I noticed that the blackness of our surroundings was no longer complete. Tiny lights appeared, first one or two, then a few, then more. They were all around us. While they shone and twinkled like stars, they were not stars. They did not stay in fixed positions but moved in unpredictable ways around us as if accompanying our flight. I started to have the feeling that we were being watched. These points of light were eyes, unblinkingly examining us – myself, the skeleton, the knight and his mount.

The number of miniscule lights increased steadily until, all at once, there was a burst of light in front of us made up of thousands of the fiery pinpoints.

"Whoa!" cried the knight above my head. He tugged on his reins and the flying horse raised its head, neighed loudly, beat its wings and brought us to a halt, hovering in the air.

The lights approached and at last I had sight of them although their brightness hurt my eyes which had become accustomed to the gloom of the night.

It was like looking through a microscope. Although each lantern was tiny, I was able to make out its form and shape. Each was a miniscule silver being with arms and legs and head and beating wings of silvern gossamer. They were fairies.

They approached, surrounding us in a ball of light that banished the knight's darkness.

A thin, high pitched but clearly audible voice cried out. "Sir Night we bid you cease your flight."

"By what authority do you command me?" boomed the knight.

"The peoples of the world are disconcerted by this disturbance of day and night. The Sun is halted in its path, and you travel north instead of from east to west. Tell us why?"

"I am on a quest," the knight replied as if that explained everything.

"A quest? What is the nature of this quest?" the fairy spokesperson said, "Pray tell us what quest is so important as to disrupt the passage of time."

"I seek a large hoard of electrum and follow the sorceress who possesses it."

"Ah, we suspected that our Queen's electrum may have something to do with these events. How do you know that it is heading north?"

An Extraordinary Tale

"I have a guide."

"The passengers that ride with you? A gnome and a skeleton!"

"That is correct. Now let me continue." The knight raised the reins as if to urge the horse into forward motion.

"Hold, Sir Night," the fairy called. The army of fairies became agitated. "We know of your desire to capture all the world's electrum, but that which you seek is the property of the Fairy Queen."

"I need to ensure that the electrum is in safe hands and its powers under control."

"That is the Queen's desire too. Please sir, return to your duties as the Knight of the Night. Allow us to apprehend this thief and sequester the electrum once again."

"Hmm." The knight hesitated, perhaps disappointed not to continue with his routine-destroying mission. "I suppose you have a point. I am certain the Sun is becoming impatient, and it is not good to arouse his fury. The disruption to my daily routine causes me discomfort as well. Nevertheless, I cannot allow electrum to be exposed willy-nilly."

"Of course, not, Sir Night," the fairy replied with great authority despite his voice being high-pitched and thin. "The Queen desires that her electrum is returned to her at once and safely deposited in the deepest dungeon where its light may not be observed. We will do our utmost to ensure that the Queen's wishes are met." The fairy waved its tiny sword and the swarm of accompanying Fairies brandished theirs too.

"You seem determined in this course of action," the knight said. "Should I return to my duties and allow you to pursue this miscreant, this thief, this witch who has stolen your electrum, how will I know if you continue the quest."

"We will keep you informed of our progress in this endeavour if you will allow the Sun to travel its course across the sky."

The knight sniffed, a noise like a gust of a gale. There was a short pause then he said, "I will comply with your suggestion."

The fairy fluttered, "Thank you, sir, that is most noble of you, but before you depart, please hand over your guides to us so that we may continue to follow the witch."

I had listened with growing anxiety to the conversation between the knight and the fairy. Now my anxiety became fully blown terror. What would the fairies do to me and my companions?

"They are no longer of use to me," the knight bellowed. "You can have them."

The knight jerked the reins. The horse folded its wings and we descended in tight circles accompanied by the glowing ball of fairies. I hung on to the horse's hair tightly until its hooves made contact with the ground with a thud. The horse tucked its wings to its sides. The knight's great hand came down and scooped up me and Bones. He leaned down from his saddle, dropped us to the ground not ungently, then kicked his spurs. The horse beat its wings and rose, soaring into the black sky.

As the knight departed so the day returned.

I scrambled to my feet and dusted down my attire. The mice too stretched, stamping their feet to remove the stiffness caused by clinging to me for so long. Bones also loosened his joints. Now that I could see again, I examined our surroundings. The knight had left us on a narrow rocky ridge devoid of plant life, overlooking the broad plain that bordered the Parting. The line of the dark impenetrable cloud was visible in the distance. We were not alone.

The swarm of fairies had spread out to surround us. Their silver brightness exceeded even that of the Sun that again shone from the sky. A fairy flew towards me, his wings buzzing like that of a bee which he resembled in size if not form.

"So, you have fallen into our power, gnome," he said, "You are an accomplice of the thief."

"No, no, no," I waved my hands to emphasise my rebuttal. "I was following the woman to recover the electrum for the Queen."

"The Queen of the Fairies has no need for a gnome to recover her electrum."

Bones turned to me. His eyeless sockets looked at me accusingly.

"You said you were commissioned by the Fairy Queen to follow my mistress?"

I puffed out my cheeks, "Yes, well, that was a slight exaggeration. I haven't actually met the Queen." Truth be told, I had never spoken to a fairy till now. I felt sharp points jabbing at my ankles. I looked down. The mice were prodding me with their swords.

"You told us a pack of lies," Major Mouse shouted. "And you stopped us from getting the electrum from her bag."

I leaned down to face the mice. "You had no chance of getting that bag open at all, and, while some of what I said was not strictly true, I would not call them lies."

"Ahem," said the fairy, "Time presses on us. I need the truth from you, gnome. You were with the sorceress, as was this heap of bones."

"I beg your pardon, sir," the Skeleton said, "I take offence at being called a *heap*. I am a revitalised skeleton, in service to the lady of whom you speak."

The fairy fluttered into Bones' face and emerged through an eye-socket a few moments later.

"Well, there is certainly no living flesh in there," he said, "so you are bonded with the woman."

"I am."

"And you know where she is."

"No."

"No? What then?"

"I know where she has been. I am drawn along her trail."

The fairy circled Bones' head. "So, which direction is she headed?"

Bones raised his hand and pointed his finger bone

towards the distant cloud of the Parting. "That way," he said as if that was the end of the matter.

"It cannot be," the fairy muttered, flying up to join his companions. "Why would she approach the Parting?"

"To enter it?" I offered.

The fairy buzzed down to me, hovering over my nose. "Enter it! What madness is this?

"I don't know," I replied, "But I cannot imagine another reason for heading in this direction."

"What will become of the electrum if it enters the Parting?" The fairy was making figures of eights now.

"I don't know," I said, "but I'd like to find out."

"We must catch her before she enters it," the fairy said. "Come fellow fairies, to the Parting. Oh, and bring them."

The fairy leader and a proportion of the swarm flew off northwards. The remainder clustered around us; under our arms, around our legs and under my buttocks and Bones' nether regions. I felt myself lifting off the ground. The mice scurried to grab hold of my trouser hems before they were left behind.

"Not again," one cried, "How many more ways can we be carried through the air?"

I had not known how fast fairies fly. With my gleaming flying suit, we soared down from the peaks and across the broad plain towards the looming cloud that was the Parting. Fast, maybe; scary, definitely. I decided I preferred the firm but soft surface of a pigeon or winged horse beneath me. Bones, borne alongside me seemed similarly terrified, his lower jaw hanging limp in a silent scream all the way.

As we travelled, the Sun passed rapidly overhead. Was time passing quickly? No, I think it was the Sun trying to catch up the day after the knight's little detour. By the time we started our descent to the ground the shadows were lengthening.

The continent-wide plain adjoining the Parting is covered largely by grassland and shrubs with the occasional village that nestles surprisingly close to the ominous cloud bank. We landed in the centre of one such community, though it was hardly more than a hamlet. The buildings on the four sides of the square, no, more a misshapen quadrilateral, scarcely deserved that term. The walls were low heaps of rubble, roofed with branches torn from the bushes. We landed amongst the rest of the fairy swarm as the inhabitants emerged from their dwellings. They formed a cluster staring blankly at me, Bones, the mice who disembarked from my clothing, and the fairies.

They were ogres, varied in size but impossible to tell their age or which were male or female. They were all a little taller than me, as broad as they were tall, with little tufts of mud brown hair sprouting from all over their round heads. Little eyes were spaced widely above a wide piggish nose and thin lips concealed a mouth filled with odd-shaped, yellow teeth. Having stared at us for a while they conversed with each other in a series of grunts that conveyed no sense to me.

"Why did we land amongst them?" I said to the gathering of fairies. I wasn't sure which was their commander.

"It was a landmark," came the reply. The fairy leader flew up and hovered a hand's breadth from my nose. I felt my eyes crossing.

I boldly questioned him. "Do we need a landmark? We can see the Parting. That's where we're headed, isn't it?"

"That is true, but we need to assess the situation and make some decisions." He flew to the skeleton and addressed him, "Can you still sense the sorceress?"

"I can feel where she has been," he said.

"Has she been here?"

"She passed through here."

"Where is she now?"

"I don't know. Don't you listen. I follow her presence but know not her location." I could sense Bones grating his teeth with annoyance.

"Hmm," the fairy mused. "So, she is still heading towards the Parting?"

"She was," Bones said, "She may have entered it by now."

"Hmm," the fairy said again.

"What are you planning?" I asked thinking that the fairies must have a plan for getting their electrum back.

"We'll let you know soon. For now, you may rest," he replied.

It seemed a good idea to catch some sleep while we weren't being chased or harried or in pursuit. I lay down on the dirt and was asleep in moments.

I was woken by a noise that was familiar but unexpected; a huffing and clanking and bell ringing. Beyond the roofs of the ogre homes, small puffs of grey smoke rose into the clear, blue sky of a new day. The noises and the smoke were approaching. In a few moments, a steam engine drawing a single carriage drew to a halt just beyond the ogre village. Why did the elf railway network include this remote village? Well, elves are inveterate sightseers so I suppose that some might like to come to gaze at the Parting. Though why they should want to view the mysterious barrier defeats me.

Doors were flung open and there came the muttered cries and groans of travel-weary elves. They appeared between two of the ogre buildings. I recognised Lord Pelladill at the front but there were other expensively attired elves, a small platoon of pikemen and a handful of the downtrodden workers. They joined the ogres, the fairies and my companions in the square.

Pelladill addressed the fairies. "Ah, I see you have captured these accomplices of the sorceress."

"I am not her accomplice," I protested. Before anyone had a chance to disagree with me there was a noisy fluttering of feathers and a giant pigeon landed on one of the roofs. It promptly collapsed and the bird disappeared in a cloud of leaves, twigs and rock dust.

The chief fairy buzzed in my face. "A friend of yours, gnome?"

"An acquaintance," I replied, "better known to the mice than myself." The pigeon flapped its wings some more and stepped through the collapsed walls of the cottage to join our growing band.

The Sun had been rising above the eastern horizon but suddenly fell from sight. Darkness spread across the sky. I felt rather than saw the arrival of the knight on his mount but there he was, amongst us, his figure almost but not quite absorbing the light the fairies emitted.

"Ah, so this is where you are meeting," the knight boomed. The elves and ogres huddled together in two groups and stepped away from the tall knight and his huge, winged steed.

"Greetings again, Sir Night," the fairy said. "I think our gathering is complete."

Lord Pelladill took a step forward from the other elves. "We responded to your invitation, fairy, but we wonder at the purpose of this meeting and the others in attendance." He glanced at the cluster of ogres with distaste. Other elves looked warily at the large dishevelled creatures who shuffled around, showing no interest in their visitors. The fairy hordes buzzed with agitation and kept their distance from the elvish soldiers who glared at them with suspicion. For eons fairies and elves had engaged in mutual distrust while relying on each other for trade. Us gnomes had profited from their disunity. The mice kept to themselves, swords at the ready and prepared to act if any party threatened. Bones stood by my side for all appearances as dead as a statue, but I guessed he was watching the proceedings intently. Of course with the sun obscured again by the knight's dark, only the fairylight illuminated the scene.

The fairy leader flew into the middle of the space between the groups.

"We are here because we are all involved in the loss of our Queen's electrum," he began, "... Although I'm not certain about the pigeon."

"She's with us," I said, without thinking.

"The damage sustained will be your responsibility then

gnome," the fairy responded. I didn't like the sound of that. I avoid responsibility if I can.

"Get on with it," intoned the knight, "I can't stay here, er, all night, not when the Sun is waiting in its course."

The fairy buzzed in a circle. "Yes, of course, Sir. We are here to decide what to do if, as we suspect, the sorceress has carried the electrum into the Parting."

"It is lost then," Lord Pelladill said.

"Not necessarily," the fairy replied, "We do not know what becomes of anything that enters the Parting, just that nothing has ever emerged from it. Is that so, Sir Night?"

The booming voice replied. "The Parting divides our world from what is beyond. But of what is beyond I have no knowledge."

The fairy continued, "Thank you, sir. Nevertheless, the Queen sorely regrets the loss of her hoard. You, Lord Pelladill, have spent your life acquiring electrum and have concerns about its influence on your nation's economy. The knight here has worries about the powers someone like the sorceress could wield in possession of such a quantity of the extraordinary metal."

Another finely dressed elf stepped up alongside Pelladill.

"And what of these other beings?" he said pointing at me and my companions.

"They were involved in the theft," the fairy said, flying around me, Bones and the mice.

"I was not," I protested, "I was pursuing the sorceress in order to return the electrum to its owner."

"That's your story now, is it?" Major Mouse said, glaring up at me.

"It's the truth," I said. Well, it was partly true, though I felt I was losing the plot.

"Ahem," Bones made a strange coughing sound. The fairies, elves, ogres, mice, the knight and the pigeon stared at him. "As a bonded, revitalised skeleton who has no control over his actions, I served my mistress as I was bound to. I take exception to being lumped in with these miscreants." He waved a bony hand across me and the mice.

"We understand your position," the fairy said, "and when we capture the sorceress you will be freed from her service and allowed to rest in peace."

Bones nodded his acceptance.

"But what are these fighting mice doing here?" Pelladill's companion said.

"Oh, they were after the electrum too. Ouch!" I said. Major Mouse had jabbed my foot with his sword.

"Well, that is everyone's position explained," the knight boomed, "What are we going to do to retrieve the electrum and return it to its place of storage?"

"Someone must follow the sorceress," the fairy said.

"But you said she has entered the Parting," Lord Pelladill said.

"The skeleton says that she headed in that direction," the fairy replied. Bones' skull rocked on his spine in agreement.

"Who will follow her then?" the elf asked, casting his gaze over the throng.

The fairy raised his tiny hand and pointed. At me.

"Why me?" I asked, thinking I had no wish to depart this world for the unknown existence in or through the Parting – if indeed existence continued.

The fairy flew around my head. "You, gnome, seem to have exhibited a certain resourcefulness in pursuing the sorceress up to now."

"That's just my luck," I replied and wished I hadn't.

"Your luck?" At least half the members of the gathering repeated in unison. The ogres added a few grunts too.

"Yes," I said, realising that I would have to offer some sort of explanation. "You see I am an adventurer. I'm no swordsman, or wizard. I don't command any forces or possess great intellect, but I am lucky. Things happen to me. I happen to be on a train where I recognise one of the passengers as a great sorceress and I just happen to overhear a conversation about a theft occurring in Fairyland. I jump out of a tower in Elfholm and just happen to fall into the path of the Knight of the Night.

These things happen. Another piece of luck gave me these." I raised my cap and the dragonflies flew up from my head. The fairy withdrew to a safe distance. I clicked my fingers and the dragonflies settled again. I replaced my cap.

The knight let out a roar of laughter that sent a gale across the square, blowing most of the gathering off their feet.

"Well, gnome, it looks like you are the ideal person to lead the expedition into the Parting. It will need a good dose of luck."

"A gnome as leader?" Lord Pelladill sneered, having regained his footing.

"He'll do," the fairy said.

"But you don't trust a lone gnome to apprehend the most resourceful mage that ever lived, do you?" Pelladill added.

"Not at all," said the fairy, "He will have companions. A fairy." The cloud of fairies contracted as each tried to hide behind another. "An elf," he added and the elves all looked at each other with dismay. "And the skeleton of course, as he follows his mistress." Bones shrugged as if he expected nothing else.

"And a mouse," Major Mouse said, "I'm not getting left out of this little jaunt."

I raised my hand to attract attention. "Um, I think you're assuming that I want to go on this mad expedition."

The fairy flew into my face. "You will go or you will take the place of the missing electrum in the most secure cell in Fairyland."

It looked as though my choices were limited. The various parties had turned in on themselves, huddling together to choose my companions. I confronted Bones.

"Are you happy with this?" I asked.

He shrugged. "Why not? Entering the Parting will either bring a blissful end to my second life or we will discover new wonders."

"Putting it like that makes it sound almost attractive," I said.

Major Mouse was jumping up and down. "We will be hailed as heroes."

I frowned at the mouse. "I think I need to remind you Major, that no-one and nothing has ever emerged from the Parting, so being celebrated here will mean little to us."

Lord Pelladill was walking across the square towards us with a young elf maiden dressed in working rags by his side. He pushed her towards us.

"This is Aelfed, the daughter of my electrum smith."

"The one rendered comatose by the sorceress' curse," I said. I observed some likeness between this fresh-faced maid and the wizened old smith.

Pelladill nodded. "She is keen to avenge her father and, as his apprentice, she is well-trained in the storage and treatment of electrum. She will join this expedition."

The fairy flew around us accompanied by another who appeared identical. "This is my deputy, Queen's Guard Tenplessium who also will join the party."

The knight leapt on to his horse, his black armour clanking. He took hold of the reins.

"That is good. The team is selected. Now I must return to my duties. Farewell." The great horse beat its wings and rose into the air. The darkness lightened as the Sun leapt into the eastern sky and resumed its path

"Go then," the leading fairy said. "Follow the sorceress and ensure the electrum is not misused."

The fairies and elves and ogres moved to create a path out of the settlement towards the Parting. I hesitated. The elf stepped towards me. She was shorter than me so looked up into my face. She smiled and I felt that having her as a companion would make the quest as pleasant as a journey into the unknown could be.

"Come gnome, let us begin." Aelfed grasped my hand in one of hers and took hold of the Skeleton's in her other. She tugged and pulled us along the track made for us. The fairy, Tenplessium, flew ahead of us and Major Mouse scampered between my feet.

Ahead was the towering, seething cloud of the Parting

that stretched from the eastern horizon to the west and rose so high that it was impossible to see if it ended. No top to the cloud had ever been found or reached.

We had not taken many steps when I heard heavy footfall behind us. I paused and turned. An ogre was pursuing us. He – or it may have been she – joined us and grunted a few times.

"You wish to join us?" I interpreted, guessing rather than translating.

The ogre inclined its head on its neckless shoulders.

"Right well, come along. The more we have for this mission the better." I had no idea what use the mindless oaf would be but perhaps his muscles would become useful.

We resumed our trudge across the plain, leaving the village and the assembled fairies, elves, mice and ogres behind. They followed us at a distance. The Parting was a grey wall ahead of us though it was impossible to say how far because its height and length defied perspective. Nevertheless, it could not be more than a few furlongs from the ogres' homes.

"We are still following her?" I said to Bones.

"Yes," he replied, "she passed this way."

"How was she travelling?"

"On a sunbeam."

"Beats pigeons, winged horses and a swarm of fairies I suppose." To be truthful I was becoming apprehensive about what would happen when we entered the mysterious cloud. Despite my words to the gathering, I wasn't enamoured with adventure, and my idea of *real* good luck would be to find myself in a comfortable armchair with a glass of malt beer at my side and a plate of jam tarts.

I was musing on whether blackcurrant or strawberry flavour were my favourite when Aelfed tugged on my hand.

"We're there."

"There?"

"Alright, here, within it. Look around."

I did as she suggested and saw that the Sun was no longer visible overhead and the sky was grey. We were surrounded by the cloud of the Parting, yet it was not completely dark. A faint grey light came to us from all sides, but there was nothing to see. I turned and could not see the plain we had just crossed. Ahead, to the sides, above and below was all the same grey although I could feel solid ground beneath our feet.

"Can you feel her path, Bones?" I said.

"Hmm, it is faint, as if spreading out and merging with the cloud."

"Great," I muttered. "If we have no route to follow, how do we know where we are going."

The fairy, Tenplessium, flittered above my head.

"That perhaps is the essence of the Parting. One must make one's own decision and follow it."

Anxiety gripped me. "Perhaps we should retrace our steps and make sure we can still return."

"I think that opportunity has passed," Aelfed said. "Can you say precisely which way we came into this fog?"

I spun around but only succeeded in making myself dizzy. Every direction was the same and I had no idea where we had come from or where we were going.

"Remember, nothing emerges from the Parting," Tenplessium said, a reminder I did not need. "Skeleton, can you still lead us?"

Bones hadn't moved since we had commenced our discussion.

"I believe it is this way," he said and took a step forward.

I hurried to fall into step with him, Aelfed beside me, Major Mouse at my feet, the ogre a pace or two behind and the fairy above our heads.

Whether the cloud grew thicker or the fog was in my head, I do not know, but in a few more steps I felt lethargic, my feet grew heavy. I felt confused, disorientated, drowsy. I just wanted to...

Part 2

Beyond the Parting

Chapter 5

An ordinary morning

Wake up. I fought off the foggy tendrils of sleep, batting aside the half-remembered memories of dreams: a pigeon flapping wildly; riding (on what?) through the night; a stabbing pain in my foot. My eyes opened to a grey dawn with an autumn mist visible through the gap in the curtains. I drew in a deep breath and lay back on my pillow reluctant to leave the warmth of my duvet. I wanted to recall those dreams but the images in my head were confused, jumbled, incomprehensible. All I had was a feeling of anxiety, of a task uncompleted.

Minutes passed as I delayed getting up but just as I was beginning to accept that perhaps it was time to move, it was gone eight o'clock after all, the doorbell rang and there was the banging of a fist on my front door. With my temper, good or otherwise, shattered, I rolled out of bed, dragged my dressing gown off the hook on the door and hurried to the hall. As I paused to pull the dressing gown around me, the banging was repeated.

I dragged the door open. "OK, OK, I'm here. Er?"

I know I am not very tall, shorter than the average, but the fellow standing on my doorstep appeared to be a giant. A very thin one, apparently lacking in any flesh at all. Although he wore a long black overcoat, it hung from his shoulders as if they were a very thin coat hanger. The legs below the coat were as thin as broomsticks though clothed in tight cloth. On his head he wore a black trilby hat that contrasted with the white skin taut on the skull.

"Good morning, Mr Hohenheim," he said in a quiet rasping voice. His almost lipless mouth barely moved.

"Um, good morning," I replied, my politeness belying my confusion. How did this ghoulish fellow know my name? I certainly did not know his, although something about his extraordinary appearance seemed familiar.

"May I come in?" he asked. "This cold mist is getting to my joints."

Again, I reacted out of habit rather than common sense. "Of course," I replied, stepping back into the hall. I did have brain enough to add, "Should I know your name?"

"I doubt it," he said, closing the door behind him, "We have not been introduced."

"Then why have you called on me at this early hour?" I was beginning to get some control of my reason.

"Is it early? Hmm, the sun has only recently risen, so I suppose that for night sleepers it is early. I hadn't thought of you as a day person."

"Oh," I responded, confused again. "But I haven't had breakfast yet, so it *is* early. Would you like to join me?" I retreated into my kitchen. My tall guest ducked under the lintel as he followed me.

"No, no, no, I couldn't eat a thing," he said.

I paused with my hand half raised to the cupboard where I keep my porridge. I turned to face him.

"Then what can I do for you? Why have you come here?"

"That is a long and complex story, Mr Hohenheim," he rasped, "Perhaps you should make your own breakfast and then I will explain."

What he suggested seemed a good idea, so I busied myself filling the kettle and preparing my porridge. The man folded himself on to the spare chair at my kitchen table and spent the ensuing period gazing around the room.

It took just a few minutes to have a steaming cup of tea and bowl of porridge in front of me. I blew on a spoonful of syrup laden oats.

"So, what is this tale of yours?"

"Have you lived here long Mr Hohenheim, in this little, low cottage under the hills?"

"Uh, yes, all my life in fact. It was my parents' house, of course, and when they died, I inherited it."

"You have never travelled, never had adventures?"

What was the fellow getting at? Yes, I know I am a bit of a stick in the mud, boring I suppose, but I don't bother other people. I get on with my life and I'm happy in my little house, digging the garden, growing my root vegetables. I shook my head.

"You recall your life here?"

What an odd question. "Of course. Not every last moment, but yes, I remember being a child here. I recall my mother cooking in this very kitchen." Using the same old cooker. "I remember helping my father to dig the new potato plot. It may not be exciting, but I do remember my life."

"Hmm," the tall, thin man looked thoughtful. "Do you have dreams?"

"Doesn't everyone? I thought I'd read that they were a normal part of healthy sleeping."

"Yes, but do you remember any dreams?"

"Well, occasionally, I suppose, there are snippets that stick in the mind." The images that had been in my head when I awoke reappeared. "Only last night there were –"

"What?" The man was suddenly alert, excited although his white face did not display the emotion. "Did you have some different dreams last night?"

I shrugged. "I don't know about different. They were a little strange; something about falling in darkness. I don't suppose that's so unusual. Then there was a pigeon. There was something about it, I can't remember what it was. And something jabbed me in my foot."

The man leaned across the table. "What stabbed your foot?"

"Um, I don't know." A memory floated into my consciousness. "No, I do remember it was… no, that's silly."

"What?"

"A mouse holding a sword."

"Yes!" He clenched his fist.

I didn't understand. "What has this got to do with your story? Why have you come here?"

"I have had dreams too," he said, "disturbing dreams."

"I suppose we all get unsettling dreams from time to time, nightmares perhaps."

"No, these weren't exactly nightmares though some were scary enough. They repeated, became clearer and they set me on a quest."

"A quest?" What kind of word was that to use at the breakfast table? I realised my porridge was cooling. I took another mouthful.

"Yes. A quest to find you."

"Me? How could I be in your dreams?"

"Oh, you weren't. Not this you at any rate. But there were clues which led me to you, and some other people."

I was about to ask the obvious question when there was another tap on the front door. This was lighter, a set of rapid raps. I sat frozen in my chair bemused by the way the morning was turning out.

"I think you'd better answer that," he said.

I stood up in something of a daze and went to the door. I opened it. There was no one there. Well, that's what I thought until I glanced down. There was a little girl. At least, she was the size of a girl no more than five or six years old, but as I examined her I saw that she was not really that young at all. She was dressed all in white and her skin and hair were as white as snow. She seemed to glow with her own light.

"Hello," she said in a soft, high-pitched voice, "Is Mr Bones, here?"

"Bones? You mean a tall, thin gentleman."

"That's him." She rushed past me and sprinted down the hallway. I hurried after her.

When I reached the kitchen, they were greeting each other with hugs. Well, she hugged his calf and he patted the curls of hair on her head.

"Does he know?" she said.

Mr Bones, as he appeared to be called, shook his head. "No, not yet."

"Well, get on with it. We have to find her."

"I know, Ten, but we mustn't rush him. He doesn't seem to have had as long as us."

"What are you talking about?" I asked feeling a bit miffed that they seemed to know about something that I didn't. "What haven't I had so long of?"

"Dreams, the special dreams," Mr Bones said. "And you believe you've lived your whole life here."

"I have."

"You only think you have. What would you say if I told you that you've only been in this universe since last night?"

"That's nonsense. I told you. I can remember spending all my life here."

"Ah, yes, memories. Those come with the universe."

It was all very mysterious. I sat on my chair, with my cooling porridge in front of me. The strange little woman stood next to Mr Bones. She was just about able to peer over the table.

"He doesn't get it," she said.

"I haven't explained much yet," Mr Bones said. He leaned forward as if examining my face. "Despite appearances and your memories, you don't belong here, Mr Hohenheim."

"Don't belong here? Me?" His words were meaningless to me.

"That's right. You, me, Tenplessium here, have all arrived in this universe from another. What is strange is that we seem to have turned up here at different times and places."

"But I've never been anywhere else. I haven't been abroad or anywhere. I've always lived here."

"I know, I know," Mr Bones said. "It is difficult to believe, especially as it's your first day."

The white girl with the strange name piped up, "Yes, I was confused for a long time, months. The dreams were so real but different to everyday life."

I wanted to know more about her. "What is your everyday life?"

She smiled. "I'm an actress. I get parts in shows where they need a little person."

"I see," I said, "I'm sure you're very popular."

"Oh, I am, but now I know it's not real. It's never actually happened, and I don't care if I never act again. I've learned I'm not supposed to be an actor."

"You learned that from the dreams?" I ventured.

"Them and the stories Mr Bones and the others told me."

"Others?"

Mr Bones nodded. "Yes, they'll be here soon."

As if on cue there was another knock on the door, a solid thump.

Mr Bones rose to his feet, "Don't get up, I'll let them in. I think I recognise that knock."

He left the room, ducking his head. The girl smiled at me. I felt she was trying to cheer me, but it seemed more a smile of pity.

I heard the front door open and an exchange which sounded more like a couple of grunts. Mr Bones returned followed by my latest visitor. His appearance was as astounding as the first two. He looked and was dressed like a bouncer at a rather sleazy nightclub, not that I have ever visited such an establishment. He was as wide as he was tall and he was taller than me, with a square head that sat on his shoulders with little sign of a neck. His scruffy suit did not seem to fit him at all and his hair was odd tufts that stuck out at unusual angles. He had a wide nose and a hooded brow.

"This is Hugo," Mr Bones said. "He doesn't say much."

Hugo stood in the entrance to the kitchen and grunted. I presumed that was both a greeting and an agreement with what had been said.

"How do you do," I said. Hugo grunted again but didn't move.

"Why have you all come to my house?" I said, beginning to feel that my little kitchen was getting rather crowded.

"It's the quest," Mr Bones said. "As I said, for a long time I had these dreams which slowly began to make sense to me. Tenplessium, and Hugo and Aelfed..."

"Aelfed?"

"She'll be here soon."

"Oh."

"They all appeared in my dreams as you did."

"And so you all came to visit me."

"Yes, but it wasn't as easy as it sounds. It has taken me years to figure out what it all meant and to follow the clues that led me to meet everyone."

"Years? What about your job?"

"I suppose you could say I was retired. I have little need for the comforts of life, so I have devoted myself to the quest, and here we are, ready to begin."

"Begin? But I thought you said your quest was to find me." It all sounded like a strange dream of its own. I pinched my wrist to check I was awake. It hurt.

"Ah, but finding you is just the start."

"The start of what?"

Before he could answer there was a ring of the doorbell. No hammering on the door this time. Mr Bones rose to answer it. I jumped up.

"No, Mr Bones, it is my front door, I shall answer it. Presumably this is your other friend. What was the name?"

Mr Bones nodded graciously and sat back down. "Aelfed."

"Ah, yes." I pushed past Hugo who was slow to move. He really was a big lump of a fellow.

I opened the front door and found a young woman standing there. She was a little shorter than me and had short straw-coloured hair. She wore a green boilersuit with a satchel over her shoulder.

"Good morning, Mr Hohenheim. I'm Aelfed," she said brightly.

"Good morning," I replied, "I understand you are expected."

"I saw the others were here already. That's good."

I guided her down the hall to the kitchen, which was filling up.

"Here she is," I said endeavouring to appear in charge of my own home, "Is that all?"

Mr Bones looked a little uncertain. "Sort of," he said.

"Right, well, perhaps you can explain what you mean by this *quest*."

"I think you had better sit down again, Mr Hohenheim," Mr Bones said. "I know it will be difficult for you to accept what we have to say."

"Oh, yes," Tenplessium piped up, "We all thought it was wild before we took it all in."

I took a deep breath. "Well, perhaps you had better get on with it. It's all to do with dreams then."

All four of them had their attention focussed on me as if looking and waiting for my reaction. Mr Bones began.

"The dreams were the start, but really they are memories overlaid with the experiences that this universe has provided us with."

"I don't understand," I said.

Mr Bones raised his hand to make me pause. "I know. It took me years to realise that the dreams were my real past, not my life here." The other three nodded their agreement. "Then I began to have some success in making sense of the dreams, following the clues that lead me to Tenplessium, Aelfed, Hugo and finally you."

Aelfed spoke, "Once we met, it all became clear. We had the same dreams, the same memories of where we have come from and what we are doing here."

"Where we come from?" I was still bemused.

Mr Bones nodded. "That is the point. You see the five of us have come here…"

"To Little Waggleford."

"I mean to this universe with its stars and planets and Earth and continents but yes, I suppose also your dear little village."

"But I've been here all my life."

"Yes, I know you think that. You said so earlier, but it's not what really happened. We came here through something which seems to be called the Parting. For reasons we don't understand we arrived at different places at different times. Some of us have been here for years, for you it is today."

"Where is this other place?" I asked.

Mr Bones shrugged. "We can't say where. It's elsewhere, but we do know it is very different to this universe and that we have all been changed by the Parting.

"Changed? How?" I felt as if my head was about to explode.

Tenplessium grinned. "In the other world I'm a fairy no bigger than a fly."

"And I'm an elf," Aelfed said.

"Hugo's an ogre," Mr Bones said. I looked up at the passive, hulk of a man.

"And you?" I asked.

"Oh, I'm just a bundle of old bones, a walking, talking, thinking skeleton."

"That's nonsense," I cried. "How can a skeleton be alive."

"Because the other world is different," Mr Bones said, "Everything you think you know about science and nature in this universe is just not true in the world we come from."

It seemed too ridiculous to be true.

"If I came from there too, what am I?"

Aelfed chuckled. "You're a gnome."

I put my hands to my bald head and laughed. "A gnome! One of those things people put in their gardens."

Mr Bones spoke quietly and firmly. "No, not a garden gnome. A noble race of beings, who mostly live in the tunnels and caves they have carved out under the mountains. Well, *They* think they are a noble race." He frowned and I wondered if he was telling me everything he knew about gnomes.

I looked from one to the other, from the tiny, glowing Tenplessium, to the broad solid, Hugo, to the dainty and earthy Aelfed and the frankly cadaverous, Mr Bones.

"You all believe this nonsense?" I asked. Each of them nodded.

"It may sound fantastic," Tenplessium said, "but we know it's true."

I didn't know what to think or why they were really all

squashed in my kitchen, but I thought I should humour them.

"So, the five of us came through this Parting thing – "

"Six, actually," Mr Bones said.

"Six? There's one more person still to come?" I said, feeling more and more confused.

"No, we believe he is with you now," Mr Bones said. I stared at him, speechless but Mr Bones was not looking at me. His eyes were on the floor.

"Come and join us, Major," he called, addressing no one I could see. Then I heard a faint scrabbling of claws on lino. I looked down. A dark brown house mouse had appeared from behind the cooker. It paused and sat up on its hind legs, its whiskers quivering.

"I knew I had mice, but I have never done anything to get rid of them," I said.

"Just as well that you didn't," Aelfed said bending down. She laid her hand on the floor. The mouse scampered towards her and sat on her hand. She lifted it up and placed it on the table. The mouse took a few paces and sat looking up at me with its red eyes.

"Meet Major Mouse," Mr Bones said. "He's the leader of a band of brave, fighting mice."

"Oh," I said, "Can he speak?"

"Of course not," Tenplessium said, "Mice can't talk in this universe, but this is Major Mouse alright. See how he recognises us."

The mouse certainly did not appear afraid of us and was content to sit, cleaning his whiskers, while we talked.

I stroked my beard. What could I make of this? It seemed to be nonsense, but Mr Bones had said this meeting was just the start of some quest. I would listen until their story fell to pieces and I would know they were having me on.

"The quest," I said.

Mr Bones nodded. "That's right, the reason why we're all here."

"The reason why we came through the Parting," Tenplessium added.

Mr Bones glared at her. "Let me explain."

I folded my arms and sat trying to ignore the mouse that was still looking up at me. "Go on, please, Mr Bones."

"We are pursuing a woman, a sorceress, a witch, who has stolen the Queen of the Fairies' hoard of electrum."

"Electrum? What's that?"

"An extremely valuable and powerful metal," Mr Bones explained. "It doesn't exist here. At least, not as the magical, glowing material that has been in my dreams." Aelfed nodded her head, apparently agreeing with him.

"What is this witch doing here?"

All of them looked sad and Mr Bones shrugged. I could almost hear his shoulder blades grinding. "We don't know, but she must have some kind of plan and that's why we must find her."

"Well, I don't know anything about a witch or this electrum stuff. Why do you need me? Why can't I just carry on with my life here, even if it isn't real?"

"Because we do need you," Aelfed said.

"You're important," Tenplessium said.

"Ergh," Hugo grunted.

The mouse squeaked.

"Because you are lucky," Mr Bones said.

"Lucky?" Am I lucky? My life had been quiet and peaceful and totally lacking in any misfortune other than the passing away of my parents at a great age in their sleep. I'd never won any lotteries or raffles, nothing to speak of. Was that good luck?

"That's the impression we have of you from our dreams," Mr Bones said. The others nodded. "With you around, things happen, perhaps not what one might expect but it turns out for the best in the situation. We accompanied you into the Parting. Perhaps it is your good luck that it's us that have had to spend all our time piecing together the dreams to find out who we really are, while you are just here now."

I wasn't convinced. "I don't believe there is anything

like luck. There is just good planning, common sense and avoiding getting into situations. Why should I join you in this silly quest? I doubt whether any of this is true. Why should I go off trying to find a strange woman?"

Mr Bones looked even graver than previously. "Because electrum is extremely powerful. We don't know what she could do with the hoard she has, but it could be disastrous for this universe. We have to find her, get the electrum and return it to the Queen."

"Hmph!" I said in disgust and laid my hands on the table. I glared at Mr Bones, struggling to find words to reply to him. I felt a tickle on the back of my hand. I looked down. The mouse had crawled onto my hand and was poking me with his right front paw.

"What is it doing?" I cried but I was too scared to move my hands.

Tenplessium answered. "I think Major Mouse is trying to tell you something."

"What?" I said.

Aelfed answered, "Well, of course, here, he's only a mouse, but in our world he is a brave and resourceful fighter and thief. I think he's showing you that he's not afraid of you."

The mouse was certainly acting strangely for a mouse. I looked up at my four visitors. They were an odd assortment of characters. Could they really be telling the truth? I thought back to my own dreams of the previous night. Other scenes came into my mind: a carriage drawn by unicorns; gleaming towers surrounded by fog, or was it smoke; and a rolling grey cloud that stretched across the horizon. They were fragments to be sure but seemed to hint at a bigger story. I thought too of my life. Pleasant it had been, and I had no desire for anything more exciting, but… yes, there was a but. The thought of an adventure, a quest, a journey, seemed strangely attractive. Why should I, homely, old Philobrach Hohenheim, be tempted by an expedition to find a dangerous witch? It was nonsense, and yet I found myself answering.

"Alright. How do we find this witch?"

"Ah," said Mr Bones, "that is the difficult bit. Apparently back in our real world, I am bound to the woman by some contract that enables me to follow her. But here I simply do not know who she is and I feel no pull from her." He looked despondent.

The fairy creature at his side spoke up. "Perhaps if we went somewhere where we could all sit down and maybe had some refreshment, we could discuss our plan or at least make a start on one."

It seemed as though I was being asked to feed the whole party. Well, a cup of tea would suffice.

"We can go into the lounge," I said. I started to stand, but as I did so, the mouse jumped onto the sleeve of my dressing gown and ran up to my shoulder. I had to stop myself from shivering and brushing it off.

Aelfed chuckled, "There! Major Mouse has taken a liking to you, Mr Hohenheim." I tried to look unconcerned as I led them all down the hall towards the lounge. I noticed that the newspaper had been stuffed in the letterbox while we had been in discussion. I pulled it out and carried it into the sitting room. The room was small and dark like all the rooms in my little cottage, but it did have seating, of a sort, for five. Mr Bones and Hugo squashed themselves onto the sofa, with Hugo taking up at least two thirds of it. Mr Bones' knees stuck up like two tent poles. Aelfed and Tenplessium sat in my armchair and looked quite comfortable together.

I dropped the newspaper onto the coffee table in the centre of the room thinking to take orders for the refreshments that were apparently required, as the paper flopped open to page two. Mr Bones leaned forward and stared.

"I don't believe it," he murmured.

"What?" everyone asked, me included.

He looked up at me. "It must be your luck. There she is," He pointed a long bony finger at the photograph in the paper. "The witch. She's in your newspaper."

Chapter 6

We go for a drive

We all stared at the picture in the newspaper. It was a colour photo of a woman standing at the entrance to a modern building. She was wearing a skirt and jacket that matched in colour her bright red hair. Men in dark suits were to her left and right and behind her, but she appeared to be confidently addressing an audience. I had no idea who she was, but she seemed rather familiar.

"Are you sure it's the witch?" Aelfed said to Mr Bones.

His head bobbed up and down. "I am certain of it. She has been in my dreams always. In our other lives, I know I was her servant. We were parted before we came through the Parting, as it were, before we all gathered together."

I was confused. "If she has just come from this other world you talk about, what is she doing in the news? You have to be a celebrity to have your photo taken like that, or a criminal or a politician."

"This universe has accommodated her," Mr Bones said, "We each have our place here with memories of a full life. It seems she has made some kind of impact that has attracted attention."

He bent closer to read the article that accompanied the picture.

Tenplessium frowned. "Do you think that is the witch's intention?"

Mr Bones glanced at the little woman. "I can't imagine that she does anything without a purpose. It suggests here that she is someone of great wealth and influence but that her emergence as a person of note occurred quite recently. That suggests that she hasn't actually been here very long."

"What is her plan?" Aelfed asked in a pained voice.

Mr Bones shook his head. "I do not know."

"But we know who she is now," Tenplessium said, "We can capture her and make her tell us how to get back home."

Hugo grunted agreement and made fists with his huge hands, but Mr Bones looked doubtful. "I am sure she will be wary of enemies. This article refers to her bodyguards who accompany her at all times."

"But we can get close to her," Aelfed said, "We can find out where she lives and works." She opened her leather knapsack and took out a very modern smart phone.

"We can do that," Mr Bones acknowledged. "It says here that she owns a company called, well, would you believe it, it's called Electrum."

"The brazen witch," Tenplessium cried almost bouncing out of the chair. "She's goading us. Why else should she name her company after that which she stole from my Queen."

I had been listening to the excited conversation and was still somewhat confused. I ventured a question, "Does she even know all of you and me are here? After all, I had no idea of your existence until you knocked on my door."

Mr Bones scratched his chin with a long, thin finger. "You are right Mr Hohenheim. She entered the Parting before us and may think that the tales of that border between worlds would prevent anyone from following her."

"What tales?" I asked.

"That nothing and no-one has ever returned," Mr Bones said. "That is a recurring theme of my dreams. They suggest we are trapped in this universe. Do you agree?" He looked around our little gathering. The fairy and the elf nodded, even the ogre grunted agreement, and the mouse on my shoulder, which I had almost forgotten about, squeaked.

I had a thought. "If this witch knew those tales but came here anyway then she must have a plan."

Mr Bones nodded. "That would seem to be a reasonable assumption."

"So, this company she runs is part of that plan," I went on. The four of them nodded again. "Perhaps we should find out what the company does."

Aelfed held up her phone. "Her wiki page says that having made a fortune in IT, she is carrying out development of innovative energy systems."

"Er, what does that mean?" I asked.

Tenplessium and Mr Bones shrugged while Hugo sat immobile and dumb.

"I think we need to investigate," Aelfed said.

"We do," Mr Bones agreed, "where does she do this innovative work?"

Aelfed peered at her small screen. "The only address is in the centre of London."

"Then we must go there." Mr Bones stood. "Are you all coming?"

Tenplessium, Aelfed and Hugo all jumped up. The mouse on my shoulder squeaked excitedly. I stayed quiet.

"Mr Hohenheim. You don't seem eager to join us." Mr Bones said, staring at me with those dark, hollow eyes.

"I've never been to London," I said, noticing a whine in my voice which disappointed me. "I've never even been out of Little Waggleford."

"Nonsense," Mr Bones said. "You are the adventurous gnome who travelled from the Kingdom of the Fairies to the Land of the Elves in pursuit of the witch and the electrum."

"I did?"

"Search your memories of your dreams – or rather the dreams of your memories. That was your true life. This homeliness is the false life. We need you. We need your luck."

"Come with us, please," Aelfed said.

Tenplessium came at me with her fists clenched. I thought she was about to assault me but she stopped in front of me.

"Don't worry, Mr Hohenheim. We'll protect you from

danger. I may have been an actor here, but back there I was a fighting fairy, a leading member of the Queen's militia."

I felt a heavy hand on my shoulder. It was Hugo. He grunted something which I think was intended as encouragement.

Mr Bones headed towards my front door with the others behind him. I followed, finding I was drawn along with them though I trembled at the thought of an exciting and dangerous quest. I had the presence of mind to grab a jacket and pull the door closed behind me.

"How are we going to get to London?" I asked.

Mr Bones paused and raised a long, thin arm. "There is our transport."

I looked to where he was pointing, to the lane beyond my front garden. Standing there was a huge black vehicle.

"In a hearse! How do you come to possess a hearse?" I said approaching the long, tall car. The black, extravagantly curved, front wings gleamed, as did the chrome bumpers and radiator grill. The huge, round headlights stared at the road. I approached the ridiculously opulent vehicle. There was a broad seat in the front and behind, a polished wood byre that was thankfully empty.

Mr Bones opened the drivers' door. "My life here was spent as an undertaker. I kept the car when I retired, but that was before I arrived. They are all false memories. Come on, get in. Hugo and Mr Hohenheim in the front. Tenplessium and Aelfed lie down in the back."

"Is the mouse coming too?" I said noting that the creature was gripping onto the shoulder of my jacket.

"Of course, he is," Aelfed said, "Major Mouse is an important member of our company. He'll find a cosy pocket I expect."

I walked around the high bonnet of the Daimler. Hugo was holding the passenger door open and indicated I get in between him and Mr Bones. The mouse did as the elven girl said and scrambled down into the pocket of my jacket.

"Are you secure in the back there," Mr Bones called

out. There were high pitched affirmations from behind me. Mr Bones pressed the starter button and the big engine rumbled into life. The hearse began to move.

"Now we just have to find our way to London and the sorceress' lair. At least we have most of the day ahead of us."

The car rolled from side to side as we turned from my lane onto the highway.

"The sooner we can get there the better," cried out Tenplessium, "Every extra hour we have to search for the witch will be a help."

Mr Bones nodded and bent over the large steering wheel. We picked up speed.

I cannot say that I have travelled in a hearse before, or indeed in any transport on motorways, but it would have been adequately comfortable if Mr Bones had not driven like a madman. He seemed determined to beat all the traffic to the city and swerved around any vehicle that had the gall to remain in front of us. At least I was securely wedged between the broad torso of Hugo taking up half of the bench seat, and the knobbly limbed Mr Bones whose hat was pressed against the roof lining. I could only imagine how the two smaller people behind us were avoiding being flung around the large space usually reserved for a coffin.

Despite the hair-raising journey, I did have opportunity for reflection. The more I thought about my dreams and what Mr Bones and the others had said, the more memories of this other life surfaced. I felt as though I had had two existences running in parallel and it became increasingly difficult for me to decide which was real. This world with its metal boxes speeding along strips of tarmac was obviously real for now, but my life in the other world was so much more exciting than my remembered existence here. It was also filled with such a wide variety of beings – fairies, elves, gnomes, ogres, plus intelligent and belligerent mice, re-animated skeletons and dark phantoms as well as malignant mages.

After a considerable time, I realised we were approaching our destination. The city closed around us, brick and concrete replacing green fields and wooded hills.

"What do you intend doing when we reach the building you saw in the newspaper?" I asked.

Mr Bones did not answer but from behind me came a breathless and high-pitched voice. "Mr Hohenheim is right. What are we going to do Bones? Don't you think we should discuss our tactics and formulate a plan?"

"And have some lunch," Aelfed added.

"Lunch?" Mr Bones cried, "When every hour, every minute is vital in our quest."

"I think eating is important too," Aelfed said. Beside me, Hugo grunted in what I presumed was agreement.

"Oh, alright," Mr Bones said, turning the steering wheel abruptly. The hearse lurched to the left. We left the main roadway, following a narrower road which led to a group of buildings surrounded by an array of vehicles some large, some small.

"Oh, good," Aelfed said with obvious joy. "A service area."

The hearse drew to a halt and we all tumbled out. Aelfed led us into the nearest building which turned out to be a collection of establishments dispensing what Tenplessium called fast food, which I had never experienced in either of my lives. We sat around a table while Mr Bones went to a counter from which he returned with a tray loaded with card boxes. My companions fell on the food which I found singularly un-nutritious.

Aelfed had her mouth filled with a mixture of fried potato, bread and grilled flesh. The fatty smell of it made me feel a little sick.

"So, what are we going to do when we meet the witch?" she said.

Mr Bones shrugged. He was contemplating a single chip that he held between a finger and thumb. "We don't even know if she will be at the building."

Tenplessium replied with a raised clenched fist. "Oh, we will find her and then we will take back the electrum that belongs to the Queen of the Fairies."

Mr Bones sighed. "You forget that we have no idea what form the electrum takes in this world. We are all changed to fit in with this world's laws; the electrum must be changed too."

All my companions stared at their food without speaking. Although all obviously human, except for the mouse that remained curled up in my pocket, we were a diverse collection of tall, short, broad and thin. Some of the other travellers looked at us with expressions of surprise. I suppose it was that, most of all, that reinforced my growing sense that we were not of this world, and that our quest was not a nonsensical flight of fancy.

"She must be changed too," I said, "even though you recognised her in the photograph. Perhaps she is still confused by this world, like I am, like we are."

Mr Bones shook his head slowly. "No, she had some reason for coming through the Parting into this world and was obviously confident that she could pursue her plan regardless of the changed circumstances. The fact that she has become a successful businesswoman, a celebrity, shows that she is adept at fitting into this world's structures." He paused. "However, she may not have expected any of us to follow her, so if we confront her, we will have the advantage of surprise." He looked at me and the thin smile spread across his face. "And who knows how your luck will help us, gnome."

"So, let us continue," Tenplessium said, "let us enter her lair and confront her."

"I'm ready," Aelfed said, jumping from her chair. She swallowed the last morsel of her meal and swept the whole collection of cardboard packaging into a nearby rubbish receptacle.

Mr Bones eased himself up to his full height. "I suspect, elf, that this delay was *solely* so you could eat one of these ghastly meals."

"That's right, Bones," Aelfed said, grinning, "but we

haven't lost much time." She turned and hurried from the building with the rest of us following.

It did not take very much longer to reach our destination. Aelfed called out directions from behind Mr Bones' head, directions which she gleaned from her smart phone. They led us to the heart of the capital, with tall towers all around us. Memories of Elfholm were clear in my mind now, though there was little similarity between the straight lines and sharp angles of the shiny metal and glass I saw from the windows of the hearse, and the fluid curves, grey stone and confused pinnacles in my head. We came to a stop in a layby alongside a golden building with the single word Electrum above the doors in large, curly letters.

"This is it," Mr Bones said, turning off the engine.

Tenplessium leaned over Hugo's shoulder. "Right. This attack requires military precision. Aelfed and the gnome should cause a diversion at the back of the building while you, Mr. Bones, the ogre and I storm the entrance."

Mr Bones shook his head, "No Tenplessium. That won't be necessary. Let us all stick together and let me do the talking. Remember that I worked with the witch in the other world."

"You were her faithful servant, Bones," Tenplessium accused.

"I was forced to be her servant," Mr Bones insisted, "In this world I am not bound to her. I want her evil plan stopped as much as you do, whatever it is. Now come on."

We got out of the car, Aelfed and Tenplessium leaping out of the rear. We stood in a line looking up the steps to the building, soaring into the sky amongst the other towers. Mr Bones strode ahead and the rest of us followed.

Our way through the door was barred by a man in a fancy golden coat. From his frown it seemed obvious that we were not welcome, and he would not let us enter. Although he was big and powerfully built, he was neither as tall as Mr Bones nor as bulky as Hugo. Nevertheless, he stood in our path.

"You cannot come in," the doorman said in a commanding voice.

"Why not?" Mr Bones asked, "Is Electrum not open for business?"

"Not to a rabble like you lot."

"A rabble? Us?" I could see that Mr Bones looked pained by the accusation. Tenplessium clenched her tiny fists. Mr Bones turned to Hugo. "What do you think of that Hugo?"

The ogre-like man approached the doorkeeper, wrapped his arms around him and lifted him up. Gold covered arms and legs flailed to no purpose. Mr Bones stepped forward. The doors opened.

"Come on." Mr Bones waved for us to follow him. As we passed through the doors, he added. "You can put him down now, Hugo."

Hugo dropped the doorman at the top of the steps. He tumbled down to come to a rest beside the hearse.

We had entered a vast vestibule which was empty except for a long desk against the opposite wall. There was just one young, pretty woman behind it. Mr Bones strode up to her. She looked a little alarmed having no doubt watched our entrance and the fate of the doorman.

"We've come to see the boss-woman," Mr Bones announced. He turned to Aelfed. "What's the name she's taken?"

"Dame Carmine Magus," the elvish girl replied.

"Of course, how obvious," Mr Bones said. Addressing the receptionist. "Her, we want to speak to her."

"Dame Carmine does not see visitors. She is a very busy woman."

"Busy? I am sure she is, but she will see us. Tell her that her once faithful servant has returned."

The girl's eyebrows rose in confusion, but she bent to look at a concealed screen.

While Mr Bones was busy, I looked around the hall. There were huge pictures on the walls showing views of industrial works. There were photos with lots of pipes and large shiny metal boxes in various settings, some by the sea, others in deserts. One picture was different. It didn't look as though it could be an actual photograph. It showed a sphere of brilliant light in a cavity built from cables and tubes. Was this the sorceress' innovative energy source? What did it have to do with electrum? Not that I really had much recall of what electrum itself was.

I was lost in my musing when the rumpus started. Doors at both sides of the reception desk opened and men in dark suits appeared. They were the bodyguards that had surrounded Dame Carmine in the newspaper picture. They quickly formed a ring around us. Tenplessium and Hugo looked prepared for a fight but Mr Bones calmed them.

"No, violence," he said. "I believe that these gentlemen are going to lead us to the witch."

One of the bodyguards spoke. "You will accompany us. All of you. Keep together."

The ring closed round us and moved us towards a lift whose doors had opened. There was room for all of us with four of the guards also squeezed into the compartment with us. I remembered the mouse and signalled Aelfed and Tenplessium to try not to press too closely to me. I peered into my pocket. The mouse was curled up, but his whiskers vibrated showing that he was alive and aware.

The lift rose so swiftly that my stomach felt it had been left on the ground floor. It stirred another memory of ascending a tower. The floor numbers flickered by on the indicator screen until we slowed to a stop. The doors opened. We tumbled out and I took in our new surroundings.

We were right at the top of the tower, rather as I recalled we had been in the city of the Elves. It was a large open room, with floor to ceiling windows giving a view over the city and the river.

Just rising from a vast white sofa in the middle of the floor was Dame Carmine. It was the first time I had seen her since the train, the memory of which had become steadily sharper and more well-defined as the day had gone on. She looked unchanged. Still a striking woman with long red hair, wearing a skirt and jacket that matched her colouration.

She came towards us but stopped a few steps away in order to take us all in. The four guards who had accompanied us were joined by the others from a second lift. They stood around us watching warily.

"So, these are the visitors who were so determined to see me," the sorceress said. "Now let me see." She paused with a forefinger against her deep red lips. She pointed to Hugo.

"You are obviously an ogre going by your grotesque body shape." Her finger wandered to Aelfed, "And you are an elf from your disgusting work attire." She stabbed her finger toward Tenplessium, "This little thing must be a fairy. Which means that you," she pointed at me, "are the gormless gnome. I believe you and I have met."

I found myself nodding in agreement but had no voice to reply. She faced Mr Bones and held out her hands in some kind of welcome.

"And you are Bones. What did you say to my girl downstairs? My faithful servant?"

Mr Bones remained impassive.

Dame Carmine carried on talking. "Not so faithful since you joined this rag tag band to pursue me. Who persuaded you all to follow me through the Parting?"

Mr Bones stood stiffly erect. "That was a joint decision of the fairies and elves and the others who had become involved in the pursuit of the electrum. Mr Hohenheim here was our appointed leader."

The woman stared at me with a sly grin. "I didn't know a gnome could lead a bee to honey, let alone an expedition through the Parting. Do you really think you could return home?"

My two lives now seemed equally clear to me, like two photograph albums open side by side. I had had enough of the sorceress' baiting. "Returning wasn't an issue, witch.

Our mission was to secure the electrum that you stole."

"Stole! Liberated more like. The fairies were doing nothing with it so why shouldn't I put it to use."

"But why bring it through the Parting?" Aelfed said. "You couldn't possibly know what it was like here."

A red-lipped smile spread across Dame Carmine's pale face. "Ah, but there you are wrong."

"How could you know?" Tenplessium cried, "No-one has ever passed through the Parting and back again."

"No person or being," the witch said, "but I used my spells to open a window through the fog. It permitted me to see into this world. I saw what I could do if I had a supply of electrum."

Mr Bones shrugged as if unconcerned, but I noticed that he had become tenser, more wary. "What could you possibly do with it. Electrum as we know it does not exist in this world."

"Now, wouldn't you like to know," the woman said, "and perhaps you will when we get to Broomholm."

"What is Broomholm?" I asked.

"It is where my plan is being put into action, where I will become the most powerful sorceress in this world."

Mr Bones frowned. "But, madam, magic doesn't work in this universe. No sorceress or sorcerer has any real power."

Dame Carmine let out a wild screech of laughter. "You will see! Bring them."

The guards crowded around us shuffling us back to the lifts.

The lift only rose one floor and we stepped out onto the roof. I was quite disconcerted by the expanse of sky and the panorama of many square miles of city and countryside. I much prefer a roof, or a whole mountain over my head. The view was blocked ahead of us by a very large helicopter.

The other lift's doors opened, and the witch emerged surrounded by more bodyguards.

"Why are you standing there gawping?" she screamed at our party. She was correct in that all of us were just gazing at the scene. "Get them on the transport and secure them."

The guards pushed us to the open hatch of the helicopter. I wondered whether Mr Bones would signal for us to attempt an escape, but he willingly stepped on board. I followed with the others. There were plenty of seats for the five of us and an equal number of guards. When we were seated, the guards fastened harnesses around us. Mine held me so firmly that I couldn't move my torso at all. I tried undoing the catch, but it was locked. I did manage to peer into my jacket pocket. The mouse was still sitting there, whiskers quivering. He looked content.

The witch and the rest of her guards were not with us but we were in the rear of the craft, so I presumed she had got into a more sumptuous cabin at the front.

The engine started and the rotors began to turn. In no time we were airborne and again my stomach felt as though it had left my body. I had never flown before; not in this world anyway. My memories of flying on a pigeon and on a huge black horse definitely seemed to belong to someone else.

There was a lot of noise, but Tenplessium tried to converse in her high-pitched voice. "So much for the element of surprise, Bones." The guards that accompanied us said nothing and sat motionless in their seats in front and behind us.

"The witch was prepared for any occurrence," Mr Bones replied. "No matter. She is taking us to the electrum, which is what we wanted. We must keep alert for opportunities to free ourselves and overpower her."

"Just let me get my hands on the electrum and I can use its power to defeat her," Tenplessium said.

"Are you sure you can do that?" Aelfed shouted, "Don't forget it will have changed too."

"What could it have become?" I asked.

"That is a very good question," Mr Bones said. "Electrum is the most valuable substance in our other world. What would have that designation here?"

"Gold?" I ventured.

Mr Bones shook his head. "No, electrum was more valuable than gold in our world and gold isn't even the most valuable substance in this one."

"Diamonds?" Tenplessium suggested.

Mr Bones shook his head again. "I don't think so. I'm sure there are more expensive and useful materials here. She said it is involved in her innovative energy project."

Something came into my head, something I had read in the newspapers which kept me in touch with this world while I lived my quiet life in my dark little cottage.

"What about plutonium?" I said. "It's very rare. In fact, scientists have to make it, and it's used in the most powerful nuclear weapons."

"I think you might have something there," Mr Bones said.

Aelfed was tapping at her smart phone. "Plutonium has a value of about five thousand dollars a gram while gold is about fifty dollars a gram."

Tenplessium laughed. "That's it then, plutonium is much more valuable."

"And it gives out radiation, just like electrum," Aelfed added.

"Does that mean that the witch is building nuclear weapons?" I said, feeling rather scared at the direction our conversation had taken."

"No doubt she will reveal her plans when we arrive at this Broomholm place," Mr Bones said.

"Where is it?" I asked. I had no idea where we were headed.

Tenplessium was close to a window. "The sun is almost behind us and it is mid-afternoon. We're travelling east. I'd say we're heading to Norfolk, or perhaps out into the North Sea."

"Broomholm certainly sounds like a suitable home for a witch," Mr Bones said.

For a while we contemplated our fate in silence but not much time had passed before the noise of the engine changed and I had the feeling of falling.

"I think we're nearly there," Tenplessium cried out, leaning as far as her restraining belts allowed across the guard at her side. "We are descending. I can see buildings. Good Gosh!" The guard elbowed her back into her seat.

"What is it, Tenplessium?" Mr Bones said. I too wondered what the Fairy lady had seen.

"There is a huge golden dome at the centre. What can it be?"

"A golden egg?" I suggested.

"There are no giant, magic geese in this world," Aelfed replied with a note of fear in her voice. "I wonder what the witch has built?"

Hugo grunted in agreement, and Mr Bones added "No doubt Dame Carmine will delight in informing us of her achievement before too long."

The helicopter came to rest and the engine whine died away. The guards removed their restraints and opened the door. We were released and shoved out onto the tarmac. We huddled in a group beside the craft wondering what would happen next.

There was a strong breeze, and I was sure I could smell the sea – not that I have been to the sea in either of my lives.

Dame Carmine stepped down from the forward cabin. She beckoned to one of the bodyguards.

"Bring that rabble along but make sure they stick together. I don't want one of them sneaking off and sticking their noses in places where they shouldn't." She strode away and, with guards shooing us along, we followed. We rounded the helicopter, and I had my first view of Broomholm. There were lots of buildings – some in traditional brick and concrete, others in modern steel and glass – but dominating the centre of the complex, as Tenplessium had described, was a vast golden sphere. About a quarter of it was invisible, presumably underground. It looked like a huge rising or setting sun, twice the height of the adjoining ten storey tower and a diameter of at least a hundred metres. What could possibly be happening in that vast space, I wondered, and where did electrum – or plutonium – come into it.

At the edge of the landing field, we descended a ramp which took us into a tunnel under the closest buildings. It was broad, well-lit and warm. The walls and ceiling were decorated with colourful patterns, which appeared meaningless. The floor had arrows in various colours and other symbols that also meant nothing to me.

We walked for about ten minutes, turning left and right at intersections before the sorceress stopped at a pair of double doors. She muttered something inaudibly and they slid apart with a soft whoosh. She entered the room.

The guards pushed us in, following her. We entered – well, what can I call it? – the control room, the witch's lair, her headquarters?

Chapter 7

The Sorceress

We gazed around in a huddle as the doors whooshed and clanged shut behind us. We stood on a broad balcony from where we had a view of the whole vast sphere of the building. I felt terrified by the enormous, almost empty, space as I peered over the parapet trying to make sense of the metal boxes, the tubes and cables and all the other stuff that occupied the structure below us. Directly beneath us, a platform ran out to the centre, but the rest was open. None of it made any sense. At the centre was some huge machine that shone and sparkled but whose shape and function I could not make out.

I felt movement in my jacket. I glanced down and saw the mouse scrambling out of my pocket. He descended my trousers, paused for a moment in my turn-up, dropped to the polished floor and scampered off. In a moment he was out of sight behind one of the large metallic cubes that were scattered in no apparent pattern around the space.

The sorceress had marched to the one recognisable collection of furniture, a wide raised desk with chairs which provided a panoramic view of all the activity in the sphere. She sat in the biggest chair and spun around to face us.

"Come and join me, you poor wanderers through the Parting. Welcome to Broomholm."

We hurried to get closer to her, still casting our eyes around, trying to take in the meaning of the apparatus. I could see no sign of the mouse.

"What is this place?" asked Mr Bones.

Dame Carmine smiled. "Once upon a time it was a site where they pumped gas ashore from under the sea."

"Gas?" inquired Tenplessium.

"Yes, natural gas, the crushed remains of their ancestors, dinosaurs and the like. The gas that they burn to keep warm and make electricity."

"Oh, that gas," Aelfed murmured.

"So primitive," the sorceress said, shaking her head. "Now it is my famous innovative energy research centre."

"Research?" Mr Bones said, "That doesn't sound like the sort of activity that you would engage in, madam."

She chuckled, "Well, it's a word the government and the media like. I suppose a more accurate description would be that it's the source of my world domination."

"That's more like it," Aelfed whispered.

"But without the magic powers you have in the other world, how can you achieve domination here?" Mr Bones went on.

"I don't need magic here," Dame Carmine laughed, "Here I have science and engineering, and power!"

I was confused and blurted out, "Do you mean to use the plutonium to gain power?"

The witch stared at me with a look of utter contempt. "Plutonium? What are you mumbling about?"

"Well, that's what the electrum has become in this world hasn't it. Plutonium, far more valuable than gold. It's radioactive and used in nuclear bombs." I tried to sound authoritative but knew I had failed.

She launched again. "Oh, you poor, ignorant, cave dweller. The electrum didn't become plutonium. It became something far rarer, far more powerful, far more exciting."

We all stared at her and I am sure we were all in the same state of confusion.

"What is it?" Mr Bones asked.

"A black hole!" Dame Carmine said, raising her arms and letting out a cackling laugh.

Now I haven't studied science – in either of my lives – but my quiet cottage memories did include reading a little bit about black holes.

"But black holes are huge," I cried, "They have the mass of thousands of stars. You can't carry one around in a bag like you do a hoard of electrum!"

She looked at me again with an expression of pity. "Yes, gnome, there are black holes like you describe at the centre of the galaxies in this universe. But I have a mini-black hole. It has the same mass as the electrum had – a few dozen kilograms by this world's measure – but it is packed into a space not much larger than an atom, less than a nanometre in diameter. It is so dense that it bends space-time near it and light cannot escape from it."

"What can you do with a mini black hole?" Aelfed said.

"I thought an elf would be interested. I could have done with a few of your sort when I set up this place. The people they have here are so incapable. Think about it. When any matter gets close to the mini black hole it's pulled in by its gravity. The atoms accelerate to high velocities and smash into each other releasing huge amounts of energy before the fragments fall into the black hole and make it even heavier."

"So, it is an energy source," Mr Bones commented.

"That's what the governments of the world think," Dame Carmine smiled, "In fact of course it's a very tiny weapon that could destroy the whole planet if I allowed it to drop into the centre of the Earth. Once they have given up all their other inferior sources of energy, I will have them in my power, and I will become the Empress of the Galaxy."

"Yeah, yeah, yeah," Tenplessium said, "we guessed that bit. We won't let that happen."

"Really?" the witch sneered. "It doesn't look as though you are in a position to stop me. Look around."

I did. The guards had formed a semicircle around us. Each of them held a weapon, pointed towards each one of us.

"Um, there's something else," Aelfed said.

The sorceress narrowed her eyes at the elf. "What is it, girl?"

"How do you stop the black hole dropping into the

world. You can't keep it in a box or your bag. As you said, anything close to it just gets absorbed by it."

The witch looked proud of herself. "That was the clever bit. The black hole is suspended in space by electromagnetic fields."

I could see that Aelfed was confused. "How do you do that. This world has nothing that could control a black hole, even a microscopic one, like that."

"Not now, perhaps," The sorceress replied. She paused and looked at us as if about to take us in to her confidence. "Why do you think we're here now?"

"Now?" Tenplessium and I said in unison. Hugo grunted.

"Yes, now. This period in this world's existence."

Mr Bones spoke, "Because we followed you. As your bondservant I was bound to you. Where you went, I followed, at least till we arrived here and were changed by the laws and rules of this universe."

"That is correct, my unfaithful servant. I came here at this time because the world needs me now. It is run by squabbling men, and is much in need of a source of energy that will not destroy the environment in which they live. In short, they need me to take control and give them what they require."

"But where did you get the means to hold the black hole?" Aelfed cried.

"From the future of course," the witch laughed and clapped her hands. "My window through the Parting looked on any time I desired and so I watched and learned how, in this universe's future, black holes and other exotic materials can be controlled and used."

Something in the witch's story seemed strange to me. I interrupted her tale. "If you had all this planned, why did you offer the electrum to Lord Pelladill?"

The sorceress laughed. "You worry about that little diversion? I intended to get the fairies to suspect the elves were responsible for the loss of their precious electrum and put them off track. I hoped to have a little more time before crossing the Parting."

"What stopped you?" I asked.

"You did, gnome. Your bumbling interference attracted others to follow you."

"And Lord Pelladill refused your offer," Bones said.

Carmine looked momentarily surprised. "Yes, I had not expected that. I thought elvish greed would have clouded his judgement."

I was feeling prouder of our pursuit. "So, we made you rush to the Parting."

The sorceress sniffed but then straightened and clapped her hands again. "My plans were made, though it wasn't easy to get these nincompoops to follow my instructions. Now it is done and we're almost ready to start energy production."

"Almost?" I said.

"Just a few adjustments to make," she said, just as the lights went out.

It was completely dark and, like presumably everyone else, I could not see a thing. But I am used to the dark. Gnomes spend a lot of their time in unlit tunnels under the mountains. We learn to use our hearing to determine our position and move around. There was plenty of sound. The witch, her guards, the dozens of workers, each cried and screamed when they lost their sense of sight. There were other noises too, hums and buzzes and clicks and screeches from the machinery that occupied the sphere. All the sounds allowed me to build up a picture in my mind of our surroundings.

"Gather round me," I whispered loudly to my companions. They responded and clustered around me. Hands, small and large, groped my torso from my shoulders down to my waist.

A bony head pressed against mine. It was Mr Bones. He said in a hoarse whisper, "We must use this fortuitous event to disturb the witch's plans and retrieve the electrum."

"The black hole, you mean," Aefed said.

"Whatever," Mr Bones replied, "We must get to the floor of the building. Mr Hohenheim, guide us to the edge of the balcony. I do not think we are very high up."

I took his hand from my shoulder and tugged him and the others to the parapet. "I think we are about three times my height from the floor below," I said.

"That's what I thought," he said, "Now, Hugo, make sure none of those guards get in our way."

Hugo grunted softly. Mr Bones let go of my shoulder and I heard him clambering over the edge. His next words came from over the wall of the balcony. His voice was slightly strained. "Each of you, climb down my body. You should then be able to drop to the floor."

"Can you take our weight?" I whispered. Mr Bones was more skin and bone than flesh and muscle.

"Yes, of course I can. Quickly, before the witch discovers what we are doing. Tell Hugo he will have to jump. He won't be hurt by the fall."

I took hold of an arm that was attached to my waist, Tenplessium's I think, and guided her to Mr Bones's hands gripping the edge of the balcony. She quickly climbed over and descended. Aelfed followed, then it was my turn. As I prepared to clamber over the parapet, I felt a tickle on my ankle, then a prickling up my calf and on up my thigh. I stood up straight, held in my stomach and allowed the mouse to clamber past my waistband. It continued up to my shoulders.

"Was that you that put the lights out?" I whispered. I got an answering squeak that I presumed was an affirmative. "Well thanks, now hold tight."

I thrust my leg over the balustrade and reached down until my foot touched Mr Bones' right shoulder, then I lowered my other foot onto his left shoulder. He grunted. I gripped his arms as I lowered myself down his gangly body.

"Hurry up, gnome," Mr Bones gurgled as I passed his head. "You weigh as much as the elf and fairy combined. I can't hold you much longer. I feel as if my skeleton is coming apart."

"That's happened before," I said sliding down his thighs.

"I know and I do not want to experience it again, especially in this world. Now just let go."

I did as he said and fell to the floor. I landed in a heap, but the fall had only been an arm's length or two. Hands groped my body and tugged me to my feet. There was a thump and groan as Mr Bones landed beside me, then a louder, heavier thud which I guessed was Hugo making his leap.

I listened to our surroundings. There were still shouts from above us demanding light and also some worried cries about the black hole. Our departure had not been noted, and the witch and her servants were still blundering around in the dark. The cries did show considerable concern, however, and I wondered if Major Mouse had overdone the gnawing through power lines. Perhaps as well as cutting the light circuits he had damaged the containment of the black hole.

"We must get to the black hole," I said.

"Of course," Mr Bones replied. "Lead us to the centre of the sphere. All of you, hold on."

Mr Bone's long hand gripped my shoulder – thankfully not the one that the mouse was sitting on – and I set off towards the centre of the dome. We bumped into a few of the odd shaped containers that occupied the floor, but soon we reached the huge machine that I had observed from the balcony. Its form and shape confused me and in the noise that continued behind us, I was unable to decide where we should go.

"We need to see the machine," I said.

"I have a torch in my bag," Aelfed replied.

"Why didn't you get it out before?" Tenplessium muttered.

"Because showing a light would have brought attention to us," Aelfed answered. "Gather round me so that the light doesn't escape too much.

A dim light appeared, shining on the lower parts of the machine. It was constructed of curved struts linked with a web of tubes and cables. There were also columns – as broad as me, twice as tall – at intervals around the thing.

We circled the machine trying to make sense of its construction but failing. We came to a structure different to the others. It was a large rectangular box.

"Is this a control panel?" Aelfed asked, though I don't think any of us could offer an answer. "Look there's a button."

There was indeed a single, large, red button in the middle of the vertical face of the box. In the light of Aelfed's torch I read the writing above the button. It said, "For Emergency Use Only."

"Is this an emergency?" I asked.

"I think so, don't you," replied Mr Bones.

"Should we press it?" I said again. Before any others of us could ponder the dilemma further, Tenplessium jumped up and hammered the button with her tiny hand.

Lights on top of the box began flashing bright red, and a booming voice filled the sphere.

"Containment chamber dimensional reduction process initiated. Evacuation of containment housing recommended within two minutes."

"What does it mean?" I cried.

"It means we have to get out of here, fast," Mr Bones shouted. "Aelfed, lead us with the torch. Move! Now!"

"Where?" the elf replied.

Mr Bones pushed us away from the machines shouting. "There must be an exit somewhere, probably under the balcony."

Aelfed set off at a run with the rest of us close behind. I hoped the mouse could keep hold of the shoulder of my jacket. Behind us the machine repeated its warning message, but the time was reducing in ten second intervals.

The commotion on the balcony had increased but it seemed that some had noticed our light and movement.

Dame Carmine's voice rose above the rest. "There they are. Stop them. Oh, let me out!"

It took us no more than two more repeats of the message to reach the curved wall of the building. The torchlight reflected from the golden surface. Mr Bones' prediction proved correct. There was a broad entrance below the balcony and thankfully its doors were wide open. We passed through and up the concrete ramp. Some of the witch's guards ran down towards us.

"I wouldn't come this way," Mr Bones shouted with some authority, "It's going to blow any second." The guards paused, listened to the warnings and looked at each other in a state of confusion. We ran past them.

I was puffing and struggling to get my breath by the time we reached ground level. We stopped and turned to look at the gleaming hemisphere.

We were joined by the sorceress and her guards. "You meddling idiots!" she screamed. "Do you know what you've done?"

"Um, no," I said, suddenly feeling that we might have achieved something. The witch continued to screech at us as she backed away.

That was when it happened. One moment we were standing a few dozen paces from the great golden sphere. The next, it wasn't there. There was a brief violent gust of wind and, there in front of us, was a bowl-shaped depression in the ground, the same size as the sphere but with a smooth stone surface.

"It's gone," Mr Bones said, as we all stared at the space where the dome had been.

"Not completely," Tenplessium said, "There's something down there."

Fairies are renowned for their fine sense of sight but I wondered what she could possibly see in the vast area of bare rock. I didn't get a chance to ask because she had set off, almost flying to the edge of the crater and down into it. We followed her to the edge and tentatively looked over. The fairy was actually running, not falling down into the bowl, her little legs a blur of movement. As the curve of the bowl flattened out, she slowed somewhat and right at the bottom she stopped, bent down and picked up an object. An object that fitted into the palm of her hand.

Her thin, high-pitched voice carried to us across the space. "It's a gold ball."

From behind us came the roar of engines and the whir of rotors. I turned around and saw the big helicopter taking off. It began to move towards us and the crater.

"It's the witch," Mr Bones cried, "She's going after it!"

That seemed a reasonable conclusion; the golden ball was obviously some remnant of the sphere.

"We must stop her," Mr Bones went on, "and protect the Fairy." He leapt over the edge of the crater and was gone. I took a step forward and saw his gangly figure, limbs flailing, sliding down the steep slope. Hugo and Aelfed dashed past me and launched themselves into the bowl. It looked dangerous and painful, but I knew I couldn't be left behind. I held my jacket pocket open and the mouse scrabbled down from my shoulder. Then I crouched down, crawled to the edge and swung my legs into the void. As I did so, the helicopter flew low over my head. Dame Carmine was at the open door looking down into the crater and shouting orders.

I pushed off and fell. The air was sucked from my lungs and I felt as if my stomach had hit my brain. Thankfully the rock where the golden sphere had rested was as smooth as polished marble. While my increasing speed scared me more than riding a pigeon or travelling in Mr Bones' hearse, I slid with ease. As I approached our little band, gathered around the Fairy, I began to slow, coming to a stop as the helicopter hovered overhead. Mr Bones leant down and pulled me to my feet. I brushed down my jacket and peered into the pocket. Major Mouse was curled up and quivering but apparently uninjured.

The witch was leaning out of the cabin door, arm outstretched, demanding. "Give me the ball!"

Tenplessium held it to her chest. "No, you shan't have it."

Mr Bones said, "It is obviously of some value."

"Some value!" Dame Carmine screamed and leapt out of the helicopter. She landed feet wide apart, amongst us. "Of course it's of value, it contains the black hole!"

Tenplessium held up the small golden sphere and examined it. "It's in here?"

"Where else? It's not boring into the Earth. That is the containment device I brought from the future."

"But we thought that was the big sphere, that disappeared," I said somewhat confused.

"It's the same thing," the sorceress said, exasperated. "The ball had to be expanded so that I could connect the power extraction to the technology of this era. I presume it was one of you that set off the emergency dimensional reversion."

The fairy looked sheepish.

"I thought so," Dame Carmine said glowering at her. "You've undone all the work that I have spent months planning and organising. Give the ball back to me."

Tenplessium shook her head and cupped the gold ball in her tiny hands.

"We're keeping it," Aelfed said, "If the black hole is what the electrum became then we're taking it back home."

"Back!" the witch laughed. It was not a very amusing noise. "You don't know how to get back."

"We'll find a way," Aelfed insisted.

Dame Carmine shook her head. A smile spread across her face, a very wicked smile. "No, you won't, because there's something else you don't know."

"Which is?" Mr Bones said, his hairless eyebrows rising.

"In this condensed state the containment device is temporally unstable."

I thought I understood. "You mean it might go back to its full size soon."

"Not temporarily, temporally," the witch sneered. "It is likely to return to when it originated."

I think we all paused to consider what that meant.

"So give it back," the witch shouted and lunged towards Tenplessium. The fairy reacted by lobbing the ball into the air, in my direction. I reached up and plucked it from its trajectory.

The witch froze with her arms extended. "Now you've really disturbed it."

The ball became cold in my hands and vibrated. Then I saw that everything was shimmering – my hand, my arm, the air around me, my companions, the sorceress, the rock we stood on, the sky above.

Chapter 8

In which we find ourselves in new surroundings

I awoke – or came to, I wasn't sure which – thinking I might be back in my comfy bed in my quaint little cottage, or else snug in my cosy nest under the mountains. I opened my eyes and found it was neither. I was lying on grass. At least I thought it was grass. It was green and thick, as soft and springy as a bed but with the addition of the fresh smell of lawn cuttings. My pillow turned out to be Hugo's thigh. As I moved, he stirred too and sat up with a grunt. The others were scattered in a heap of comatose bodies. I say the others, but I noticed that the sorceress wasn't amongst us.

I looked around. We were in a small meadow surrounded by towering trees that climbed a ridge. The Sun shone in a sky that was dark blue but for a few small cotton-wool clouds. It was warm.

"Hey, everyone," I called, "Are you awake? We're somewhere. Not where we were."

Aelfed sat up and rubbed her eyes. Tenplessium yawned and stretched her arms. Mr Bones kicked out his long legs and hauled himself to his feet. I looked at each of them and at myself. We were as we had been; human, sort of.

"We haven't changed or adapted to this new world," I said, "not like when we crossed the Parting."

"A sound observation, Mr Hohenheim," Mr Bones said, "That can mean only one thing."

"I know. We're still in the same universe," Aelfed said, standing up and looking around.

"But it did seem like passing through the Parting," I said. "Everything went blurry and hazy and we fell asleep, just as I did before."

"Similar, perhaps, but not the same," Mr Bones said. "The witch told us – the gold ball returned to its own time, the future, and drew us with it."

I had a sudden anxiety. Where was the gold ball? I had caught it just before everything changed. I did not have it. I looked around. It was nowhere to be seen.

"The gold ball, the black hole, it's not here!" I cried.

"Neither is the sorceress," Tenplessium pointed out. "What are the chances that she recovered first and has taken the ball to wherever she has gone."

"That is a reasonable assumption," Mr Bones said. "The question is where? Where are we and where is she?"

"In the future," Aelfed said.

Mr Bones nodded. "That is probably true, but what period of time lies between then and now?"

I shrugged. "It is impossible to tell."

Mr Bones' eyes seemed to pierce me. "You think so? Look around. What do you see?"

"Well, I can see that we've moved," I replied. "We're not at the witch's place, Broomholm. That was flat and the sea was nearby. Here the land is hilly and I detect no odour of saltwater."

"Correct my fine gnome, but have we moved across the world or has the world changed?"

"Surely we must have moved," I insisted.

"Look more closely at our surroundings." Mr Bones spread his arms hands pointing to the meadow.

"You mean, the grass?" I asked.

Aelfed was already crouching, her fingers plucking at the blades of grass. "It looks like grass, but isn't," she said in an amazed voice.

"How is it not grass?" I said stooping to look closely. I had been something of a gardener in the life spent in my little cottage. I knew plants. A close examination provided the answer. The grass while green and covering the ground was, as Aelfed had noted, not grass. There was no vein running up the centre of each blade. Each blade was exactly the same length and width and it felt more spongy than true grass. The colour too was not quite right – darker, bluer.

"Is it artificial?" I asked, "Perhaps we are in a future garden, where natural plants have been replaced by something?"

Tenplessium had also picked up some of the grass. She put it in her mouth and chewed.

"I don't normally eat grass, so I couldn't say if this tastes likes grass but it is definitely living. There is water, sugars, and other flavours almost like nectar." Since fairies consumed a great deal of nectar, I presumed she knew what she was talking about.

"Look at the trees," Mr Bones commanded, flinging out his arms at the trunks climbing to the sky. "Can you identify them, any of you?"

I know well the pine trees that covered the mountains under which I was born and grew up. I was familiar with the trees of all kinds that flourished around where my cottage was set. These trees did look a little odd, and resembled none of my memories. They were tall, with perfectly straight, smooth trunks and boughs that thrust out at right angles at very regular intervals. The leaves seemed to have a blueish tint to their green.

"They do look different," I said, "Perhaps we are in the tropics. I've never seen tropical trees, and it *is* warm." In fact, I realised how hot I had become. Sweat dripped from my beard and my jacket felt thick and constricting around my body. I shrugged it off, taking care to look in the pocket. Major Mouse was awake and took the opportunity to scamper up the cloth and onto my arm. He brushed his ears with deliberation.

"You make an important observation, Mr Hohenheim, but I think your conclusion is incorrect," Mr Bones said. He too removed his coat revealing his thin arms and almost fleshless body clothed in a white shirt.

"Look at the Sun," Tenplessium said. I did as she said, lifting my spare hand to shield my eyes from the glare. There was something different, but I couldn't quite decide what it was.

"It's larger," Aelfed said.

"And redder," Tenplessium added.

"And, therefore, it must be older," Mr Bones concluded.

"Older?" I repeated. "What do you mean? How much older?"

"Millions of years, a billion or two," Mr Bones said.

"What?" I cried. "But that's, that's, er, a long time."

Mr Bones nodded, "Time enough for the Sun to start to swell and give off more heat. Time for new grass and trees and other lifeforms to evolve. I doubt whether there will be people that we recognise here in this time."

"But, but, but," I was having trouble making sense of what he had said. "How do you have such knowledge, Mr Bones. This is not our world."

Mr Bones nodded. "That is true but in my long career as an undertaker I had plenty of time to read up about this world, this universe, which is markedly different to our own. The Sun is not a glowing ball hauled in a chariot across the heavens. Here it is a vast sphere of incandescent gas which exists for billions of years, but undergoes change."

I felt quite embarrassed at my failure to note all the changes that Mr Bones had spotted, but our reason for being here was at the forefront of my anxiety.

"Dame Carmine told us that she brought back the black hole and the gold ball thing from the future to whatever you want to call the time where we were. I presumed she meant a few decades, a century or two perhaps, from a time when humans had developed their sciences even more."

The others nodded, even Hugo grunted.

"That is what she seemed to suggest," Mr Bones agreed. "But I think we'll find that this time is very different to the one that we just left. I will be surprised if it was humans who mastered the handling of black holes."

"So where is she?" Tenplessium said spinning on her toes and glaring into the trees. "And what has she done with the black hole or the electrum or whatever it really is in this time."

We all looked into the forest that appeared to enclose our little meadow. There was no hint of which direction the witch had left us. As we stared, I saw movement.

I pointed. "Look over there. Someone is coming."

Two figures emerged from under the trees and approached us across the meadow. At first I thought they were two people in white suits, but as they got closer their appearance became more confusing. Like humans, and indeed the five of us, they had a head on top of a body, two arms and two legs, but that was where the resemblance ended. Their legs bent as they walked but not in the same way that the bones in legs usually bend at joints. They were not wearing white suits but were naked. Their skins were smooth, hairless and uniformly pale white with no hint of gender. Their arms swung at their sides, but like their legs, apparently lacked bones. The faces were blank – no mouth, no nose, no eyes nor ears. No hair either. They walked side by side, in step, like identical twins or like two identical dolls.

They reached our group and stopped. They were a little taller than me and slimmer than Hugo. They seemed to be examining us but, lacking eyes, I did not know how they were doing it.

Mr Bones spoke. "Greetings. We are visitors."

There was no reply.

"What are you?" Tenplessium demanded, placing herself in front of the newcomers. "You're not from any peoples of which we are familiar."

"We wish you no harm," Aelfed added. Unnecessarily I thought, since I didn't think we presented a belligerent appearance even though Tenplessium had adopted a defensive pose.

"We are following another, the sorceress. She has red hair," I said, somewhat pointlessly.

One of the creatures stepped forward and took the grass blades that Aelfed was still holding from her hand. It closed its palm over them in a way that no hand with bones could manage. After a few moments the hand opened again. The grass had gone.

"That's a clever trick," I said.

"I think it absorbed the grass," Aelfed said.

A hole formed in the centre of the other creature's face. There was no evidence of teeth or a tongue or even of lips. It came as a surprise when a sound emerged from it, a flute-like tone. The sound modified in tone and timbre until it became speech-like.

"Follow," was the word I recognised.

We looked at one another, each no doubt wondering what these strange creatures were. They turned and moved away.

"I see no reason why we shouldn't obey them," Mr Bones said. "Maybe they'll lead us to the witch."

We fell into step behind them heading back the way they had come.

"What type of being are they?" I asked.

"Not human, fairy, elf, gnome, ogre or mage," Tenplessium replied.

"Not even any resemblance to a mouse," Aelfed added. Major Mouse on my shoulder, squeaked some kind of agreement.

"I am wondering if they are even animals," Mr Bones said.

Following behind the two strange creatures I had a whiff of an odour that they emitted. It seemed familiar. It took me back to dark, damp chambers under the mountains and moist, shady patches of my garden.

"They smell like fungus," I said.

Tenplessium frowned. "You mean they're mushrooms?"

I wasn't sure what I meant, but the idea seemed ridiculous.

"Hmm," Mr Bones said. "That's not such a silly idea. Fungi have many unique attributes and perhaps in a billion years from the time we are familiar with, they may have evolved to move, to speak, and to think." That seemed a most extraordinary theory, but I had to admit that he might possibly be correct.

We had now passed from the open meadow into the shelter of the trees. Far overhead the canopy made an almost complete shield for the fierce, reddish Sun. It was dark as dusk amongst the smooth, upright trunks, and the air felt damp and cool. The dark brown soil was bare of plants, but that smell was stronger. I had no doubt that beneath the surface there were tendrils of fungus. I began to have the feeling that we were being watched, sensed, and not just by our two guides.

Generally, the trees were uniformly spaced in a hexagonal pattern a few arm spans apart, but we reached a clearing where there was more room between the trunks. The boughs still bridged the space however, meaning that it was no lighter. We peered through the blue-green gloaming. In the centre of the space there were indeed a group of mushrooms. Each was traditionally shaped with a stem and cap, but they were far larger than the mushrooms I had picked from the fields or the chambers within the mountains. They were uniformly white, and their texture was so similar to our two guides that Tenplessium and Bones' fanciful theories were obviously correct. The two creatures stepped within the patch of mushrooms and stood still. Their feet and legs seemed to become one with the soil – or rather, what lay beneath it.

The one that had developed a mouth spoke again. "Sit," was all it said.

We each settled to the ground, the fairy and the elf cross-legged, the others of us, less agile, in a tangle of legs. Major Mouse remained on my shoulder, whiskers twitching.

I had barely made myself vaguely comfortable, resting my hands in the earth, when I felt a tickle on my ankles and wrists. I looked down and saw fine white fibres twisting around my limbs.

"Ah, what is happening?" I cried. Tenplessium and Aelfed were wriggling while Hugo seemed confused.

"Do not struggle," Mr Bones said. Already his lower legs and arms were encased in the white threads. "I think this is the fungal mycelium, of which our guides form a free-moving part. I am assuming it wishes to communicate with us."

"Are you sure it doesn't want to consume us?" I said, finding my legs and arms becoming more tightly bound to the ground.

"We will be captive, if we do not break free soon," Tenplessium said. She wriggled her legs but was unable to free them.

"I hope that will not be necessary," Mr Bones added.

I wondered if we would soon be encased in the fungus like a spider's victims bound in silk, but the fungus stopped wrapping our limbs. We were each held to the ground, but I felt that with a bit of force I could break free. That was when I started feeling drowsy.

My head swam and my eyes closed but I did not fall into a sleep. Instead, it was as if I and my companions were joined by an incorporeal other, like a spirit or cloud, that covered us and filled us. I felt emotions in addition to my own. I was apprehensive, anxious, not a little afraid, but these other feelings were curiosity, wisdom, authority. I realised that these feelings came from outside me, from the mycelium which, I now understood, was spread beneath us in the soil throughout the forest and the meadow and indeed across the continents of the world. I was sharing its thoughts and those of my companions.

<<The mycelium is communicating with us>> Mr Bones thought. I was only slightly surprised to find myself sharing his and the others' thoughts and feelings.

<<How?>> I asked.

<<I do not fully understand, but I think it is blending its fluids with our blood, sharing compounds. It is a language of chemistry.>>

<<You are like the other.>> The statement popped into my head, but I felt as though it was in every part of my body.

<<You mean the witch, who came here before us.>> I thought. Somehow my thoughts were carried in my bloodstream to mix with the fluids in the fungal mass.

<<Witch? That is a new compound with no meaning to me. The other has a composition like your own and an independent consciousness. My deep memory knows it as an animal, a consumer, a destroyer. Creatures such as those that were once our enemies.>>

<<Once? Do you mean in the past?>> That was Tenplessium's thoughts, <<Are there no animals now, no insects, worms, mammals?>>

It occurred to me that we had seen none of these creatures since we arrived. No birds had flown over the meadow nor called through the trees, no insects had fluttered near us or been seen creeping through the grass.

<<No more,>> said the mycelium, <<They attacked us and the producers which provide me with sustenance.>>

<<Producers? You mean the trees and the grass?>> Aelfed asked.

<<All plants. Animals threatened them so I disposed of them.>>

<<You destroyed all animals?>> I was struggling to understand the power of the organism that had captured us. It was only a fungus. Only? Who was I fooling?

<<They were unnecessary. Plants provide the nutrients I require and I supply them with the minerals they need and disperse their material when they have ceased to be of use.>>

It was clear that the world was very different in this future time.

<<Hey,>> Tenplessium exclaimed. Well, it felt like it. <<We're animals!>>

<<I am aware of that. Eons have passed since I last sensed the presence of consumers such as yourselves and the other.>>

Mr Bones shared his thoughts. <<The witch told us she had looked into this world. Why did she decide to come to this time when only you are sentient?>>

<<The other brought something I desired.>>

<<What could the witch give you?>> Tenplessium said.

<<Surprise. Challenge. Insight.>> I felt an excitement

in the fungus but what that meant it was capable of, I didn't know.

<<What did she want?>> Mr Bones asked.

<<Technology.>>

<<What do you know of technology?>> Aelfed seemed to be sneering, <<We saw no technology here, just grass and trees and your mushrooms. What do you need technology for?>>

<<To grow.>>

<<You said the plants give you sustenance.>> That was Tenplessium again. << Isn't that enough?>>

<<I also need space.>>

<<But you have the whole world>> I cried.

<<I fill the whole world. I need more room to grow.>>

Mr Bones joined in <<You want more than one world?>>

<<Yes.>>

<<You mean to expand to other worlds?>>

<<Yes.>>

<<The witch helped you?>>

<<She promised.>>

Ah, that was when I became worried. When had the sorceress ever kept her promises.

<<So, she promised to take you, or part of you, to other planets,>> I began.

<<Yes.>>

<<What did she want in return?>>

<<Containment for the materials she possessed and a means to transport it to other times.>>

<<The electrum?>> I said excitedly.

<<The black hole,>> Mr Bones corrected.

I was fully occupied with the silent conversation between us and the fungus. It seemed the natural thing to be aware of the thoughts and feelings and memories, yes, the memories, of my companions and this strange creature that had us bound. I had become detached from our surroundings and even from my own body.

The scratching came as a surprise.

I became aware once again of my arms. Or rather, one

arm. There was a prickling around my wrist of what felt like a dozen sharp pins. They irritated me enough to cause me to open my eyes. I didn't take in everything at once, but I did see the mouse gnawing away at the fungal thread that bound my wrist. Its tiny claws pressed into my skin as it tore at the tendrils with all the strength the small creature could muster. My contact with the others had been interrupted and I had recovered enough of my independence to look around. I think that what was what Major Mouse intended.

I was half buried in the loose soil, my legs and my other arm encased in the fungal stuff. Alongside me my companions were also wrapped liked mummies. I realised what was happening. The fungus was absorbing us, sucking not only our thoughts from us but our lives. It had lulled us into a false sense of calm with its conversation and explanations while attacking us as it had no doubt done to those long extinct animals. The fungus though huge, was however weak and Major Mouse had stirred me.

I tore my other arm from the fungus' grip, snapping each thread and I helped the mouse tear the remaining strands of fungus from my wrist. The mouse ran up to my shoulder squeaking frantically.

"Yes, Major, thank you for coming to our rescue again. I will rouse the others." First though I had to retrieve my legs from the fungal mass. Feeble though the mycelial fibres were there were a lot binding my ankles and calves. I had to use all the force I could muster to pull my legs from the earth. As soon as I was free, I went to Mr Bones. I could only tell it was him because it was the longest of the cocoons that lay in the ground. I tore and pulled at the fungus freeing his arms and legs and neck. He started to come round. I urged him to move while I went on to free Hugo, Tenplessium, and Aelfed.

Before I had them all free and aware, I realised that a change was taking place in the fungus. New threads appeared above the soil, spreading and groping for us. No doubt the fungus was disturbed by the breakdown in communication. Perhaps it was getting angry.

The others were rising to their feet, rubbing their heads, brushing the remaining fungal fibres from their bodies, examining their wrists. I looked at mine. There was a rash of tiny blood blisters where the fungus had first made contact.

"Thank you, gnome," Aelfed said. "I think you saved us from being absorbed by the fungus."

"It was Major Mouse we have to thank, again," I replied.

"Indeed, he has my gratitude," Mr Bones said. "The fungus would soon have ingested all our knowledge and experiences as well as our bodies."

As he spoke a mound appeared in the earth. It quickly grew, the soil sliding off to reveal one of the mobile mushrooms. It may have been one of the two that had met us or a new one. Once it was free of the buried mycelium it lurched towards us.

Its speaking-hole opened. "Return. You will be absorbed."

"No, we won't," Tenplessium shouted. She leapt forward and took a swing with her short arms. Her hand connected with the white creature's head. There was sharp 'snap' and the head broke off and fell to the ground, but the body did not fall. It stepped forward with its tentacle-like arms groping for the fairy. Hugo stepped up and pummelled it with his fists. Bits of mushroom flew in all directions till there was nothing left.

"That's got rid of that one," Mr Bones said, "but there will be more. I am sure the fungus has other means of destroying animals."

"Where can we go?" I cried. "The fungus is everywhere, under the trees, the meadow."

"There's possibly once place it isn't," Aelfed said. "Follow me." She ran off up the slope through the trees. We all followed.

"Where are we going," I gasped. Already the incline was taxing me.

"I think the top of the ridge is bare. Perhaps the fungus doesn't grow on exposed rock."

"A good idea," Mr Bones said. With his long legs he had already outpaced the elf and was climbing through the trees.

I sneaked a glance behind me. There were more of the mushrooms emerging from the soil. That sight was enough to get me moving faster. Soon I was puffing and panting hard.

My heart was thudding in my chest and my beard was soaked with sweat as I climbed, following my companions. I was only able to keep going by what my occasional glances behind showed me. A growing band of the mushrooms – dozens, hundreds – was following us. They emerged from the soil between the trees and joined the fungal army. They voiced no cries but the squelching of their broad foot pads in the soil and the strange creasing of their limbs produced a noise like a sponge being squeezed that grew in volume as their numbers increased.

Having experienced the mycelium's charm once I was not about to be fooled again. I was not going to be captured by a regiment of toadstools. I kept moving though my legs ached and my lungs struggled to suck in air.

At last, I emerged into the red sunlight on the ridge. Aelfed had been correct. There was bare rock where neither trees, nor grass, nor fungus grew. With my last dregs of energy, I hauled myself onto the grey crag, and stood alongside my companions.

We had reached the highest peak and looking out over the canopy of the nearest trees we could see the forest stretching in all directions, up and down the hills and valleys. The uniform carpet of blue green was only broken by small meadows where the sort-of-grass had a slightly different shade. I was wondering if there would be a similar view from every hilltop on the planet, when Aelfed tugged on my arm.

"They're coming. Look!" She pointed down to the trunks from which we had just emerged. The horde of walking mushrooms were climbing towards us.

"There's nowhere else for us to go." Tenplessium stated calmly. "We're going to have to fight." She raised her fists. I was worried. Although the mushrooms had been shown to be fragile, there were a lot of them coming for us. Then Mr Bones let out a cry.

"Look at the treetops. What's happening?"

A haze had formed over the crowns of the trees surrounding our eyrie. First in wisps and then in thicker clouds a vapour was rising and spreading up the ridge towards us. It looked like a natural occurrence, but I guessed that it was a response to our attempt at escape. The fungus through its contact with the roots of the trees could control everything they did including releasing the mist from the leaves of the trees. At first it seemed harmless, nothing more than a rain cloud forming below us and drifting up to us. As the first tendrils of vapour crept over the edge of our promontory an odour reached my nostrils. Almonds.

"It's poison!" I cried, "Cover your faces!" I hooked my elbow across my nose and my companions copied me. It was hardly enough to stop the gas. We needed fresh air to breathe.

Chapter 9

In which breathing is a relief

I held my breath until my lungs felt they would burst. Then I felt the grip of Major Mouse's tiny feet on my shoulder loosen. He slid down my chest, his fall only slightly slowed by his claws catching in the threads of my shirt. I grabbed him with my spare hand and held him in a loose grip. The mouse appeared to be unconscious, and I feared that I would be soon. The others were staggering, their legs buckling. Tenplessium and Aelfed, being shorter leaned against Hugo. The mist was growing thick around us and only Mr Bones' head remained above it. My eyelids felt heavy and my head felt it was going to roll off my shoulders.

"Quickly. Get on board!"

I looked up and while my vision wavered, I could see a craft hovering beside the cliff. It was egg-shaped and constructed from a translucent glass-like material. That was about all I took in other than the open hatch in its side and the sorceress beckoning us to step from the rock. One by one each of us, staggered, fell and collapsed into the vehicle. I was last, my head spinning as my legs turned to jelly. Then the door closed. Were we safe?

The air smelled of lemons. I breathed deeply, sucking air into my aching chest. My head began to clear. Major Mouse stirred in my hand. I unfolded my fingers to see him sitting up and brushing his whiskers. All of us were sprawled on the floor of the cabin, holding our heads, coughing, spluttering, groaning.

The witch stood with her legs apart and hands at her waist. Her holdall rested on the floor beside her.

"Well, are you going to thank me for rescuing you," she laughed.

Mr Bones hauled himself to his feet. His head brushed against the low curved roof of the craft.

"I am grateful, Madam, but I also wonder why?"

The witch laughed again, "Why? Why should you thank me?"

"No. Why did you rescue us? I am sure it would suit your plans, whatever they may be if your pursuers were halted."

The sorceress' mirth subsided. "I suppose I could do without your pathetic but persistent efforts to recover the electrum, but I could not allow you to be absorbed into the fungus."

"Why not?" Tenplessium said, joining Mr Bones in facing the witch.

"Because everything absorbed by the fungus becomes part of its memory. After a billion years it has a lot of knowledge stored across the whole world."

Aelfed added a question. "So? What are our lives and memories to you?"

The sorceress shrugged, "Your lives mean nothing to me but your memories and knowledge of our own world are very important."

I had got as far as sitting up. "It's that promise you made to the fungus isn't it."

She looked confused as if she struggled with the meaning of the word, promise.

I explained, "You told it you would help it to expand off this world."

"That was its request."

"Where were you proposing to take the fungus?" Mr Bones asked.

The sorceress shook her head vigorously. "Nowhere. There is no place suitable here. None of the planets that circle the Sun would sustain the fungus and the plants it uses as a source of sustenance."

"I see," Tenplessium said, nodding, "You tricked the fungus into giving you what you wanted by making a false promise."

"I made no promises."

"The fungus seemed to think you had," I said. Carmine shrugged showing little concern.

"What did you want from the fungus?" Aelfed asked.

"Technology," she said.

I recalled our own conversation. "It said it provided you with containment for the electrum, er, the black hole. The gold ball?"

The witch nodded, "That's it. I knew that when I brought the electrum into this world it would change and I needed something that would hold it safely."

Aelfed was shaking her head. "I don't get it. How could the fungus provide you with a gold ball? It lives off the trees and the grass."

Dame Carmine had recovered her chuckle. "Oh, it does a lot more than that. It has grown to cover the whole world, and evolved to not just extract minerals from the soil that the plants need but to excavate the rock beneath it and extract and dissolve compounds. In its billion years of existence, it has learnt all about the properties of different elements and the forces of nature. It learned from the civilisations it displaced and can do all sorts of wonderful things, such as build this craft for me."

For the first time I looked around. The craft wasn't very big, about the same size as the lounge of my cottage, with a lower ceiling. It was like what I had seen from the outside, a glass egg.

"So, the fungus can make a glass flying machine," I said, masking how impressed I was with the craft that had rescued us.

The witch laughed again. "This isn't glass. It's diamond and it's powered by my black hole. To get you as far away from the fungus as possible we are currently heading towards the Sun at a quarter of the speed of light."

There was no sensation of moving at all. I couldn't believe it. Neither apparently could the others.

"Madam, you are telling tales," Mr Bones said.

"See for yourself," the sorceress said. She didn't move but a portion of the eggshell behind us turned from translucent to clear. The sky was dark – black in fact – and there in the middle was a glowing blue globe, sporting continents I recognised from my memories of living in my cosy cottage. Well, almost recognised; some of them seem rather misshaped. The disc was getting visibly smaller as I watched.

"The fungus made a spaceship for you?" Aelfed said, her eyes wide open.

"Yes. I explained what was required and the fungus used its knowledge to grow it, no problems."

I could see that Mr Bones was frowning. "Why hadn't the fungus built its own ship and taken itself elsewhere?"

The witch looked impatient. "Because while it has immense knowledge it has little imagination. It hadn't thought to build a spaceship till I suggested it."

Bones persisted with his questioning, "Where then did the fungus think you were going to take it?"?"

Dame Carmine snorted, "I suppose it thought I would take it to an Earth-like world but as a solitary being it has no expertise in negotiation. It was easily manipulable and gullible. I had no intention of doing anything at all. You lot however, would have given it what it wants."

We all stared at her.

"What do you mean, Madam?" Mr Bones said.

"The reason why I rescued you," the sorceress said, "If you had been absorbed, the fungus would have found out about our home, our world and it would have gone there."

"It doesn't know where you are from?" Aelfed said.

"No. I let it think I was from another time or another place in this universe."

I was still confused, "But why did you enter into any agreement with the fungus at all?"

For a moment the witch looked sad. "There's no magic in this universe. I had no powers. I needed the fungus' abilities to control the black hole and to send me back in time to establish my dominion over the civilisation of the humans."

Mr Bones spoke. "What was the point if the civilisation passed away and all that was left was the fungus."

"I planned that under my control, the future would be changed and I would reign for ever." The sorceress's voice rose in pitch and her eyes gleamed. She really was mad.

"We stopped that silly plan," Tenplessium said.

"Oh no, you haven't," the witch screamed.

We were all focussed on the witch. All except Hugo. I glanced down and saw that he was still lying on the floor of the craft. Then I let out a cry and knelt down to examine him.

"What is it?" Mr Bones said.

"Look at Hugo," I replied. Hugo's face and hands were covered with fine white threads. They were spreading across his body inside and outside his clothes. Some were growing into the air like tiny fingers feeling for something.

"It's the fungus!" Aelfed cried.

Dame Carmine laughed but it wasn't out of good humour. "It is indeed. You've brought it with you."

"How?" I asked.

"You must have had contact with one of the fungus's sprouting bodies."

"You mean the walking mushrooms?" I said.

The witch nodded, "They were a new product of the fungus, modelled on you and me. But just like mushrooms they're packed with spores. Spores which can grow and develop into a new form of the fungus."

Aelfed said, "They must have got on him when he smashed that mushroom."

"But I hit it too," Tenplessium said. She held out her arm. More of the fine, white, strand dangled from her hand. "Ugh, get it off me." She shook her hand violently but the fungal threads remained stuck to her."

The witch cackled. "They'll grow into your body, digesting your flesh, and turn your substance into itself."

"You've got to stop it," I cried. I knelt beside Hugo watching him become covered by the mass of mould.

"Hmm, I suppose so," the sorceress said. "I don't want any of the fungus with me wherever I am. Get away from the ogre, gnome. You, fairy, you're contaminated. You lie next to him.

I scrambled away from Hugo's inert body. Aelfed and Mr Bones moved to the back of the craft. Tenplessium lay beside Hugo. The fairy looked exceedingly worried – I felt the same. Could the witch be trusted? I didn't know.

Dame Carmine stepped back and muttered something.

"What was that?" I said

"Shh, I am commanding my craft. Keep as far from them as you can."

A radiance appeared in the diamond walls; a ring over and under the two prostrate figures. It became brighter and bluer until I could not look anymore. I closed my eyes and turned my head away but still I saw the blue light through my eyelids. It shone for moment after moment until it began to fade.

The dazzling light had gone but when I opened my eyes everything looked dark. It took a while before I could see anything clearly again. Hugo and Tenplessium still lay on the floor, but I could see no sign of the fungus on their bodies.

"They'll probably have a severe case of sunburn," the witch said, "but that should have got rid of the fungus."

"You killed it with ultra-violet light," Aelfed said.

"Yes. The fungus can't stand bright light. It lives in the dark and has grown used to a redder Sun."

Hugo and Tenplessium stirred and sat up. The fairy examined her hands. "You're sure it's all gone?"

"It shouldn't have had time to penetrate beneath your skin. Your immune system should be able to handle any fragments that did."

"I suppose I should thank you," Tenplessium said. She sounded reluctant.

"Oh, don't bother," the sorceress said. "I've got rid of one problem. Now I have to deal with another."

"What problem?" I said.

"What to do with you."

I saw Tenplessium tense as if about to fly at the witch.

Dame Carmine held up her hand. "Don't think of

attacking me. The craft will protect me from anything that you can do."

Tenplessium did not relax, but stood her ground.

"What do you intend doing with us?" Aelfed asked.

The witch raised a hand to her chin as if pondering her plans. "There are endless possibilities. Bones, of course, is my servant. Should I take him back into my service, or punish him for deserting me?"

"You have no power over me in this world," Mr Bones said.

"Don't I?" She muttered again. Mr Bones was slammed against the wall of the craft by an unseen force. "You forget that the fungus gave me control of the forces of this world through the mechanism of this craft."

Mr Bones picked himself up and tested his joints. There were several ominous clicks. "You have power over the forces, enough to harm us, but no control over my mind. You cannot make me want to serve you as you did in our own world."

She sniffed, "Well, perhaps I don't want your miserable assistance here. I'll just have to dispose of you, Bones, with the rest of your companions."

"Um, hold on a moment," I said trying to think of some way of stopping the witch. She glared at me as if daring to speak at all was a great offence. "What are you going to do when you've got rid of us."

She snorted. "I shall return to the time where we met and re-run my plan."

"Why go to that time?" I persisted, still trying to think of a way out of our predicament.

"The humans of that time were easy to turn to meet my desires. They were desperate for a form of energy that did not harm their precious climate. They were grateful for my initiative. I would soon have been Empress of the World."

"No, you wouldn't," I said.

The witch stared as if I had slapped her. "And why not, gnome? I have all the powers needed."

"But you forget that we followed you through the

Parting. We would arrive again to disrupt your plans."

The witch's mouth opened and shut as she tried to find something to say but no words came out.

"You would be stuck in a timeloop," Aelfed said, "forever going round and round, never achieving your goal. Who knows, perhaps you have done this before, perhaps many times."

"That's right," Mr Bones said joining in. "Even if you went to an earlier or later time to avoid getting stuck in a never-ending cycle, I would be drawn by my bond to you and we would arrive through the Parting whenever you were. We'll always be there to stop you."

I could see that our arguments, whether true or not, had made her think. She glared at us, fury in her eyes.

"So, you see," Tenplessium added, "killing us will do you no good at all." Hugo gave a grunt of agreement.

"You must break out of the loop," I said, "Do something different." I didn't know what. I was just trying to goad her into doing something, preferably something that didn't harm us.

"Such as returning to our own world," Aelfed continued.

"And handing over the electrum to the Fairy Queen," Tenplessium concluded.

"Never!" the witch screamed and turned away from us to face the front end of the craft. She muttered and waved her arms.

"I think you went a bit far then, fairy," Mr Bones whispered. "What is she doing now?"

"Giving the craft instructions, I think," Aelfed said.

The sorceress turned to face us. "There is some truth in what you say," she grumbled, "and anyway, those people were such a bore, so lacking in imagination. But I'm not going back, never."

"What are you going to do?" I asked, feeling nervous.

"We're moving on!" she said, her voice rising with a note of triumph. "I'll find a new universe to conquer. Watch!" She pointed to the front of the craft. The diamond turned transparent and there was the Sun dead ahead of us, growing larger with every breath I took. It was bright but not unbearable to look at, so I guessed that the material of the spaceship was filtering the light somewhat. Nevertheless, we could see that we were heading straight for the Sun at great speed.

"What are you doing? Tenplessium cried, "We'll be burned to cinders!"

"How does falling into the Sun get us out of this universe," Aelfed asked, far more calmly than I felt.

The sorceress smiled at the elf. "You can't get out of this universe, but you can go somewhere else by diving into it. I told you that the fungus gave me power over all the forces of nature. Well, when we reach the centre of the Sun the craft will reverse all the forces that bind the fundamental particles of this universe together. They will fly apart leaving nothing in between and we can slip into another reality."

Her words confused me entirely, but her eyes glowed in triumph.

Mr Bones asked, "What will happen to the Sun?"

"Oh, it will blow up. A rather satisfying supernova I think."

"You will destroy it and the life on the planet," Mr Bones frowned.

"Yes, the fungus will be frazzled," the witch cackled, "that will make sure it doesn't use my plan for its own purposes."

There was no time for any further discussion; we were already inside the Sun.

"Here we go!" the sorceress cried.

The walls of the craft blew out and I was floating in an ocean of light. I felt no heat, no hurt, just wonder. I saw my companions and the witch floating with their arms and legs flailing. They were moving away, spreading out, becoming smaller and smaller as they became more distant. Each moved frantically trying to grab something, anything, but nothing remained in reach. Except, that is, for the witch's bag, which she grasped tightly.

I was getting bigger and bigger. I could see my body

swelling but still there was no sensation of pain. The light became less intense and continued to fade as if it too was being stretched. Twilight descended and then darkness. By this time, it felt as if my body was as big as a planet and I had long lost sight of my fellows. Slowly even my own body faded from sight and I, or what was left of me, floated in the total blackness of nothingness.

How long I floated there, just a mind or a soul, I don't know. It could have been a few breaths, which I wasn't taking, or eons. Eventually though, I became aware of something happening around and to me. I felt I was becoming enclosed as if my surroundings were taking on a solidity. Some sense of possessing a body returned. I could feel my heart beating and I took breaths. That meant there was air around me. I had the familiar and comfortable feeling of being underground as if I was back home in the caverns beneath the mountains of my birth with the dense rocks enclosing me. My body also felt as if I had regained my original gnomish form. I had short legs, a slight pot belly, strong arms, and a curly beard that covered my chin and cheeks. Had I, after all, come home?

Part 3

The Land of Dreams

Chapter 10

I find home is not quite as it was

"My Lord, you appear distracted."

I was indeed distracted. For some reason my surroundings and dress seemed unfamiliar. I have long become used to wearing fine silk shirts in brightest blue next to my skin, and vibrant red woollen breeches, but today they felt strange and new. Not as strange however as the robe of gold and platinum threads that I wore over them or the heavy golden crown, with its speck of electrum at the front, that rested on my bald head. Surely, I had become used to the trappings of kingship, but for a moment they seemed incongruous. I glanced at the young woman who had spoken to me. A most attractive gnome she was. Nicely plump with a rosy-cheeked face and a wispy beard tied with ribbons. She was, of course, my wife and Queen but at this moment I saw her with fresh eyes, the love of my dreams made real.

I replied, "Pardon me, my darling. I was just thinking."

"Of course, my dear. You are always thinking. You carry the burden of all Gnomeland, to which you must apply your noble thoughts."

"Um, yes, of course."

"The delegation of the elves approach."

I had forgotten that I was standing on the dais in the Great Cavern of the Mountain Palace, looking down at the assembled throng. I looked at them now, seeing them as if the view was new to me.

The cavern was huge, and so filled with my fellow gnomes that they merged into a swarming mass. The rocky roof was lost in the darkness high above the hanging chandeliers of glowstone. The people in the crowd, even those closest to me were unknown to me, except for one. Could that really be my mother, as young and spry as I remembered from my childhood – but surely it could be none other. How had she retained her youthful look? Didn't I recall that she had died when I was a youngster? I felt confused, but my thoughts were disturbed by a fanfare of unicorn horns. The ethereal notes filled the vast space and produced an immediate reaction from the crowd.

The noisy chatter ceased. Everyone turned to look towards the great doors that were now opening at the distant end of the hall. The gnomes made haste to move to the sides of the cavern. The reason for their speed was soon apparent. The doors had barely opened when a double line of soldiers marched in.

I had never seen such a fine collection of warriors of gnomish descent. At least, part of me hadn't. Their attire and orderly drill impressed me anew. They wore chain mail coats of silver steel, with conical helmets that shone like beacons. They marched two by two, in step, until the leaders reached the dais on which I stood. Then they turned to face to the crowd, marched a few paces outward, then did a quite remarkable about face, stamped their booted feet as they came to attention and raised their ornamental weapons; hammers, pickaxes and boring poles, each polished to perfection. It was a display that I had never expected to witness from a group of gnomes. I did not know gnomes were capable of such cooperation and immaculate timing. But of course, I did; I had trained their trainers before I seized the kingdom. Why was part of me in conflict with the rest of myself?

The hall was silent. Everyone was apparently waiting for something to happen, as indeed was I. Then others appeared, entering the hall and making their way to the dais between the lines of the honour guard. This was not an organised and synchronised march, but a motley collection of elves sauntering along, looking around with no obvious sign that they were of one mind. To the fore were half a dozen opulently attired individuals. They wore bejewelled gowns in various shades of green that swept the floor. On their heads they wore feathered hats that made their height approach that of the gnomes around them. At least I had some experience with elves of this calibre. They were Lords of Elfholm. With them were other green-clothed elves, their servants and workers.

These guests of my kingdom halted below me, with all their eyes on me. One of them spoke.

"King of the Gnomes, we bring greetings from Elfholm and all elves. We are honoured that you give us audience."

The speaker was familiar – a fat, short, lavishly dressed elf. Could it be that he was Lord Pelladill?

"You are welcome, Lords of Elfholm," I said, though I could not at that moment recall why the elves had come to visit me in my palace.

"Thank you, your Majesty. We present you with a gift as a sign of our lasting friendship with your kingdom." Lord Pelladill raised a hand and flicked his fingers. A lesser elf stepped forward, legs buckling from carrying an obviously heavy object that was covered by an emerald-green silk cloth. The object was tall enough to obscure the elf's features.

The elf advanced to the edge of the dais. The two nearest gnome soldiers closed in as if to restrain the elf. I raised a hand to halt them. Arms shaking with the effort, the elf lifted the object onto the dais a couple of arm's lengths from my feet, then stepped back. For the first time I saw her face. She was Aelfed. Now why should that name come to me? How could I know a lowly worker elf? She looked at me with surprise. The surprise of recognition.

"Thank you for your gift," I said, somewhat half-heartedly. My thoughts were on the mystery of how part of me could have memories of a subordinate elf, while the rest of me was unconcerned by the lives of such creatures.

"Would you like me to remove the cloth?" Aelfed asked.

"Yes, please," I said, with what I realised was uncharacteristic politeness.

The elf gave a gentle tug to the silk and it floated off the object revealing it in all its resplendent glory.

It was a statue of a gnome in silver-white platinum wearing a crown of gold and holding up a sword with its blade of glowing electrum. It was obviously a representation of me, the King of the Gnomes, and while it was but a tenth of life size the sliver of electrum in the blade was the largest piece of the metal I had ever seen. That was true for both sets of memories that were competing in my mind.

I had to respond. "That is indeed a fine gift, Lord Pelladill. Please tell me about it."

The leading Lord of the Elves stepped forward. "It symbolises your heroic career as King of the Gnomes, your Majesty, and the esteem with which all elves hold you."

I nodded in acceptance of his flattery. "The workmanship appears superb," I said, "I know how hard it is to work electrum."

Lord Pelladill smiled as if I was praising him. "It is the work of my leading metalsmith, Aelfed, your Majesty." He pointed to the young female elf. His leading metalsmith? The Aelfed I knew was but an apprentice... The Aelfed I knew?

"I would like to discuss her work with her in person. Please bring young Aelfed to the banquet. I will talk with you and the other Lords of Elfholm while we eat. Now please go and take your rest."

Lord Pelladill, the other lords, Aelfed and the accompanying elves bowed low and backed away. The gnomish soldiers encircled them and escorted them from the great hall.

My wife stepped to my side. "You didn't mention the reparations."

My head seemed fuzzy as conflicting memories clashed. "Reparations?" I muttered.

"For the damage caused to our armies when we subdued the elves."

"Ah yes, my darling," I said. I made up a response. "We'll discuss that at the banquet. They will be more amenable over good food and ale."

"They do not have to be amenable, my Lord. They just need to do whatever you order them to do."

"Yes, my dear. But they gave me a very nice statue." I pointed to the likeness of myself at my feet.

"A mere bauble."

"But look at the electrum. Have you ever seen such a quantity? It is many times the size of the fragment in my crown."

"It may be all that the elves had," the queen said, "But it is no more than you deserve for putting an end to their dominance and their discrimination against gnomes."

The memories of my army of gnomes defeating the motley forces of Elfholm were strong in my mind but now seemed to have fresh impact.

I saw my queen looking at me with some concern on her face. "Are you well, my Lord? You appeared distracted earlier and now you seem self-absorbed. What concerns you?"

I shrugged. "Nothing at all, my dear."

"Well, let us return to our rooms to get ready for this banquet. I'm not looking forward to sitting down with a bunch of elves. All they can talk about is their wealth and means of making it."

"Ah, but now they are in our power, their wealth is our wealth."

The Queen sniggered. "That's more like my King talking. Come on." She ordered our servants to escort us from the cavern leaving the throng to get on with whatever activities filled their time when I was absent – talking and plotting no doubt. My spies would be amongst them listening and noting who said what. I amazed myself at the degree of intrigue that lay at the heart of kingship. Was this what I had dreamt of all those years ago before I began my rise to power?

I found myself alone for a few heartbeats. After a brief

period of kissing and cuddling with my darling wife she left me to dress for the banquet. I had removed my platinum and gold cloak but had paused in the act of removing my underclothes. The act seemed both familiar and strange. Familiar because of course everyone undressed from time to time, but strange because, for some reason, the richness of my clothing seemed wrong.

What was the cause of this clash of memories and personalities? Who was I? The victorious King of all Gnomes, or a wandering adventurer? One part of my life seemed unquestionable – my early years living under the mountain, a poor miner, like many of my sort. Then, on the one hand I had left to seek my fortune in the world beyond the mountains, and on the other I and a group of loyal friends had tried our luck and we had risen to power. Set side by side both stories seemed equally incredible but somehow both felt true. There only seemed to be one common factor and that was the young elf, Aelfed. In the one thread she was a servant of the elf lord who had made a gift for me, in the other she was a companion with whom I shared adventures. I needed to speak to her, and I couldn't wait for the banquet. I called a servant and told them to bring the elf to me.

Chapter 11

Aelfed and I converse

The knock was hesitant but audible.

"Come in," I commanded.

The door opened revealing one of my servants.

"The elf you asked for, Your Majesty, is here."

"Good. Show her in, then leave."

I had had time to change my clothing while Aelfed was being collected. Now I was in my finest banqueting outfit of satin and silks. I was attired not unlike those elven lords in fact, though while they preferred shades of green, I ransacked the rest of the colour pallet for reds and blues. As I looked at myself in a silver mirror my two selves were agreed that it was ostentation gone wild. But my people required that I display the fruits of my success as their conquering hero.

The door opened again, and the elf took a step into my dressing room, but only one step.

"Come in young elf. I wish to speak with you." I beckoned her to approach me as I settled into a gold leaf encrusted chair. Aelfed stood in front of me looking at the floor. It was covered in an elegant carpet liberated from some elven lord's tower.

"You are a metalsmith of some talent," I said.

She whispered something.

"Speak up, elf," I said. It came out rather harsh which was not what I intended.

"Thank you, your Majesty," she said.

"Have you been a metalsmith for long?" It was a silly question, but I wanted to get her talking. I wanted to find out how it was that I knew her.

"All my life, your Majesty. My father has taught me everything I know about all the metals, how to shape them and mix them together."

"Your father?" Something in my mind told me her father was dead or injured. "Is he with Lord Pelladill's entourage?"

"No, your Majesty. He is home in Elfholm. He is old now and not strong enough to travel."

"But he lives?"

"Oh, yes, your Majesty."

"Good, good. Um, now, elf, Aelfed, that is your name."

"That's correct, your Majesty."

"It is strange, but it seems that I once knew an elf by that name."

Aelfed looked up into my face and her eyes sparkled.

"I feel that I know you too." She covered her mouth with her hand, "Oh, I am sorry your Majesty, please pardon my impertinence."

"Do not worry," I really did want to reassure her. "Of course, everyone knows me, I am the King of the Gnomes and victor of the war with the elves." Her eyes dropped to the floor again. "But no-one really knows what I look like unless they have seen me close, and only a few elves have done that. So why should you think that you know me."

She looked at me again, her eyes searching my face for certainty. "It is true your Majesty. Your appearance is familiar. I seem to have a memory of accompanying you on a journey, a quest. But that cannot be true. All my life until now has been spent in Elfholm. It has been my dream to surpass my father as the best metalsmith amongst elves and I felt that I had achieved that with the statue we presented to you. So how can I have been with you on some wild quest?"

"A quest? Ah yes, to recover a quantity of electrum."

"That's it," Aelfed was excited, "stolen by a sorceress."

It was as if a curtain had been opened and I looked out of a new window on an expansive view. Another part of my memory had been revealed. A chase, across the world, no not just one world. Different worlds and times. And dragging us along on this convoluted trail, the red-haired sorceress. The very sorceress who issued threats from her island fastness in the Southern Ocean.

I was confused but curious. "How can the two of us, from such different backgrounds and races, share memories of something outside of our normal existence. I am King and you a creator of elvish goods, yet we share memories of a quest. It is most puzzling."

"It is your Majesty."

Another knock came on the door. A firmer, more urgent knock.

"Come!" I called.

A senior member of my guard appeared, in full armour. He blurted out, "Your Majesty, a squadron of fairies has appeared at the North Gate."

To say I was shocked by his announcement was an understatement. We had had no dealings with fairies for years. They had not interfered with our war with the elves and I had not taken any interest in any of their actions.

"What brings them here now? What size force?"

"There must be a million of them beyond the gate, your Majesty, all armed. Their leader, a General Tenplessium, demands you speak to her."

Tenplessium. Now that was a name that tingled my memory. I noticed Aelfed react too.

"You know that name, Aelfed?" I said.

"Yes, your Majesty. It is another name mixed up with my memories of the quest."

"Me too. Strange that she turns out to be a top military leader of the fairies, and strange too that she should come here now."

I addressed the guard. "Arrange for an escort to accompany me to meet this fairy general. Make sure the North Gate guard is reinforced. This elf will be joining me." It was difficult to see the guard's eyebrows rise under his helmet, but I am quite sure they did. Nevertheless, he left at speed to do my bidding.

Aelfed spoke without waiting for permission. "You want me to come with you to meet the fairies."

"Hmm, yes. There is something unusual going on and

you and this fairy, Tenplessium, are part of it."

Although dressed in my banqueting garb I grabbed my sword belt and buckled it around my ample middle. The scabbard hung down to my ankle and tugged me to the left. It was an encumbrance, but I felt happier with a weapon to defend myself. I put my crown on my head and ushered the elf in front of me through the door. A platoon of six guards was already waiting for me.

"Lead on," I commanded, "To the North Gate."

The North Gate was more than a thousand steps from the royal quarters. We soon left the plush corridors of my palace and entered the tunnels that passed through the dwellings and workplaces of ordinary gnomes. It was places like this where I had started my life before I set out on the path of military might and power. As we neared the gate, we entered the fortifications and quarters of the gnomish soldiers who defended this entrance to my kingdom under the mountains. We came to a cavern as wide and tall as the Great Hall. There, a thousand of my troops were lined up in phalanxes awaiting my orders. Another thousand occupied the battlements beside and above the gates, no doubt keeping watch through the firing holes on the fairy swarm outside.

"Show me this force of fairies that has arrived without warning," I commanded. The leader of the Guardians of the Gate led me to the stairway that zig-zagged up the wall that blocked the entrance to the mountain. Aelfed followed. We reached the sentry room above the gates. A dozen gnomes jumped to attention when they saw me, or rather, recognised my crown.

"Resume your duties," I said, "But let me see these fairies." One gnome remained standing beside the viewing slit. I stepped forward and peered through. It was dusk in the valley beyond the North Gate but it was lit up by the glow of a million fairies. They hovered in formation, a cube as high and as wide as the gate, each point of light a fluttering, heavily armed fairy. Aelfed also peered out at the scene.

"Where is General Tenplessium?" she asked.

"A good question," I replied, "Captain, can you answer?"

"She is at the gate itself with her guard," The commander of the Guardians said.

"Open the gate to let her in. I will go and meet her," I said.

"But the fairies," the Commander flustered. "If we open the gate just a little their whole force could be inside in moments."

"I'm not sure why they are here," I said as soothingly as I could manage, "But I do not think they intend to invade. Nevertheless, close the gate as soon as the General and her guard enter and keep watch."

"Yes, Your Majesty." He called to his junior officer who called to another down the stairway. The cry got repeated a few times before I heard the great mechanism of the gates begin to move. Dozens of worker gnomes were turning the wheels that opened the massive gates. There was a great clanking of chains, grinding of gears, grumbling of stone rubbing against the ground as the gates began to move.

I hurried down the stairs with Aelfed and the guard behind us. We reached ground level just as a shaft of dim light pierced the gap between the gates. Immediately a dozen sparks came through and hovered over us. I squeezed my eyes to make out the tiny silver body and the silver wings of the leading fairy.

"Greetings, King of the Gnomes," the fairy said in a high pitched but clear voice.

"Greetings to you, fairy. General Tenplessium, I presume. To what may we owe this unexpected visit of your sizeable force?"

"We bring you a dire warning, great King, but...but," The fairy flew into my face and circled around examining my features. "We have not met, previously...have we?"

"I hadn't thought so General, at least, not in our current positions. Why do you ask?" I felt I knew what her answer would be.

"You are familiar to me. I have memories – or are they dreams, I do not know – in which you appear, though I did not know that the gnome in my mind was the *King* of the Gnomes. And who is this?"

The fairy fluttered off to examine Aelfed who stood impassive at my side.

"How strange that the King of the Gnomes is accompanied by a lowly elf. Can your name possibly be Aelfed?"

"It is," the elf replied. Tenplessium flew off in a frenzy of figure eights and loop the loops. Eventually she flew back to hover in front of me.

"It is too much of a coincidence," she said in a whistling whisper.

"It is," I agreed, "I was surprised when the elf and I shared strange memories of each other, but it is beyond chance that the three of us should have similar remembrances. Tell me, what is the context in which you recall us being together."

The fairy did not hesitate. "We were in pursuit of the sorceress, the Magus Carmine, and the electrum she had stolen."

"That's right," Aelfed said excitedly, "We crossed the Parting to a new, strange world, then leapt into the future and then, and then…"

"Yes," I said, nodding in agreement, "what happened then?"

"We're here," Aelfed said.

"But I have always been here," Tenplessium piped. "I grew up a fighting fairy, but I had a dream that one day I would lead the forces of Fairyland in the service of the Queen of the Fairies, and so it has turned out."

"I dreamt of being the heroic King of the Gnomes," I said, "And my dreams too have been realised."

"Me also," Aelfed, "I dreamed of being a great metalsmith."

"Which you undoubtedly are," I agreed.

The fairy fluttered back and forth between Aelfed and myself. "So, all three of us have achieved our greatest dreams while sharing memories of a completely different life in which we pursue the witch."

She had stated what was in my head. "How strange," I said.

"And the reason why I am here must be connected," Tenplessium said.

I had forgotten the great force of fairies hovering outside the gate.

"What reason is that?" I asked.

"We have news that the sorceress is launching a bid to overcome all the peoples of the world and establish herself as Empress of all of creation."

"She's doing what?" I cried.

The fairy seemed to let out a sigh. "We have information that she has recited a spell of extermination. It is expanding from her island fastness at hundreds of furlongs per day. When it reaches the southern coast of the continent it will begin to wipe out all sentient life in its path."

"She must be mad," I muttered.

"We have long known that, King of the Gnomes," Tenplessium said, "That is why we have kept watch on her."

"But why kill every gnome, elf, fairy and the rest?"

"Oh, I don't think she intends to kill us all," the fairy replied, "It is a threat which she is capable of carrying out, but she has also issued an ultimatum."

"She has, has she," I wondered what the red witch wanted.

"We are to hand over all wealth and power to her or the spell will do its worst. Obviously, we have until it reaches land to give in."

I was seriously troubled. "What has given her the power to launch such a destructive spell? She has often made threats in the past but her powers have been limited."

The fairy answered, "We believe she has acquired a significant quantity of electrum."

"Where did she get it from?" I asked, "We have little."

"And so do we," Aelfed added.

"The Fairy Queen's hoard is intact." The general said, "We don't know where Magus Carmine could have obtained this new supply."

A thought had entered my head. "I think I do." I looked around us. My guards were standing staring at us, looking worried, and not without justification.

"We must discuss this further in my war room," I said. "Come with me, General Tenplessium and you Aelfed. What about your fairy army, General? Are they going to remain at our gate?"

"I will tell them to disperse but stay close and alert," the fairy said. She flew to her escort. Some of them soared up to the wall above the gate and were gone, presumably through one of the gun ports.

We set off at once back to the royal quarters deep under the mountain. My mind was in torment. The sorceress' action threatened my people, who I had spent my life turning into a civilisation to be honoured by fairy and elf instead of being despised as hole dwellers and simple miners. Alongside that was my memory of another life as a plucky adventurer who somehow had gone on a quest chasing the same witch across universes.

We arrived at the room where I planned all my campaigns, my war room. It was really rather a small office hacked out of the rock containing maps and plans of the world and all its major cities and resources. I immediately drew out a map showing the whole world from the icy wastes in the south to the Parting in the north. The sorceress' island sat alone in the Southern Ocean. I quickly measured the distance from it to the nearest point of the continent that filled the northern part of the world. Tenplessium gave me a more accurate figure for the speed of expansion of the witch's spell. It worked out that we had about twelve days before the spell made landfall and started killing sentient folk. Twelve days was not long to organise a forceful response to the sorceress.

Tenplessium and Aelfed had watched me in silence as I

performed my calculations. When I stopped, looked up and stared into nowhere, Tenplessium spoke.

"So where do you think she got the extra electrum from, King?"

"It's obvious isn't it. She stole it from your Fairy Queen."

"But she didn't. We've checked. The Queen's electrum is still in safekeeping."

"Here yes, but not where we came from."

"The quest!" Aelfed cried. "You think it was real."

I looked from the elf to the fairy. "We each have the same memories of another life, two other lives in fact. We became humans when we crossed the Parting."

"We actually crossed the Parting," Tenplessium said, as if to confirm it to herself.

"Yes," I said firmly, "Everything we recall happened, but somewhere else, and we ended up here. Don't ask me how."

"And the sorceress…" Aelfed paused as realisation dawned.

"Yes, she has come here too, and brought the electrum from that other world where we began the quest."

Tenplessium fluttered in a circle. "But the other place and here are the same. A land inhabited by fairies, elves, gnomes, ogres, mages and so on."

"Not quite the same," I said.

"What is different?" the fairy general asked.

"Us," I said. "Here, we have each achieved our dreams."

Chapter 12

We make plans to defeat the sorceress

There was a tap on the door quickly followed by my Queen walking into the War Room. I had never insisted on privacy although she rarely joined me in "my room".

"Hello, my dear," I said.

Her reply was abrupt. "What are you doing in here with the elf? Have you forgotten the banquet?"

"Ah, the banquet." It had slipped my mind completely. Tenplessium decided to circle my crown.

"Oh, there is a fairy here!" my Queen cried, "What's going on, husband? The elven lords are becoming agitated and not just because they want to eat. There is talk of a fairy army outside the gate."

Tenplessium moved to orbit the Queen's head.

"This is General Tenplessium, commander of the fairy force which, as you say, is outside the North Gate," I said, "But it is nothing to worry about. Well, there is a lot to worry about, but the fairies are here as our allies. You had better get Lord Pelladill in here. I hope he will speak for all the lords of the elves. There are things he needs to know."

Various expressions passed over the face of my wife and Queen – surprise, annoyance, concern, agreement. She retired from the room.

I addressed the elf and the fairy. "We must find a way to stop the sorceress' spell. It will take all of our peoples to do so, I think."

"And all of our fellowship who were engaged in the quest," Tenplessium said hovering over the table on which the map of the world was spread.

"All of our fellowship?" I felt I was forgetting something.

"That's right," Aelfed cried, "it wasn't just us three. There were six."

I felt the curtain over the window of my memory parting further. "Of course, the skeleton, the ogre and the mouse. Where are they?"

"We must guess at what their dreams of fulfilment may have been, in order to suggest their locations," Aelfed mused.

"What do ogres desire?" Tenplessium twittered as she flew a search pattern over the map,

I shrugged, "A dirt filled hole to sleep in and a steady supply of turnips to eat, perhaps."

Aelfed nodded agreement. "What about Bones? He served the sorceress alive and dead but happily joined us in opposing her when we became human."

"That's right. I remember now," I said, "but he told me all he wanted to do was rest in peace."

"A quiet grave then," Aelfed said.

"And those pesky renegade mice." Tenplessium flew in agitated spirals. "What do they want other than to steal from whomever they can?"

"What else is there?" said a squeaky voice.

I looked down at the floor. Emerging from the space under one of the map chests was a sturdy mouse with a sword buckled at his side.

"Major Montgomery Mouse!" Memories flooded into my head. "You saved us, twice."

"Only twice? Well, we can always try again if necessary." The mouse stroked his whiskers.

"Where did you come from?" I asked.

"Oh, I've been here for a long time, ever since you gnomes started to become successful. You provided rich pickings for me and my merry band of fighting mice."

"I've had no reports of armed mice in my mountain," I said rather put out that the mice had escaped detection.

"Oh, we kept out of your way, but I listened and watched of course, and then just now I started getting flashes of other memories. Overhearing your discussion, I became aware of who I am – and what is going on."

Tenplessium flew right down to the floor and stood in front of the mouse. "And what is going on?"

"It's obvious isn't it. This world isn't real, well, not as real as our original home. For example, how did he become King of the Gnomes and you commander of the Fairy Queen's forces? Don't you see. It's a world where dreams can come true, our dreams, because it is us who made this world when the witch flew us into the Sun. By *us* I include the sorceress, whose dream of world domination she is apparently close to fulfilling."

I was troubled by the mouse's analysis of our situation. I bent down and laid my hand on the floor. "I think you are right, Major, but what was your dream?"

The mouse stepped onto my hand. "To live somewhere where there was a generous supply of food and beer with comfortable places to sleep amongst my fellows, and plenty of valuables to appropriate."

I lifted the mouse up to the table. "You mean steal?"

"That's a serious word to use amongst friends, but yes, we have amassed quite a hoard of gold and silver and jewels which you have never missed."

"Well, I'll be…" I was astounded by the mouse's confession.

"But none of that matters, does it," Major Mouse went on, "We have to defeat the witch once and for all and get back to our real world, don't we?"

"That is indeed our intent," I said.

"Even though it means giving up our dreams," Aelfed said with a sad note in her voice.

I thought of the years I had spent in achieving my goal of ruling the Kingdom of the Gnomes. I had been successful, but it had been long and hard struggle. Did I want to give all that up and return to being a poor, wandering, sometimes lucky, gnome. Also, there was the love of my life, my Queen, who had been at my side for nearly all of my rise to power. She was only of this world and, as far as I knew, did not exist in my original life. Nevertheless, according to the fairy's reports, none of us would live for much longer at all if the sorceress' spell spread across the continent. We had to defeat her.

The door opened again, and the Queen re-entered. Her eyebrows rose at the sight of the armed mouse standing on the map of the world, but she addressed me.

"Lord Pelladill is here, my King. The other elf lords agree that he can speak for them."

"Show him in," I said.

The Queen turned and crooked her finger. The dumpy figure of the elf lord appeared, dressed in the finest silks and jewels. He had obviously set out to impress at the banquet.

"So, King of the Gnomes, what is this news that has delayed your great dinner?" Lord Pelladill eyed the fairy suspiciously.

"The fairies have brought news of a deadly spell released by the Magus Carmine from her island stronghold. It endangers the lives of every conscious being on the continent."

The elf lord's face lost its green tinge. "Every being?"

"Yes, elves, fairies, gnomes, everyone, unless we give into her and make her Empress of all."

Defiance replaced shock on the elf's face. "By what power is she able to make this threat."

"By the power of a considerable quantity of electrum that she has acquired."

"How did she acquire it?" The elf lord was furious now.

"That is too complicated to explain," I said. "The point is that General Tenplessium here, and I and your metalsmith Aelfed…"

"And me," Major Mouse squeaked.

"Yes, and the mouse, must confront her and disperse the spell."

The elf lord's eyes surveyed each of us in turn. He did not look impressed. "The four of you must confront her? Why not an army of fairies, gnomes, elves, ogres and whoever else we can summon?"

"Well, that may be useful," I said, "But it's the four of us who, if you like, form the advance party."

Tenplessium, Aelfed and Major Mouse nodded agreement.

Pelladill was not convinced. "You are a formidable leader of gnomes, King, and I have heard the name of General Tenplessium described as a celebrated commander of fairy forces. I know from personal experience that Aelfed is a metalsmith of stunning skill, but a mouse?"

Major Mouse drew his sword and brandished it at the elf. "You'll soon see how I got my reputation as a fearsome fighter."

"Really?" Pelladill said with a chuckle, "I have heard of no such accolade."

I raised my hand to stop the dispute, "I think your reputation is elsewhere Major."

The mouse dropped his sword hand to his side, "Perhaps you are correct, gnome. Here my dreams have been realised without a need to fight."

Lord Pelladill transferred his attention to me. "Regardless of the qualities of this mouse, how do the four of you plan to oppose an undoubtedly powerful sorceress who has come into a stock of electrum by whatever means."

"Er," I began, not knowing how to answer.

Tenplessium however flew at the elf lord. "We will defeat her and recover the electrum."

Pelladill shook his head. "You seem to have little idea what to do. I suggest you locate the other powerful wizards and witches in the land and see how they can resolve this threat."

I nodded. "Yes, yes, that's something. Why don't you handle that, Lord Pelladill. I am sure you know the whereabouts of mages of note."

"I may," the elf lord hesitated, "but wizards and witches are notoriously greedy. They will require some incentive to oppose the Magus Carmine. Riches such as are no longer at my disposal, King of the Gnomes."

I could see where the scheming elf was heading. "Of course, our treasury will provide whatever is needed to achieve a satisfactory result, Lord Pelladill. My Queen will oversee your efforts."

The elf looked at my Queen with a look somewhere between distaste and horror. My darling wife smiled.

"We will commence the task," she said. "Come Lord Pelladill, let us leave this company to their planning." She took the short elf's arm and dragged him out.

Tenplessium flew at me. "Is there a chance that this elf lord could be right?"

I shrugged, "How many mages do you know are capable of matching the Magus Carmine in a trial of spells?"

Tenplessium hovered at the end of my nose. "Er, none."

I looked at Aelfed and the Major.

"Don't ask me. I haven't been outside your stronghold for a long time, King," the mouse said.

Aelfed shook her head. "Most wizards and witches deal in feeble magic, mild curses and ineffective cure-alls. No doubt the offer of gold will attract them to Lord Pelladill but I cannot foresee them threatening the sorceress' supremacy."

"So, it is down to us, again, to disrupt her plans."

The others nodded. "We must confront her and force her to give in." Tenplessium said.

Major Mouse replied, "How do we get to face her if her spell kills all conscious beings."

Aelfed frowned with concentration. "We could protect ourselves from the effect of the spell."

"What?" I said excited but doubtful, "Protect everyone?"

Aelfed shook her head, "That won't be possible, but we may be able to protect our fellowship."

Tenplessium buzzed her. "How?"

"I could make armour that could withstand the witch's deathspell."

"You could!" the other three of us chorused.

Aelfed nodded, "Yes, but it would require a lot of electrum."

"Electrum!" I cried, "But all I have is the tiny chip in my crown and the strip that you used for the blade in your sculpture. That won't be enough to make armour for us all."

Aelfed nodded agreement, "I know, but…"

Tenplessium interrupted, "But the Fairy Queen maybe has sufficient."

I stared at the fairy and suddenly felt a lot more confident. "That's it! You and your fairy force must go and collect the electrum from Fairyland. Aelfed, you must prepare to make the armour. I will place our furnaces and forges for your use. I must make preparations for our voyage across the Southern Ocean to meet the witch."

The Major butted in, "Which leaves me to find the whereabouts of the ogre and the skeleton."

"How will you do that?" Tenplessium asked circling the mouse. "You said you have spent your life in this mountain."

"That is true, but there are mice everywhere, in Elfholm, Fairyland, across the continent. They pick up titbits of food and information. I am sure I will learn the location of a content ogre and a skeleton at peace."

"Well, I hope you are right, Major Mouse," I said, "Time is short, we each have our tasks, we must get to work."

"What about the banquet?" Aelfed said.

"The elves can eat and drink themselves to a stupor. I have work to do."

Chapter 13

Tenplessium flew off to the North Gate to meet her force and return to Fairyland. Hopefully she would convince the Fairy Queen to release her hoard of electrum. Major Mouse disappeared back under the cabinet. I left Aelfed scribbling in a notebook and looking very thoughtful. My first destination was the banqueting hall. There was quite a party going on, but I saw that it was all the elf servants who were making merry. They had probably never seen so much food or drink before in their poor, overworked lives serving the notoriously selfish and miserly elf lords. The lords were clustered around one table shouting at each other, while my wife stood close by looking bored.

"What are the elf lords doing?" I asked.

"Arguing about which mages are worth summoning," she replied.

"They have a list?"

"No, my King, they do not. They haven't yet agreed that a single one has power sufficient to oppose the sorceress."

"As we suspected. But keep them at it. I don't want them in my hair. Agree to any money and valuables that they demand but do not let anything out of the Treasury until we have results. I don't imagine there will be any."

"What are you doing, husband?"

"Organising an expedition to the coast and thence to the witch's island."

"But what of her spell?"

"We hope that between them, Aelfed and Tenplessium will have some answer to that question by the time I have transport organised. I must make haste my love. I leave the Kingdom in your hands."

I left my Queen speechless as I hurried to our private quarters. I lifted my crown from my head and stripped off my fine silks and satins. I dressed instead in the more common dress of a gnome, good quality though it was – linen shirt, woollen breeches and socks, leather jerkin and clogs. As I lifted my long conical hat off the hook it had spent most of the recent years upon, I had a thought.

In a recess in my bedroom was a large glass jar. In it were my dragonflies. They had not accompanied me since I became King but now I thought it expedient to take them with me on the next stage of our quest. I unscrewed the perforated tin lid, generating an agitated humming within. Then I held my cap over the opening of the bottle and slid the lid aside. The dragonflies flew into my cap. I whipped it on to my head. Instantly the tiny creatures settled. Their presence on my bald scalp felt surprisingly reassuring.

I buckled my sword and dagger around my waist and was about to set off when I saw Aelfed's figure of me standing on the dressing table. I stooped to examine it again. It really was a fine likeness of my kingly form. I noticed something that I had not seen before. The electrum bladed sword was separate to the rest of the sculpture and could be removed from my miniature hand. I very carefully pulled it off taking care not to cut my fingers on the glowing blade. The sword made a very small but exceeding sharp stiletto, a useful addition to my weaponry. I removed my dagger from its scabbard at my hip, tossed it on to the bed and replaced it with the electrum blade. It was held perfectly and would not cause me any danger.

Now it was time to leave. I called my personal guard and we set off through the corridors of the palace and then the tunnels that led to the great metal foundries of the gnomes. Most of the furnaces were burning red hot, belching flame and smoke, continuing their unending task of refining the metals that we dug out of the mountain. I hoped they would soon be used to turn the fairy electrum into whatever Aelfed was designing. I wasn't interested in the foundries now but headed to the railway that travelled south under the mountains to the coast. There was a train of wagons ready to leave, loaded with bars of steel, lead, zinc and silver. I instructed my fellow gnomes to get on board. I climbed onto the lead wagon next to the silver-bearded driver and told him to release the brakes.

There was no engine and no magic but the train began to move, very slowly at first but soon picking up speed. The track ran down through the mountains until it emerged just before reaching its terminus in the coastal town of Oldport. It was downhill all the way.

Very soon the air was tugging at my hat and I had to hold it firmly to avoid it and the dragonflies from being blown away. The wagons clattered and rattled though the narrow tunnels, the rough-hewn walls unseen in the dark but barely an arm's reach away. There were scarcely any bends, so the driver rarely operated the brakes. His long years of experience told him how much speed was required to carry us to our destination.

The journey through the mountains took two or three hours. When we emerged for the final stretch across the narrow coastal plain it was, of course, night-time. Clouds covered the sky obscuring the Moon and stars but the feeling of space after the constriction of the tunnels was pleasant even for me, a gnome who had spent most of his life underground. The train continued to rumble along the tracks, slowing very gradually. At last, silhouettes of buildings appeared against the coastal sky. The track took us directly to the harbour and the train finally drew to a halt on the short stone pier that jutted into the Southern Ocean.

I thanked the driver for delivering us. He answered a little grumpily as he had a few hours to wait until the ogres who were employed to unload the train would awaken. My guard uncovered a glowstone lamp to illuminate our exploration of the harbour and we set off along the cobbled pier.

There were three large cargo vessels moored up. They didn't interest me, as they were unsuitable for the journey we planned to make. I hoped there would be other ocean-going craft available and I was not disappointed. Moored right at the end of the pier, almost invisible in the darkness was a small wooden boat, perhaps twenty times my height in length. Its narrow girth showed that it was designed to move swiftly through the water. There was no cargo hold, but a cabin ran its whole length from bow to stern. A gangplank was set at the middle of the boat. I stepped onto it and shouted as loudly as I could manage.

"Ahoy, there. Is anyone on board? The King of the Gnomes wishes to speak."

There was no reply, so I repeated my call. At last, some sounds came from the cabin, mainly muttered cursings. A porthole in the superstructure was flung open.

"Who is that making all the noise? Don't you know some of us are trying to sleep."

The head of the speaker revealed it to be a merman, his scaly cheeks reflecting the light of our torch. I was wondering why a merman was apparently master of a boat when he continued his tirade.

"What nonsense was that about the King of the Gnomes? Are you having a joke?"

"No sir," I replied, "I am King of the Gnomes."

His expression told me he didn't believe me.

"And why would the King of the Gnomes be waking me up in the dead of night? What could possibly bring the King of Gnomes to Oldport anyway?"

He was right to be sceptical. I had perhaps made two visits to the port town in my life and only once as King. Being on the border between land and sea it was hardly part of my kingdom. Its inhabitants owed no allegiance to me or any other.

"I assure you I am King of the Gnomes and I wish to hire your vessel."

"My ship is not for hire. I don't care if you are the King of the Gnomes, leave me in peace, at least until daylight." He slammed the porthole shut and that was the end of it. My repeated calls went unanswered.

"It seems we are not going to make progress till

morning," I said to my guard captain. "You stay here with a few of your squad, and I will go with the others to find somewhere to spend the remaining hours of the night."

With a reduced guard of three gnomes, I strode back to the town. A few short streets of buildings were clustered right on the shore. It appeared that the town was partly flooded but that was because some of the buildings, occupied by the sea-people, were below the high-water line and their basements were permanently flooded. I headed towards a street that was above the high tide where I recalled there was an inn run by gnomes.

A knock on the door soon roused the innkeeper. Initially almost as grumpy as the merman, his manner changed when he discovered that I was the King of the Gnomes accompanied by guards. I tossed him a gold coin and asked for a bed for the remainder of the night. He brought malt beer and cheese for me and my fellow gnomes in the bar while he roused his wife and prepared a room. It was just a few breaths before I was able to leave my guard snoozing and take my rest on a lumpy, but thankfully clean, mattress.

One of my guards woke me at first light. I'd had an unusually restful few hours of sleep. Maybe it was because I was now in full possession of my memories of two – no, three – lifetimes, and despite recalling three periods of growing up they all seemed to slot together to bring me to my present self. I was an adventuring gnome, a reclusive human, and King of the Gnomes. Most importantly, as all three, I was still on the quest to save us all from the sorceress.

I grabbed the stuffed croissant offered by the innkeeper and stepped out of the inn. There seemed to be a lot of bustling occurring on the street for such an early hour. The people – gnomes, elves, ogres and others – seemed agitated and most were making their way to the lapping waters of the ocean a few steps away. We too headed towards the shore. The reason for the crowds soon became apparent.

Dozens of sea-people, mermen and mermaids, were thrashing around in the shallows in and outside the half-submerged buildings.

I took a couple of steps into the water until the gentle waves lapped over my clogs.

"What is going on here?" I asked. The sea-people all appeared distressed, wailing and thrashing their tail fins against the water.

"Death, death!" cried one.

"Death is coming," screeched another.

I grabbed the shoulders of a mermaid and made her look at me. She tossed her blonde hair, and her tail thrashed the water as she tried to escape but I held her firmly until she calmed.

"Have you heard what causes the death?" I said.

"Magic, fearful magic," the mermaid said, sobbing and shedding tears from her large blue eyes.

"Do you know where it comes from?"

"The island of the red witch."

"You escaped. How?"

"We heard of the death spell from other sea-people who passed the message across the ocean. Those caught by the spell die. We swam for our lives."

The sorceress' spell was evidently effective and doing what she wanted in creating terror amongst the sentient beings in its path. The sea-people were the first to experience it, and many of them would die before the spell reached land. The sooner we set out to stop the witch the better.

I released the mermaid and she sank beneath the water. I turned to the growing crowd at the water's edge.

"Help these people," I commanded, "Comfort and feed them and spread the word to other communities of sea-people." Some people listened and moved to help the refugee mermaids and mermen. Others stared, wondering who I was. I did hear a murmur going round saying "It's the King of the Gnomes." Perhaps I should have warned them that every sentient creature was threatened, but that would have created even greater panic. Instead, I stepped back on to dry land and signalled my guards to follow.

We marched back to the pier where the rest of my guard were surrounding the merman who owned the little ship. He was flopped on the pier like a beached seal.

As I approached, he cried out. "I have heard the appeals of my people. They are dying."

"I know. That is why I need your boat." I said, stepping between my guards. I crouched down to get closer to the merman.

"Why do you need it?"

"To get to the witch's island and stop her murderous magic."

His blue eyes opened wide.

"You wish to confront her."

I shrugged, "Well, something like that."

"But how will you get near her? The messages from my people say that the ring of death is expanding and no thinking being may survive its passing."

"That is true, but my fellows and I think we might have an answer to that involving the Fairy Queen's electrum." I hoped that by revealing our plans a little, I might give the boat owner some encouragement.

He examined me closely. "You really are the King of the Gnomes?"

"Yes, and I will pay you well for the use of your vessel."

"Payment will not be necessary if you save my people from the witch."

"That is unnecessarily generous," I replied. "When will you be ready to leave?"

He raised himself up on his lower body. "As soon as you wish. I can call my team to return immediately."

"Your team?"

"To tow my ship, *Seaskimmer*."

"*Seaskimmer* is it. That sounds like the name of a fast craft. Good. Make ready, but we must await my companions who will bring the means of penetrating the witch's spell. I must inform them that you will be joining us. Are there any other members of your crew?"

"Not if you and your fellow travellers can perform simple seagoing tasks such as releasing mooring ropes."

"I think we can manage that," I replied, "Now make ready to leave as soon as we are ready."

The merman hauled himself over the gunwales and wriggled along the deck to the rear where I saw now, in the daylight there was a wheel to steer the craft. He started to sing a song. I couldn't understand the words, but the tune was beguiling. Its pitch was such that the sound carried across the water.

I addressed my guard captain. "Send a message to my Queen. Tell her I have transport and await the others joining me. We leave as soon as the elf has completed her work." He stood to attention as only a gnome can, turned and hurried off to a building beside the railway track.

I stepped on to the boat. It rocked slightly and I felt momentarily nauseous. I may have travelled by train and carriage and car, flown by pigeon and fairy and starship, but this was my first time on an actual floating boat. I wondered what terrors there were to come.

Chapter 14

Our Voyage begins

The merman continued to sing while I inspected the deck of the boat peering through portholes at the interior. The timbers of the craft appeared well looked after and I felt confident that the vessel would serve us well for our quest. There was little to see of the interior but through one window I thought I saw movement.

I reached the stern of the boat just as the merman finished his song.

"You have company on board?" I said.

"A friend who has travelled with me many times," he said smiling, "Come and meet him. He doesn't say much."

The merman slithered along the deck using his arms and tail muscles to move. An open hatch allowed entry to the rear cabin. It was almost the full width of the boat and took up about a third of its length. The most obvious feature was a rectangular tin bath that occupied the centre of the space, at least as long as the merman. Its purpose was obvious as it was half full of water. Next to the bath was a bed on which lay an ogre.

The merman flopped into the bath and rolled around splashing water in all directions.

"That's better," he said. "My skin was drying out."

The ogre had got up as we entered the cabin and was making cheerful grunting noises at the merman. All ogres look alike, wide, fat, with random bunches of hair sprouting from their heads. This one wore a threadbare tunic that covered his blotchy brown body. I couldn't point to any particular distinguishing features, and yet this ogre seemed familiar.

"Hugo?" I asked tentatively.

The ogre's smile spread across his broad face. He approached me and flung his arms around me, bending his tree trunk like legs to do so.

"What are you doing here, Hugo?" I said pointlessly. Hugo grunted something unintelligibly.

"He has a name does he?" The merman said, wallowing in his bath, "I just call him friend."

"Have you known him long?" I asked, wondering how an ogre and a merman became acquainted let alone friends.

"He appeared on the harbour one day and seemed eager to come on board. His help was welcome since I lost my wife. He can perform tasks which us sea-people find difficult, even though he has little means of communication. He has accompanied me on my voyages for several years now."

"Well, fancy that," I said, still quite astonished to have found our companion. "Who would have thought that sailing the ocean was an ogre's greatest dream." That was the only reason I could think for this chance meeting, but Hugo nodded to confirm it.

"What's that about a dream?" The merman said.

"Oh, nothing important. We all have our desires don't we."

"Well, if you desire to take a voyage with me, I must make preparations for our departure," the merman said, hauling himself, dripping, from his bath. "I'll see that Hugo prepares cabins for you. How many of you will there be?"

"Four, perhaps five, but two of our number take up very little space." I wondered if Major Mouse had been able to locate Bones so our company would be complete.

"That is good."

"I'll leave you to your tasks," I said and left the merman and Hugo.

I returned to my guards on the pier. "Let us return to the inn and see if there is any more news of the fate of the sea-people."

I spent the day at the inn, carrying out my ablutions and catching up on meals missed. While I was relaxing, I handed out gold coins to the residents of Oldport to administer to the refugees. Many more were arriving by the hour from all parts of the Southern Ocean. None had direct experience of the horror initiated by the sorceress, but all had tales of leaving their homes and making long journeys to what they thought was safety. I was reluctant to inform them that the imminent landfall of the witch's spell would not end the terror and that all land dwellers were under threat as well as the sea-people until we gave into the mage's demands. That is, unless I and my companions were able to stop her.

I waited patiently for news from my home while sending frequent messages for more guards to come, bringing gold and supplies to assist the townsfolk and the refugees. When it was dark and the town had fallen quiet, I went to bed, still with no news. More than two days had passed since the witch had invoked her spell. The circle of destruction must now extend thousands of furlongs, growing ever faster as it spread.

I slept fitfully, dreaming of screaming merfolk and elves and fairies and gnomes and bodies piling up on a beach which extended further than my eyes could see. A voice was calling.

"Your Majesty, wake up."

I opened my eyes to early morning light. The curtains of my bedroom at the inn had been thrown back and one of my guards was beside my bed.

"Yes. What is it?" I asked, rubbing the sleep from eyes.

"There is news, your Majesty."

"What news?"

"A train is on its way from the mountains carrying the elf, the fairy and the mouse you were in conversation with and also another squad of guards."

"Good," I cried leaping from the bed. "That is the news I wanted to hear. I must get to the pier and aboard the ship as soon as possible."

I dressed quickly and put my cap, dragonflies safely inside, on my head. With my guards we marched from the inn. It was obvious that many more sea-people had arrived through the night, but my gold had enabled the townsfolk, from both sea and land, to organise reception of the refugees and to lessen their heartbreak at having to flee from the sorceress' spell.

We hurried to the harbour. Looking inland, I could just make out the train of wagons slowing as it approached the pier. I strode out to the ship moored at the end of the jetty. The merman and the ogre were on deck. The sea around the vessel was churning as a dozen huge golden tuna leapt and dived.

"What is happening?" I shouted, "What are these fish doing?"

The merman answered cheerfully, "They are my team."

"Your team?"

"They will tow my boat. How else do you think we would make our journey?"

I hadn't considered what he meant by 'team'. I had assumed it meant the crew to row or raise sails, but I now noticed there were neither oars nor masts. Hugo was however throwing ropes into the sea. Each had a loop at the end and as it hit the water a tuna dived into it so that it formed a tight fit around their smooth, muscular bodies. In no time each fish was hitched to the ship, and they had calmed, floating idly in the sea.

"We are ready for you now," The merman said. "We can start when you have explained how we are to survive the mage's spell."

"My companions are arriving within a few breaths," I said, "and I hope that Aelfed the elf will have the answer to your question, which is indeed on my lips too. Before then and as we are about to become fellow travellers, please tell me how we may address you."

The merman smiled as if pleased to be asked after his name. "Some call me Voyager as I voyage across the ocean far more than most of my fellows. Those that have known me since my youth swimming the oceans with my brothers and sisters use the name I was given by my parents, which is Wavecatcher."

A hail from down the pier prevented me from replying to the merman. Coming along the pier was a platoon of my gnome guards escorting Aelfed. Above her, sparkled the fairy. Also in the party, to my surprise, was my wife.

The Queen and I exchanged greetings and we hugged briefly.

"Why are you here, my darling?" I asked.

"I couldn't let you set off on this dangerous quest without saying goodbye, my King."

"Well, setting off is indeed what we will be doing very soon. Nevertheless, it is a pleasure to see you my dear." I looked at the elf, "Did you succeed in your task, Aelfed?"

The young elf frowned. "I hope so, but I am afraid that proof will only come when we meet the sorceress' spell."

I nodded. "Of course, that is to be expected." I could see that the Queen was very anxious. "Don't worry, my dear, Aelfed is the greatest metalsmith in the land. What have you devised?"

Aelfed pointed to a couple of gnome guards you were carrying packages wrapped in brown paper. "Being magic itself, electrum acts as a shield against spells. I therefore used your machines to turn the Fairy Queen's electrum into the finest thread which I then wove into cloth on your looms. I have made cloaks which will envelop our whole bodies and protect us from the witch's curse."

That the elf had done so much in so short a time seemed more than exemplary.

"You have made cloaks for us all?"

Aelfed replied. "I made one for each of our fellowship, although I did not know if Bones or Hugo would be joining us."

Major Mouse was sitting on Aelfed's shoulder but was somewhat forlorn rather than his usual ebullient self.

"Unfortunately, I have not been able to locate either of them," he squeaked, "Although I did hear from some coastal mice a strange rumour of an ogre wandering the seas. It did not sound much like the Hugo we knew."

"Ah, there you are wrong, Major Mouse. Here is our transport to the witch's isle and its crew, merman Wavecatcher and his friend." As I spoke, I turned and beckoned to the two sailors to meet my companions. Hugo grunted and thudded across the deck to join us.

"Hugo!" Major Mouse squeaked with delight.

"It is indeed," I said. "Who would have thought that an ogre's greatest dream would be to sail the ocean, but apparently it was – and is – Hugo's."

I saw Aelfed and the Queen looking at Wavecatcher with curiosity.

Aelfed spoke, "Wavecatcher is the master of the vessel?"

"He is, *Seaskimmer* is her name," I replied, "and we must get on board and set off. The sorceress' spell grows more destructive by the heartbeat." Wavecatcher beckoned us all aboard.

"I have been remiss," Aelfed said as she looked at the merman. Her voice was full of remorse. "I have not made a cloak for a member of the sea people. How can he be protected when we pass through the spell?"

I thought for a moment. Our journey so far had involved just our company, but to sail across the sea required the expertise of Wavecatcher. Then I had an idea.

"But you made a cloak for Bones?"

"Yes," Aelfed said.

"But we have no idea where he is?" I asked.

Major Mouse shook his head, "I have received no word of sightings of a skeleton formerly in the employ of the witch."

"So, we will have to set off without him," I went on, "Therefore his cloak will do for Wavecatcher. They are after all a similar length of body, though Bones has legs and Wavecatcher a tail."

Aelfed agreed. "Yes, yes. I can make minor alterations. It can be done."

"But what of my tuna? Will they not be harmed by the deadly spell?" Wavecatcher said.

For a moment I was at a loss wondering if our mission was doomed before we had even started. Then I recalled Tenplessium's description of the sorceress' curse.

"Do not worry for your tuna, Wavecatcher," I said as cheerfully as I could. "Only sentient creatures are threatened by the witch's spell. I do not believe that harming fish is part of Magus Carmine's wicked plan."

Wavecatcher appeared relieved. "You are certain, King of the Gnomes?"

"Yes," I said while crossing my fingers behind my back. I did not want harm to come to the tuna as they were our means of reaching the mage's island but certainty was in short supply.

"Well, then come aboard and let us be underway."

Aelfed stepped on to *Seaskimmer* while Hugo took the packages from the two gnomes. Tenplessium fluttered overhead and landed on the roof of the cabin.

I embraced my wife. "This really is farewell," I said. "Who knows what will happen." Indeed, I did not know whether we would remain in this world of dreams if we overcame the witch or not.

The Queen wiped tears from her beard and lifted her head. "I will await your return and ensure that the Kingdom is ready for you to resume its leadership."

"Thank you my dear, and please look after the people here in Oldport, especially the sea-people who have been displaced from their homes. If we are not successful in stopping the witch's spell soon, you may have to organise an evacuation."

"Don't worry, my King, it will all be done."

A call from Wavecatcher indicated that he was ready for us to leave. I gave my wife a last kiss on her furry cheek and stepped onto the little ship. Hugo untied the last of the mooring ropes, then with a creaking of the timbers, *Seaskimmer* began to move away from the pier and towards the open sea.

It was Hugo gripping the wheel at the stern while Wavecatcher was in the bow. He sang and the golden tuna leapt from the sea, hauling on the ropes. Slowly we pulled away from the shore. I looked back to see my wife standing with the platoon, her hand raised in a final farewell. She had been beside me for most of my life, my greatest support as I ascended to my position of King of the Gnomes. She was my one true love, and she was a figment of my dream. I knew that now, but wherever we were headed I would remember my years with her.

The ocean was beneath us, and the tuna were weaving beneath the surface, drawing us at such a speed that the hull of *Seaskimmer* created a white froth of a wash. Still Wavecatcher sang, urging the fish on and directing us southwards. Hugo at the wheel merely had to steer the boat to follow the tuna, a task he seemed completely adept at.

As the coastline disappeared from view, I took Aelfed, Tenplessium and Major Mouse into the forward cabin.

"This will be our home until we reach the island," I said. I pointed to the two bunks which took up most of the space along with the narrow galley. Major Mouse leapt down from Aelfed's shoulder and explored the cupboards, quickly discovering the supplies that my guards had brought on board. He nibbled on a biscuit.

"I presume the witch's spell is still spreading," Aelfed said, as she sat down on a bunk. The young elf looked exhausted as she deserved to be after her efforts of the last two days.

"Oh, yes," I replied, "More and more sea-people are arriving in Oldport with messages from their fellows who are fleeing from the curse. We must stop the sorceress as soon as we can."

Tenplessium buzzed around my head. "And how do you propose to do that?" she said.

"I don't know," I replied, "But assuming we pass through the spell unscathed I don't suppose there will be anything to stop us confronting her. Again."

"We will have to wait and see," said Aelfed yawning.

Chapter 15

The sorceress's spell is upon us

For more than two days we travelled across the water without a break. Wavecatcher never stopped his singing, urging the tuna on. The fish themselves did not seem to tire but continued to haul the *Seaskimmer*, which lived up to its name. From time to time the tuna's smooth bodies surfaced and then there was a brief flash of gold before they sank again beneath their own wake. While Wavecatcher and Hugo worked ceaselessly, the rest of us had little to do. We rested in our cabin or stood on deck feeling the saltwater air on our faces. The flow of air was almost too great for Tenplessium to fly so she stood on the palm of my hand as we looked towards the horizon, wondering how soon we would see sign of the witch's spell.

It was on the third afternoon while I was relaxing on my bunk that I felt the change. I had become used to the buffeting of the waves as the ship sped southwards although I cannot say that my stomach had become accustomed to it. Nevertheless, when the *Seaskimmer*'s motion changed to a rise and fall with the swell and Wavecatcher's voice fell silent I knew that something had happened.

I hurried onto the deck where I found Aelfed staring over the side, with Major Mouse clinging to her shoulder and Tenplessium fluttering above her.

"Why have we stopped?" I asked.

Aelfed pointed forwards. Many things drew my attention. Wavecatcher was lying in the bow; the tuna were floating idly on the surface of the sea their towing ropes slack; and streaming past our boat were sea creatures of all descriptions – dolphin, whales, shoals of fish. Above us there were seabirds of various species flying in the same direction. All the creatures were fleeing from something. It was not too difficult to guess what it was.

The horizon provided the clue. There the air appeared to shimmer and glow even though the Sun was shining from behind us.

"It is the sorceress's spell," Aelfed said. "All creatures are trying to escape from it even though the witch said only sentient beings are threatened."

"Who knows how sentient dolphin and whales are," I said, "We have no business with them so cannot know what or if they think." Aelfed nodded in agreement.

Tenplessium hovered in front of me. "But we have our sign. The spell is not far away. We must prepare."

"You are correct," I said. "Aelfed, get our cloaks ready." The elf returned to our cabin.

I moved along the deck uneasily, looking for places to grip hold of. Now the boat wasn't moving forward it was bucking wildly in the swell. I reached Wavecatcher slumped with exhaustion.

"Thank you," I said, "You have brought us to our first objective but now we must get protection from the mage's spell before we proceed further, if indeed that is possible."

The merman stirred, his muscular scaly body wracked with sobs. He pointed to the fleeing creatures in the water, "These terrified animals fear for their lives. Are you sure my tuna will not be affected by the deadly spell?"

"I believe it is only us that the sorceress threatens. Simple animals should be unaffected. We will find out soon enough because the curse is approaching." As I looked ahead it did seem that the mysterious glow in the air was closer.

A figure appeared from the cabin. It was slightly shorter than me with its features hidden inside a cloak that glowed pale blue. It was carrying a bundle of the same luminous cloth.

"I have brought cloaks for you and Wavecatcher,"

Aelfed said. She handed me one of the garments and took the other to the merman.

I could hardly feel the electrum cloak at all. The threads were so fine that the cloak itself hardly weighed anything despite electrum being the densest metal known. I unfolded it until it became a shining blue but incredibly faint ghost. Then I pulled it over my head. The hem fell to my feet. The cloth clung to my body but I was almost unaware that I was wearing it. While it covered my face, it was so thin that I could breathe and see through it, though it gave everything a blue tint. There were no arms to the cloak but as I stretched out my hand, the cloth fitted snugly around my arm and fingers and did not impede me at all.

Enthralled though I was in exploring the garments Aelfed had created, I nevertheless became aware that she was struggling with Wavecatcher. With him stretched out on the deck she was having difficulty getting the cloak to completely cover his torso and long, broad tail.

I knelt to help the exhausted merman move and allow the elf to manipulate the cloak into place. The merman was heavy and I was having little success in raising his buttocks until he regained his senses and with some wriggling allowed me and Aelfed to pull the cloak down to his tail fin.

"That just leaves the ogre," Aelfed said, pointing to the one folded cloak remaining on the deck.

"I'll take it. You make sure that Wavecatcher is recovered and is comfortable."

I picked up the cloak and made my way down the heaving craft till I got to the stern. Hugo was leaning against the wheel as if he was at rest. I think he was actually asleep, but he stirred when I approached. I held up the cloak and gestured for him to tuck his head inside. He caught on eventually and the cloak fell to his broad hairy feet.

Two tiny glowing blue cones approached me across the deck. The smaller I presumed was Tenplessium. She could not fly with the cloak over her wings.

"Stay with Hugo and make sure he remains covered by his cloak," I said and set off back to the bow of the *Seaskimmer*. Ahead of us it looked as though the sea was boiling. The line of broken water was approaching us. In it I could see the bodies of sea creatures leaping into the air, contorting and falling back again.

I bent down to the prone merman, speaking urgently. "Wavecatcher, we must get moving again. Are the tuna exhausted?"

He stirred, rolling to face the prow. "My fish never tire," he said. "They swim as long as I sing."

"Sing then," I begged, "We must pass through the spell."

"But my fish…"

"We cannot be certain of what will happen to them, but if we don't move the spell will be upon us."

The merman understood my argument, raised himself up and began to sing. The tuna immediately took up the strain of pulling the boat and hauled us forward towards the sorceress' spell. Terrified creatures continued to stream past as the blue glow in the sky bore down on us.

Then we were within it. The air itself sparkled blue and violet. I felt a sharp pain in my head. Aelfed curled up and cried in pain and Wavecatcher paused his singing.

The boat slowed as the tuna relaxed. "Sing, Wavecatcher," I cried, "We must move on."

In almost a whisper, the merman resumed his tune with a tremor that indicated he was feeling the same agony as I. The ship juddered as the fish pulled on the ropes and we moved on through the waves.

The ache in my skull began to fade and Wavecatcher's voice became stronger and more confident as he realised that the tuna were responding and still pulling us. I glanced back and could see Hugo at the wheel, appearing unaffected by the witch's spell. The faint blue shimmer in the air was now behind us but extended from horizon to horizon on both sides of our vessel.

Aelfed unfolded and stood up. "Are we through?" she gasped.

"Yes," I replied, "unscathed."

"Not quite," the elf said, "that pain was intense. Perhaps I made the cloth too fine, but I used all the fairy electrum to make the cloaks."

"You served us well," I replied, relieved that my head now felt clear and free of pain. "The cloaks have protected us from the sorceress's spell. Which cannot be said for those poor creatures." I pointed into the ocean. Instead of the torrent of swimming creatures, now there were corpses floating motionless. I made out bodies of dolphins and whales and one or two sea-people, but few fish. The flash of gold beneath the water showed our tuna were unaffected or at least recovered.

"Onwards, Wavecatcher," I said, "The sooner we reach the Isle of the Magus the sooner we can stop this slaughter." His voice grew in power and strength and the ship leapt at the waves at an even greater pace.

It was another day and a night before we had sight of land. Dawn had broken, the sky was clear and the sea calm. We were making good speed as the tuna raced through the water and Wavecatcher sang his everlasting song which never seemed to repeat.

We had kept our cloaks on, uncertain whether being within the sphere of the sorceress' spell meant we were in danger if we exposed ourselves, but in any case, Aelfed pointed out, they could protect us from any other magic the witch threw at us.

As the island grew in front of us, I became more and more apprehensive of the coming confrontation with the sorceress and wished that we had Bones to accompany us.

The dark cliffs of the island glowered over us and the merman slowed our approach as we looked for somewhere to make land. We followed the coast until the sun was approaching its zenith before we saw an opportunity for landfall. It was a narrow inlet with a jetty on one side and steps in the cliffs all the way to the top. Wavecatcher urged the fish to draw us into the mooring and he and Hugo made the *Seaskimmer* fast.

"Stay with your boat, Wavecatcher," I said. "We will go and face the witch."

"I will await your return," he said.

I did not answer as I was unsure if we would return, successful or not. I climbed from the deck onto the pier taking care not to trip over my long cloak. Aelfed followed with both Tenplessium and Major Mouse in her hands. Hugo joined us.

"Ogre, are you leaving me?" Wavecatcher cried.

Hugo moaned in reply. It was a sound full of regret, but he stood with Aelfed and me.

"I think he feels that, as one of our company, he must come with us," I said as way of explanation.

"Farewell then my friend," the merman called and waved his hand.

We turned away from the water and commenced the long climb up the rocky stairway. There was no other movement. No birds nested in the cliffs or wheeled in the air above us. There was no sign that the sorceress was aware of our arrival.

After many steps and feeling rather breathless we at last reached the top of the cliffs and looked out across the island. It was largely flat, covered in grass with a few stunted trees. Ahead in the middle of the isle was a building as dark and grey as the cliffs themselves. It was, presumably, the home of the witch. We set off towards it.

We walked in silence, perhaps not wanting to discuss what lay ahead of us, and perhaps the eerie quiet around us made us reluctant to make a noise. There was no rustling of creatures in the grass, no buzz of insects, no whisper of the wind in the branches of the trees.

As we neared the building, I noticed that we were passing through a cemetery. There were gravestones and some quite grand tombs. Most had names and epitaphs celebrating past lives of the owners of the isle and their servants. I wondered if one of the graves contained Bones' bones, remembering his tale that he had died and had been buried before the sorceress had him dug up to resume his duties.

At last, we came to the door of the building. It was ajar. I pushed and it swung open. We stepped into a large vestibule, with a grand stone stairway to the upper floor and doors to other rooms.

"So, you've got here at last." The witch's voice came from the top of the stairs. There she was, looking exactly the same as she always did in her red skirt and jacket and waves of red hair.

"You were expecting us?" I said.

"I felt you pass through my spell. I see you found a way to mitigate its effects. I wonder where you got the electrum from."

Tenplessium stood erect on Aelfed's shoulder. "My Queen donated it to us so that we could confront you and stop the destruction your spell is causing."

"Ah, of course, in this world the Fairy Queen still had her meagre hoard, but don't think that you will prevent me from realising my dream."

"Your dream?" I called out.

"Of course. My dream of ruling this whole world with my powers."

"In this world, all of our dreams have come true." I replied.

"*Your* dreams," the witch replied with a snort. "Only here could you possibly be King of the Gnomes. Come on up, and I'll explain before I dispose of you."

We had to get close to her, so there was no point in refusing. Aelfed, Hugo and I climbed the stairs. On reaching the broad landing the sorceress beckoned us into a room. It occupied one side of the building with windows on three sides. On the north side the expanse of glass gave a panoramic view out to the ocean. The Sun shone brightly, as high in the sky as it could be in these southern latitudes.

I took but a glance out of the windows then looked around the room. There were bookcases on the wall on either side of the door through which we had entered but otherwise the room was largely empty of furniture. A table occupied the very centre on which stood a sphere. It was solid electrum, but it shone with a violet light, far brighter than the metal alone. It wasn't just glowing but radiating magic.

"That is the source of your spell?" I said pointing to the luminous ball.

"That is correct," The sorceress replied, herself glowing with pride, "It magnifies and projects my power."

"To kill all sentient life," I added.

"Well, that is not its purpose," she said.

"What is its purpose then?" Aelfed asked.

The witch gave one of her wicked smiles. "To persuade all the leaders of the peoples of this world to hand rule over their subjects to me."

"They won't do that," Tenplessium piped.

"In that case they will all die and I will rule anyway."

"But it will be an empty world," I said.

"As if I care," the sorceress replied. "My dream will be fulfilled."

"And what of our dreams," I said.

"They are incidental," she retorted. "When I dispose of you, they will not matter."

"Are you sure?" I said, "Each of us has achieved our dreams because this world came into existence for just that purpose when you took us into the Sun."

The sorceress snorted. "Dreams! What are you? A worker of metals, a commander of fairy armies, a sailor, a lazy mouse, a tinpot king and a crumbling pile of bones. What are those dreams compared to mine?"

"Hey, you mentioned Bones," Major Mouse squeaked.

"Of course," the witch said, "He was one of the founders, like you, who created this world around us."

"Where is he?" Aelfed asked.

The witch pointed to the end of the room. Beneath the western window was a wooden box, which I had not noticed before. Now I saw that it wasn't a chest but a coffin. I ran across the room to it, bent down and pulled at the lid. The nails gave easily and with a creak of splintering timber the lid opened. A skeleton was laid out inside. It looked complete except that the left hand was missing a little finger.

"Bones?" I whispered.

There was no sign of life. Of course not, it was just a skeleton.

The jaw moved. "Not again. I was enjoying a good rest."

"Oh good. It is you."

"Who else could I be." Bones sat up and looked around. "What am I doing here? I dreamed of being laid to rest in a nice deep grave, with grass growing over it so that I could be forgotten."

The sorceress snarled, "Did you think I'd let you have all of your wish. You, my servant who deserted me."

Bones stood up in his coffin. "You left me, my lady, when you crossed the Parting alone."

"That is by the by," the sorceress screamed, "You will obey me. Now dispose of these irritants."

Bones stepped out of the coffin and staggered towards me. I backed away.

I heard the fairy cry. "If Bones can survive without a cloak, I'm going to give it a go. I need to fly."

I turned to see Tenplessium pull off her tiny cloak, unfurl her wings and take to the air.

"Me too," cried Major Mouse, removing his cloak and dropping to the floor from Aelfed's shoulder. Hugo too had begun pulling the cloak over his head.

There wasn't time to remove mine. Instead, I hitched the cloak up to my waist so that I could draw my sword. I brandished it in front of me and rushed at the sorceress. Before I had taken a pace, Hugo launched himself across the room at the witch.

He didn't reach her. She flicked her finger and Hugo flew through the air to slam into one of the sets of bookshelves.

Now I ran at the witch, sword arm outstretched. I'd taken two paces before the sword was wrenched from my hand and sent skittering across the wooden floor. I pulled up, at a loss what to do without my weapon. I heard a rattling of bones behind me. I spun around. Bones was looming over me, his bony hands reaching for me.

P.R. Ellis

Aelfed, still in her cloak, crashed into Bones, toppling him to the floor. The elf lay on top of the skeleton holding him down.

"Thank you," Bones said. "I do believe your cloak is shielding me from my mistress' commands."

"Why are servants so unreliable?" the witch muttered.

I turned to face her again to see Major Mouse running towards her and Tenplessium diving from the ceiling, both with their miniature swords held out in front of them. They got no closer than the ogre or me. One flick of the witch's finger sent each tumbling the length of the room.

I took a step towards the sorceress, wondering what I could do to overcome her.

"Have you thought what will happen if you kill us all?" I said.

"Oh yes, I've looked forward to the time when I dispose of you interfering nincompoops," The witch said glaring at me.

"But you forget that this isn't our home world," I took another step towards her. "This world is a copy created from our collective dreams. It only exists because all seven us were present when it formed."

I didn't know if I was right. Perhaps if the six of us were killed the sorceress would live on in her own private paradise. I didn't want that. If we were to die, then she must as well. Without my sword I didn't have anything with which to attack her, did I? I took another step closer to her.

"It will be my world," the sorceress replied, "mine alone."

I remembered something and slipped the electrum dagger from my sword belt. I continued to taunt her, hoping that I could distract her. "What a hollow victory that will be. A world empty of sentient beings. No elves, no fairies, no gnomes or ogres or sea-people. Not even any other mages. What will you do to pass all the time that you will have?"

That seemed to give her pause for thought. She stared

164

over my head, thinking. I reached under my cloak and lifted my cap. The dragonflies took flight and swarmed out dipping under the hem of the cloak before heading to the sorceress. They puffed out tiny gouts of flame that singed the witch's hair. She tried to fend them of with dismissive spells, but while single dragonflies were flung aside, others came back to attack her. With her attention diverted, I took one final step forward and stabbed at her with the tiny electrum blade that Aelfed had made. The blade cut through her tweed jacket and silk shirt and pierced her abdomen.

The witch screamed. It wasn't just a scream of pain but of anger. It was the scream of fingernails on a blackboard, of metal scraping against metal. It went on and on. I let go of the handle of the miniature sword, leaving the blade stuck in her. She fell to the floor, writhing.

"The spell is broken," Bones said from beneath Aelfed. I looked at the electrum ball. It had lost its violet intensity and now gave out the dimmer blue glow of electrum. I tugged the cloak over my head and called the dragonflies back. They settled in my cap which I pulled onto my head.

"Are you free of her, Bones?" I asked.

"It appears so, gnome."

"Let him get up, Aelfed. What do we do now?" I was trying to think while the witch's tortured screaming continued.

The ogre and the mouse had picked themselves up and were feeling their bodies to discover if they had any injuries. Tenplessium was back circling in the air. Aelfed stood up allowing Bones to scramble to his feet.

"I suggest you take possession of the electrum now," Bones said. I followed his suggestion. I stepped to the table and took hold of the ball of electrum with two hands. I could not lift it.

"Why is it so heavy?" I said.

"Because that is a far bigger quantity than the Fairy Queen gave me to make the cloaks," Aelfed replied.

"How do we carry it then?" I said, striving again to lift the sphere and failing.

Bones stood at my side. "The sorceress had a bag which enabled her to carry the electrum easily."

"Where is it?" I said, looking around the room for the witch's holdall but it was nowhere to be seen. I attempted again to lift the electrum ball but still was unable to shift it a hair's breadth.

"I have a suggestion, my friends," Bones said, "But you are not going to like it."

"What suggestion?" I said frowning at the skeleton.

"It will take magic to move that quantity of electrum and it will take magic to take us from here back to our own world."

"Do you want to go back?" I said. "Here, our dreams are real."

Bones looked at each of us in turn including the witch still wriggling on the floor and screeching. "We were happy until we recovered our memories and realised that we were living a dream. Do you really think that you will be satisfied with a future continuing to live that make believe?"

Aelfed spoke "But you were at peace were you not. Isn't that what you want?"

"I was at peace," Bones replied, "But now knowing that my mistress was wielding her powers somewhat disturbs the anticipation of the pleasure of eternal rest."

I had to admit that knowing that being King of the Gnomes was just a dream come true rather spoiled the pride I felt. A return to reality, even if it meant being a poor, wandering gnome again, had some appeal.

"You didn't finish your suggestion, Bones," I said. "How do we get the magic to move the electrum and go home."

"Ah, that's the bit you won't like," the skeleton said, "You're going to have to use her." His skull nodded at the squirming figure of the sorceress. She was still screaming in pain.

"You mean, allow her to use her magic," Tenplessium said, flying angrily around Bones' head.

"Yes, but under your control," Bones replied.

"How do we do that?" I asked, as confused as ever.

"Retrieve that splinter of electrum you poked her with," Bones said, "But first bind her in the electrum cloaks that you have. That will keep her subdued."

Major Mouse strode up to Bones' foot and poked a toe-bone with his sword. "How do we know that you're not still in her power and trying to trick us."

Bones folded his bones to lean down to the mouse. "You will have to trust me, Major. I do not want to be in her power any more than you do. I understand your doubts but do as I say and she will have to obey you."

"We'll give it a try," I said. The Magus Carmine struggled and twisted but together, Aelfed and I bound her arms and legs with the three larger cloaks. When we were certain we had her secured, I reached inside her jacket, found the handle of the tiny dagger and drew it out. Thankfully, her screaming ceased. She also stopped writhing. For a few moments she panted and then fixed her gaze on each of us.

"You will let me go," she said in a commanding voice.

"No," I said, "You will do what we say for a change."

She glared at Bones. "You are my servant, release me."

Bones didn't move. "No, Madam. I feel no debt to you. I am a free being."

"Free being, be damned. Who gave you shelter and sustenance when you were alive? Who cleaned your bones and restored you to a semblance of life?"

"You did, Madam, but only for your purposes not for my pleasure. The years of service I gave you more than make up for those kindnesses, if they can be called such."

The sorceress wriggled and struggled against her bonds. "When I get free, I shall make sure to separate every single one of your bones, then grind each to dust."

Bones looked at us. There would have been a smile on his face if he was capable of it. "I think that proves it. I am no longer in her power. While bound in the electrum she is under your control."

I crouched down beside the bound sorceress. "Are you

going to help us get home and get the electrum back to the Fairy Queen?"

"No!" she spat back.

"Then we'll just have to wait until you decide to help us." I spoke as kindly and politely as I could, but from the look in her eyes she wasn't intending to give in to us. "We've got plenty of time," I added.

"Um, I don't think we have," Aelfed said. She was staring out of the north window. I saw that the sky was turning dark. Surely the day wasn't ending this early, even this far south.

"What's happening?" I asked.

"The Sun has gone," Tenplessium replied.

"The horizon is shrouded in a dark mist," Aelfed said.

"I can't see," cried Major Mouse. I stooped to pick him up and he too stared out of the windows.

"Ha, ha," the sorceress laughed, "You still don't understand do you."

"Understand what?"

"By allowing all our dreams to die you have destroyed this world," the witch screeched.

"What do you mean?"

"You have all decided that your dreams weren't real, so you no longer want to pursue them in this world. You, gnome, have given up on being King. The fairy no longer aspires to lead her armies. The elf sees no future in being hailed the greatest metalsmith, not of this world anyway. You've all lost your hold on your positions in this world. Trussing me up like this has interrupted my dream. But it was because we lived those dreams that kept the day turning to night and night turning to day. Now the world is fading away."

I thought of my home under the mountain with my guards, miners and foundry workers, and my beloved Queen. Had they already passed out of existence?

"What will happen to us?" I said.

"Who knows?" the witch crowed again. "Perhaps we will just fade away too."

"Look here," Bones said, "I may have wanted to end

my existence, but you don't. If you have any way of stopping this, or getting us back home then tell us how to do it now."

Tenplessium flew down to hover over the witch's face. "Yes, tell us or I shall make sure you die before we fade away."

The witch sighed. "Well, of course, there's a way. And, of course, it takes magic. My magic."

"You'd better tell us quickly," Aelfed said, "I can't see the edge of the island anymore." I glanced out of the window. It was quite dark now, the sky only light directly above the house. The ocean had disappeared in a formless mist.

"Let me hold the electrum ball. I can make a magic bubble that will protect us while this world disappears."

Tenplessium flittered in agitation. "How do we know you won't just leave us to disappear with the world?"

The witch sighed. "That, of course, is on my mind."

"We won't let you touch the ball until you tell us how we will be saved," I said.

"Of course, you won't," the sorceress spat out. "You may all be fools but I presume you are not as stupid as to do that. If you hang on to these electrum cloaks with which you have bound me, you will be within my magical sphere and will go wherever I go."

"Can we trust her?" Aelfed asked.

"I don't think we have any choice," Bones answered, "Look the walls are going."

The windows no longer looked out onto the island but were themselves becoming a grey nothingness.

"Loosen her hands," I said to Aelfed. "We'll carry her to the table so she can touch the ball. Each of us must grab hold of the electrum cloth."

Hugo and I lifted the bound witch on to her feet as Aelfed released her hands. The Fairy landed on her shoulders and knelt to grasp the electrum. Major Mouse scurried across the floor, climbed her calf and inserted himself in a fold of the cloak that bound her legs.

We got the Magus to the table. I took a firm grip of the electrum cloth binding her arms.

"Have you all got a good hold on her?" I asked. Every one of us clustered around her affirmed that they had.

We were now standing in a diminishing circle of floor. The grey fog enclosed us and was closing in.

"Right, witch. Grab the ball and get us out of here," I said.

We pushed the witch towards the glowing sphere. Her hands touched it, gripped it, lifted it. Its blue glow expanded to surround us, just as the grey swallowed us.

Part 4

The land of forgotten histories

Chapter 16

We meet some threatened elves

Hitting the ground was quite a shock, but I must have fallen less than an arm's length as I was unhurt. I sat up and looked around. We were on a grassy hilltop. Unlike the far future, this was grass that I recognised. There were daisies and clover mixed with it, recognisable from my home. I examined my hands. They were a gnome's hands; thick, stubby fingered and hairy. I knew who I was and had memories of my life, including the two extra lifetimes that I could recall. That pleased me. It seemed I was myself and the world we had landed in was my home.

The others were also recovering but we had scattered a few paces apart. The sorceress was still bound in the electrum but had released the ball. It sat in the grass, glowing faintly. Bones was a pile of bones that slowly unfolded into the familiar skeleton. Aelfed rubbed her head and stood up. She looked around, particularly at the Sun which was low in the sky but, happily, yellow in colour.

"I think this is our homeland," I said.

Aelfed answered, "I agree, but where? The Sun is lower than anywhere I have been. Yet we cannot be in the far south. There is no land there but for islands."

I stood up and looked around too. We were not on a small island. Away from the Sun the land was hilly as far as the eye could see. Behind us there were high mountains on the horizon.

Tenplessium had taken flight and was hovering several arm lengths above us. Her thin voice just reached us.

"You are correct Aelfed – but if this is the northern continent then we must be very far north, beyond the Parting."

173

"Beyond the Parting?" I cried. "There is nothing of our world beyond the Parting. We've been through it."

"But when we went through the Parting, we found ourselves in another world where we weren't quite ourselves," Bones said. "Here we are still us, so if this is indeed our home we must be, as the Fairy says, north of the Parting."

I wasn't convinced. I shouted up to Tenplessium, "Can you not see any sign of the Parting? It does stretch far into the sky, after all."

Tenplessium called down to us. "No, I see no dark barrier, but in the valley, I do see signs of habitation. Smoke is rising."

"Somewhere to find food perhaps," said Major Mouse. The ogre grunted agreement and rubbed his ample stomach.

"Maybe we can obtain information from the residents," Bones said. "Let us go down there."

"What about me?" The sorceress wriggled on the ground still trussed up in the electrum.

"Should we release her?" I enquired of my fellows.

Tenplessium flew down to head level. "She mustn't be given the chance to escape. Just undo her legs so she can walk and keep her on a lead."

"A good idea," Aelfed said. She untied the bindings around the witch's calves and thighs then reconfigured the electrum into a rope which she tied around the magus' waist leaving a couple of arm lengths to hold. The sorceress struggled to her feet.

"You are so kind," she said witheringly.

Major Mouse was leaning against the ball of electrum. It was at least twice as high as he was. It was not moving at all.

"Hey, what are we going to do with this?"

I bent to lift it. While it was not as heavy as it had been, I could only just lift it from the ground. I couldn't possibly carry it.

"It is too valuable to leave it behind," I said, straightening my back after the effort.

The fairy circled the ball. "Definitely not. We must return it to my Queen."

The witch sighed. "I suppose you need a bag to carry it. Feel in the pocket of my jacket."

It only seemed a small pocket but when I slipped my hand into it, my arm sank up to my elbow. It seemed there was a vast empty space in there. I moved my hand around and felt something flexible. I grabbed it and pulled my arm out. My hand came out of the pocket grasping the handles of the holdall. The bag unfolded itself until in moments it was as large as I recalled it.

"Oh! There it is," I said feeling some surprise.

"Open it up and roll the electrum into it," The sorceress ordered. I placed the bag on its side on the grass and rolled the electrum ball towards the opening. The ball slipped inside the bag and disappeared from view. I found that I was able to lift the bag and its contents with ease.

"How useful," I said hefting the bag and wondering at the power of magic that could make the bag feel no heavier than it had been without the electrum.

"It is," the sorceress said, "That bag is precious, so don't lose it."

"Precious?"

"Exceedingly!"

I wanted to question the sorceress, to find out what it was that made the bag so valuable to her other than its ability to swallow heavy objects, but the others were eager to start moving. We set off with me swinging the bag from my hand and Aelfed tugging the witch along by the length of electrum. Bones lurched along behind us with Hugo, who had Major Mouse on his shoulder, at his side. Tenplessium flew overhead giving us directions.

As we descended the hill we had glimpses of our destination, but most of the time it was obscured by trees. At least these were trees I recognised, not like the strange plants tended by the fungus.

We joined a stream which gurgled and babbled down the valley towards the village, or whatever collection of buildings it was that Tenplessium had seen. Although we were beneath the canopy of trees, I had the impression that the landscape was opening out. Abruptly we came to the edge of the wood and I found that was indeed the case. We stood on a meadow overlooking a broad lake. On the bank was the village. Village? It was hardly that. It was like no villages that I knew from my journeys around my homeland, not even the scruffy tumbledown homes of ogres. It was a collection of a dozen or so huts constructed from branches with roofs of thatch cut from the lakeside reeds. Some of the huts were smoking, their roofs smouldering. Running from one hut to another were elves. Well, physically they were elves but unlike the elf lords or indeed Aelfed and her fellow servants. These were dressed in scraps of poorly knitted cloth and even wearing what looked like pieces of animal skin.

"What kind of place is this?" I said.

"They are my kin," Aelfed said, "but not such as I have come across in my life."

"They look barely civilised," Bones added.

"But they must have food," Major Mouse squeaked. The sorceress grunted but did not offer an opinion.

Tenplessium descended to our level. "I think some of them have noticed us. They are coming to meet us."

Five of the elves were marching across the grass towards us. Four of them carried long wooden sticks carved to a point.

"Step forward and speak to them, elf," Bones said. "They'll recognise you as one of them."

"Really?" Aelfed replied, "I hope I don't look like them."

The elves did appear to recognise Aelfed as one of their race and stopped a few paces from us. The one without a spear spoke but the words made no sense to me at all. We all looked at Aelfed to translate for us.

"Um, I don't know," she muttered, "I recognise some words but they are from the old speech, before all peoples adopted the same language."

"Can't you make any sense of it?" Bones said with some irritation.

Aelfed shook her head, "There was one word I recognised, 'death', but nothing else."

The group of elves were staring at us and beginning to look impatient.

"Oh, stop faffing around," the witch said, "let me help."

We looked at her. "You can translate?" Bones asked.

"Yes, just as soon as you free my hands so that I can use a spell."

We looked at each other, shaking heads, shrugging, gesturing. Without any discussion we reached an agreement. Aelfed undid the electrum binding the witch's arms and removed the electrum cord that we had led her by. She shook her hands then approached me.

"I need something from my bag," she said, "Open it."

I did as I was told without thinking. I undid the clasp. The sorceress tugged the bag open and thrust an arm into it. She felt around then let out a gasp of delight and pulled her hand out. She was holding a seashell and a gold chain and pendant. She settled the chain around her neck, then held the seashell to her ear. She listened for a few moments.

"That's it, now I suppose each of you wants it." Without waiting for a reply, she grabbed Aelfed's pointed furry ear and pressed the shell against it. After a heartbeat she released the elf who shook her head and looked surprised.

The sorceress came to me. Her hand reached out for my ear. Now gnome's ears are well-known to be sensitive as well as large. I pulled back.

"Do you want to understand or not?" she said.

"Er, yes."

"Well, stand still then and let me perform the spell."

Her hand reached for my ear again. I braced myself. She wasn't rough but I can't say she was gentle either. She grabbed my earlobe and pressed the shell firmly against my ear. I heard a rushing noise like waves on a seashore and then, nothing. She released me and performed the same action on Hugo's small, trumpet shaped ears, the side of Bones' skull and the tiny ears of Major Mouse and Tenplessium.

"There, now have your conversation again, elf," the witch said, dropping the shell back in the bag.

"I'll try," Aelfed said, not sounding at all certain. She handed to me the electrum that had been used to bind the sorceress. I shoved it in the holdall while Aelfed took a few steps towards the group of elves and spoke.

"Please repeat what you said."

The leading elf looked annoyed but started to speak. "You are not known to us. What brings your strange band of beings to us now? Do you bring death and destruction like the hoo-mans do, though you do not resemble them?"

I understood every word except perhaps one. Looking at my fellows who each had an expression of surprise on their faces, well, except for Bones who couldn't show any expression. I could see that they understood the speech.

"We mean you no harm," Aelfed said, "We have travelled a long way and will not be staying long. My name is Aelfed. What is yours?"

The elf drew himself up to his full height, which was less even than Aelfed's own. "I am Lord Ifanstor and these are my guards."

"He doesn't look much like an elf lord," I whispered.

Aelfed turned to me and whispered back, "I'm not sure he used the word 'lord' in his own language. It just came out like that. But it does seem as if he is in charge here."

She faced the elf again. "We would like to visit your village. Perhaps we can offer you help to recover from the attack you have suffered."

"Well said," Bones remarked. The scruffy elf lord seemed to like what Aelfed said too.

"Please follow us," he said. He turned and urged his five soldiers to lead us to the village. We followed on behind.

We passed through a rough fence made of sticks that encircled the village and then we were among elves. There were far more than I expected. Many must live in each of the huts. Most of the elves were grubby with just scraps of clothing. A few, like Ifanstor, looked slightly cleaner and better dressed. As we approached the huts, another character emerged from one. He had to duck his head coming through the elf-sized entrance. When he straightened up, he was considerably taller than the elves and me. He was taller even than the sorceress and rivalled Bones for height. He was covered by a black gown and hat which I saw were made entirely from rook's feathers and he carried a rough wooden staff. Noticing us he approached our host.

"Who are these people, Ifanstor?"

"They say they are travellers, Modrib. They are obviously not Hoo-mans so perhaps are no threat to us."

The black-robed fellow sniffed. "We shall see. They are a motley band and dressed strangely." He approached us, me in particular. He bent to examine the shiny buttons on my jerkin. They were a relic of my royal wealth.

"What is that material?" he said.

"It is silver," I replied.

"Silver?" he repeated as if he had never heard the word before. "What is that?"

"It is a metal, like copper and iron, not as precious as gold or electrum."

"Electrum, ah." That was the only metal he seemed to recognise. "Silver is magic, too?"

"No," I said. "It's just useful and pretty. You have magic?"

He drew himself up. "Of course. I am the Wizard Modrib of Elvenwick. I have electrum." He lowered his staff and pushed the end towards us. There was a tiny glint of blue in the tip. A piece of electrum no bigger than a poppy seed was embedded in the wood.

The sorceress was excited by the sight of the electrum however miniscule. She pushed past me. "This place is Elvenwick is it?"

"It is," the wizard said. There was a note of pride in his voice.

"What sort of magic do you do?" the witch pressed him.

"I do not discuss my magic with others unless..." Modrib said haughtily.

"Unless they are mages too?" interrupted the witch. She lifted the pendant that she had just put around her neck. It was a gold star in the centre of which gleamed a tiny sphere of electrum. It was just the size of a pepper corn but many times the amount that Modrib possessed. He stepped back in shock.

"Where did you get that?" he said.

"Oh, it was passed down to me by my mother. She got it from her mother. Tell me, how do you use magic to help these elves?" She dropped the pendant onto her breast and waved her hand to include the whole village.

While the wizard was surprised by Magus Carmine's manner and evident status as a witch, he was obviously proud of his own prowess.

"I reinforce the elves' spirit when they fight the hoo-mans; I make their spears fly to their targets; I cause the hoo-mans' arrows to fall short and their fires to be doused."

Looking around the village I had already seen at least one dead elf with an arrow in its heart and two of the large huts were still burning. It didn't seem that Modrib was too successful with his spells despite his pride.

"You must explain how you cast such powerful magic," the sorceress said, "Come, let us talk away from these people who lack the skills of spell-making."

Before I could intervene, the sorceress had taken hold of Modrib's elbow and was walking him away from the group. They disappeared into one of the smaller huts which was intact.

I nudged Bones, "Should we let her go just like that."

He shrugged. "You freed her and she has gone now, but you still have her bag. She won't go far without it."

I took a firmer grip on the handle of the holdall. Nothing was going to cause me to let go of it or lose sight of it. I had an idea and spoke to Major Mouse, still sitting on Hugo's shoulder.

"Follow the witch, Major. Listen to what she says to the wizard. Make sure you're not seen."

The mouse's whiskers twitched. "A sound idea, gnome. I will do it." He scrambled down from the ogre and scampered across the dusty ground to follow the witch and the wizard.

Aelfed addressed the elf lord. "What are these hoo-mans that attacked you?"

Ifantor replied, "You do not know of them? They are tall creatures, as tall as the skeleton who accompanies you. They are wild and vicious and covered in hair. They steal what we have striven to grow and make, destroy our homes and kill us."

These hoo-mans did not sound much like the humans we had met; but were they related? The name was immediately reminiscent of the humans we'd become when we passed through the Parting – but there were no humans in our own land. Neither were there beings called hoo-mans in the world of our dreams. Modrib and Carmine, and the rest of the mage race somewhat resembled humans, though the way Ifantor described these hoo-mans seemed a far cry from both races.

"Where do they come from?" Aelfed asked.

The elf lord pointed to the north. "From beyond the hills, from the land of snow and ice."

"They have attacked you before?"

The elf nodded. "It used to be a rare event but the attacks are becoming more frequent and the bands of hoo-mans are getting larger. My people wonder whether we can live here any longer, but there have always been elves in Elvenwick."

He was quite upset. I wondered what we could do to protect the elves from these raiders. They were apparently unable to help themselves with or without the assistance of a wizard.

Tenplessium flew close to me. "I shall take a look. See if I can spy out where these hoo-man monsters are camped." She soared up into the sky, a tiny spark of light which quickly disappeared.

Lord Ifantor was speaking again, "But I am not being a good host to guests who come from the south. We have little to offer you, nevertheless, come and rest."

We followed him to one of the large huts that seemed to have survived the raid undamaged. Some elves stopped their work to watch us, but most were so exhausted they hardly noticed us.

The empty hut was a simple circular space with a fire pit at its centre. It was dark and smelled of wood smoke. Its floor was no different to the ground outside. There was a pile of grass and reeds on one side which the lord directed us to. Hugo looked as though he felt at home, dropped onto the heap and smiled with contentment. Bones folded his long legs and settled into the grass. Aelfed and I sat beside him. I made sure the holdall was tucked between my legs.

The lord left us, shouting orders to other elves.

"What kind of elves are these, Aelfed?" I said.

She shook her head, "I do not understand. They lack many of the materials and skills that I and the people of Elfholm know well – metals, building materials, cloth. They seem so primitive."

"Perhaps that is it," Bones said. "They appear primitive because this is what the world was like then."

"You mean…" I began, understanding creeping up on me.

"We are in the past," Aelfed beat me to it.

"The past of the world where we originated," Bones said, nodding his skull.

"How far in the past?" I said.

Bones shrugged, "Thousands of years, I would guess. Before recorded history."

"You must be right," Aelfed said, "I have no knowledge of these hoo-mans or a time when elves lived like this."

I too had heard no tales of such beings as threatened the elves. "We must find out if other peoples, such as gnomes and fairies, perhaps even ogres, are being attacked by the hoo-mans."

Ifantor returned followed by two female elves carrying rough wooden cups which they offered to each of us.

They contained a liquid which had no smell. I stuck out my tongue to taste the liquid. There was no taste; it was water. I drank eagerly. The water was cool and clean.

My thirst quenched, I spoke to the Lord. "Are other elf villages being attacked, and what about the settlements of those such as myself, and the ogre here?"

The elf had little to say. "There was an elf village a few days walk north of here. It was destroyed by the hoo-mans months ago. We have not heard from other elves for longer still. I have not met a gnome in years though we know that they live in the mountains far to the south. We tell stories of times when ogres lived alongside us. It is a long time since we had any visitors at all and never have we welcomed a group such as yours. Why have you come to us?"

"We are travellers," Bones said, which was certainly true but gave the elf lord little information. Nevertheless, his eyes brightened.

"Are you able to help us against the hoo-mans?"

"Er," was Bones reply.

Aelfed stepped in. "We need more information about the hoo-mans. Perhaps you can show us the weapons they used. The wizard mentioned arrows."

The Lord was excited. "Yes, yes, I will ask my guards to find some of the hoo-man arrows." He hurried out of the hut.

"What are you doing, Aelfed?" I said. "We don't want to stay here, particularly if these hoo-mans may attack at any time. We need to find a way to get back to our time, and get the electrum back to the Fairy Queen."

"I know," she replied, "but I cannot think of leaving here without helping my fellow elves, even though they are so primitive."

"Hmm," was Bones comment, "I don't know what help we can provide for these elves. We are not fighters, although Tenplessium led the fairy forces and you, gnome had armies under your command when you were King."

"Yes, I recall leading my gnome soldiers," I said,

"though I know it is not a real memory, merely one created by my dream. Even so, I planned battles but didn't fight in them. Actually, there weren't many battles at all. Other gnomes were pleased to have me lead them – that's the way of dreams isn't it."

Aelfed nodded. "I'm no fighter either."

Bones added, "Hugo is a useful bodyguard but I doubt he would be much use against an army of hoo-mans." The ogre who had appeared to be asleep gave a grunt of what may have been agreement.

"But," the elf said, "Perhaps we can help these elves, improve their defences, support them somehow."

I shrugged, "Perhaps."

The elf lord returned carrying two arrows. He offered them to us. Aelfed took them and examined one closely. Then she looked at the other and finally back to the first.

"These are well made arrows," she said, "They have metal tips, iron I think. They're well crafted, the shafts and feathering too. The tips look identical, so I'd say they are made in moulds and then filed to sharpen them."

"That is interesting," Bones said scratching a bony finger against a bony cheek. It made a horrible noise.

I wondered what Aelfed had said that intrigued him. He went on, "It seems these hoo-mans have a higher degree of technology than the elves. The hoo-mans have smiths turning out metal for weapons which are crude by our standards but deadly compared to the elves' sharpened sticks. I wonder what else they have in addition to iron-tipped arrows."

"The elves don't stand a chance," I said. "From what the lord has said, the hoo-mans are bigger and stronger than elves. If they are also better equipped for fighting then they'll destroy the village in no time."

Bones nodded. "All the elves have is a wizard who doesn't seem capable of much magic."

"We've got to help them," Aelfed said. Her face was an expression of grief.

Lord Ifantor had been listening to us. "Can you?" he appealed.

"We must discuss your problem," Bones said. "Some food may enable my companions to assist you."

"Ah, yes. Much of our store of food has been burned or spoiled by the hoo-mans, but I'll see what we can locate." He left us at speed.

"I feel quite hungry," I said, "but you don't eat, Bones, so why did you ask him for food?"

"Just to get him out of our way so we can discuss the matter," Bones said, "although I am sure you all could do with a meal – it's been a long time since you last ate, I think."

"A few thousand years ago, it seems," I answered. "But what can we do to help the elves?"

A flash of light revealed the return of Tenplessium. She hovered in front of us.

"It's terrible," she cried. "There are so many of them."

"Calm down," said Bones, "Tell us what you saw." He held out his hand.

The fairy fluttered and settled on Bones' fleshless palm.

"I headed north. Over the first two hills I came upon the hoo-mans' camp. It was obviously only temporary – a fire with about two dozen of them sitting around it. They're big creatures with long unruly hair, wearing clothes of coarse cloth and hides. I recognised them."

"Recognised them?" I repeated.

"Not individually, but the kind of people they are. They are the people we met and became when we passed through the Parting."

"Of course they are," Bones said.

"But we had smart clothes and technology like, what was it called … a car. Humans didn't fight with arrows." I said.

Tenplessium hopped up and down on Bones' hand. "No, I don't mean exactly the same. These are primitive humans."

"From pre-history," Aelfed added. "We have worked out that we are thousands of years in our past. It's the past of the hoo-mans, or humans, too."

"Go, on, fairy," Bones said, "I don't think you have finished yet."

"No, I haven't. I flew further north and found more of them. A lot more. Over the next line of hills. I flew over lots of camp sites each with hundreds of the humans. Some of the settlements looked quite permanent. There were buildings of wood and stone with smoke coming from them almost resembling your foundries, gnome, and the elvish workshops where you work, Aelfed."

"That is where they must be making their weapons," the elf said.

Bones succeeded in looking grave even without eyes. "This isn't just a matter of raids on elvish homes. This is a full-scale invasion."

"What can we do?" I said, lost for ideas.

There was a rustling in the dust. Major Mouse hopped onto my leg.

"You have to come!" he squeaked.

"Why? Where?" I replied.

"The witch is taking over. She has that fool wizard, Modrib, in her power and now she is sweet-talking the elf lord."

Chapter 17

"What do you mean taking over?" I said, anxiety gripping me.

The Mouse was hopping with agitation. "She has put a spell on the wizard so that he now does anything she asks."

"But she only has that small bead of electrum in her pendant," I replied.

"That's more than sufficient to entrance one such as Modrib," Bones said, "and us too. She talked us into releasing her with no trouble at all. She could easily have the elves following her in no time. We must stop her before she sends the elves to capture us."

"What can I do?" I asked.

Tenplessium flew at me. "You still have that electrum dagger. Threaten her with that."

"But you must avoid falling under her power," Bones said.

"Put on your electrum cloak," Aelfed said, "That will protect you."

"It's in the holdall," I muttered. I opened the catch on the holdall and thrust my hand in. It felt like a large empty space but then there was the slightest of caresses on my skin. I grabbed whatever it was and pulled it out; it was the cloak that we had used to restrain the sorceress. I shook it and it billowed out to its full size. I pulled it over my head and felt for the scabbard at my belt. The electrum blade was still there. It was but a toothpick compared to the sword I once had at my side, but it had inflicted pain on the mage once and could do so again.

"Take the holdall," I said to Aelfed. "Keep it safe. The witch must not regain control of the Fairy Queen's electrum."

"Definitely not," Bones said. "We will remain here. Go now and take Hugo. He could be useful."

Bones had a point. I urged the ogre on to his feet and to follow me. He lumbered along behind me as I left the hut.

Some of the elves were still performing tasks in a desultory fashion but others were looking towards the hut where the witch was. Some were even making their way towards it, drawn by something or other.

I pushed past a group of elves that were clustered by the entrance. They drew back when they saw me in the faintly glowing cloak. I thrust my way inside with Hugo close behind me.

The hut was similar to the other but smaller and better lit by the flames of the fire that burned smokily. The sorceress was sitting beside it, cross-legged on a bed of reeds with her skirt hitched up over her knees. Her hands rested on her thighs with her eyes closed. On her left stood Modrib in his black feather gown, and on her right was the elf lord. Both of them appeared to be in a trance.

At the sound of our entry, the mage opened her eyes. A smile spread across her face.

"Ah, here they are my elves, the gnome and the ogre. They say they'll save you from the vicious hoo-mans but they have no power, no means to assist you, unlike me. Sit down, ogre!" She flicked a finger. Hugo fell on his broad bottom and let out a grunt of surprise.

"See. He obeys me." The witch chuckled.

"You won't try that on me, will you," I said, "You know that your spells have no effect when I am cloaked."

"I have no need to act against you at all, gnome," Magus Carmine said with a thin-lipped smile on her face. "The elves will do my bidding."

"No, they won't," I cried and ran towards her. The electrum blade was already in my hand. I thrust it through the cloak as I launched myself at the witch. Her mouth opened in surprise as I tripped over a log and fell into her lap with the point of the blade in her navel.

The witch screamed and fell back, writhing.

"Help me, Hugo," I cried. Released from the spell the

ogre scrambled to his feet and ran to my assistance. He grabbed the witch's shoulders, hauled her on to her feet and held her in a bear hug.

I got to my feet, reached forward and grabbed the pendant that dangled from her neck. I gave a tug and the gold chain snapped. The witch renewed her screams and oaths, promising me all sorts of dire curses.

I found that I was puffing with the exertion, but I managed to say, "You won't be casting any more spells, witch."

Beside her Modrib and Ifantor shook their heads and looked around as if unsure where they were.

"What has happened?" Ifantor asked.

"You fell under the spell of the sorceress. Without her electrum she will no longer have power over you or your people."

"But she promised to protect us from the hoo-mans," he said with a little bit of doubt in his voice.

"I doubt that she could do that with the little power she had control over," I said.

"But who will save us? You?"

"We will think of something," I replied, though I had no idea what that might be.

Modrib had also woken up and looked at the witch in Hugo's strong arms, "She is a powerful mage. If she could cast a spell on the hoo-mans as she has on us, then we could be saved."

"But you allowed yourself to be entranced by her," I said, "She talked to you. The hoo-mans are not going to stand around and be lectured to sleep."

"The gnome has a point," Lord Ifantor said. "The witch beguiled us with her promises but you, Modrib, are our wizard. It is you that we trust."

It wasn't the moment to explain that Modrib had considerably less power than the sorceress.

"I suggest you continue your preparations," I said. Preparations for what I wasn't sure – another attack by the hoo-mans, or evacuation of the village.

"Darkness will be upon us very soon," Ifantor said,

"We must make sure that the village is as secure as it can be for the night."

"We will discuss how we can help you," I said as authoritatively as I could manage, "Hugo, carry the witch back to the other hut." The ogre lifted the sorceress up and effortlessly carried her out of the hut despite her shaking her arms and kicking out her legs.

"I will see that you receive the food intended for you," The elf lord said.

"Thank you," I said, turning to follow Hugo.

Aelfed, Bones and Major Mouse greeted us enthusiastically and Tenplessium looped a loop.

"You can put her down now, Hugo. Thank you," I said. The ogre did as I asked, dumping the sorceress beside the fire.

"Should we tie her up again?" Aelfed said, gripping the holdall tightly.

"That's up to her," I replied. I showed them the pendant with its tiny gleaming drop of electrum. "She does not have any power now, except her powers of persuasion, but perhaps we've learnt to ignore what she says."

"You fools," the witch growled. "What are you going to do when the hoo-mans attack again. They will, you know. The elves are expecting them in the morning."

Bones stood over the witch and looked down at her. "Well, what were you going to do?"

She snorted. "I was going to use them to protect me of course. What else can you do with these primitives?"

Aelfed cried, "You would have let them die to save yourself."

"Of course, and they would have done so too."

"Only because you had them in your spell." I said. I was angry, as angry as I had ever been with Magus Carmine. "And what would you have done then. There are not enough elves to protect you from the might of the hoo-mans who are waiting beyond the hills."

She stared up at me her eyes wide in disbelief. "More?"

"Yes. Tenplessium has seen thousands of them

gathering and preparing to overrun not just this settlement but perhaps everyone on the continent."

"Well, that's it then," the witch said, "We can't stay here. We have to leave."

Bones spoke coldly, "And leave these people to their fate."

"Why not? They're not our responsibility. I don't know about you but I'm leaving." She got on to her knees and was starting to stand up. Bones shoved her with his bony hand. The witch fell back in the dust.

"You're not going anywhere," he said, "And you couldn't get anywhere without your holdall anyway."

The sorceress glared at him with red-eyed hate. "To think I gave you life after you died."

"Don't expect me to be thankful for it. I never wanted to be dug up."

Major Mouse was hopping, trying to get our attention. "She does have a point though. If the hoo-mans do attack tomorrow, how are we going to help the elves? I am assuming we are staying put?"

We looked at each other, lost for words. I for one had no ideas of how to defend the village. By lucky chance just then, Lord Ifantor arrived with a party of elves carrying food laid out on wooden platters. It wasn't a lot, mainly brown, rough bread, a yellow lump which I decided was a cheese and some fruit.

"I am sorry we do not have much to give you. Most of our food has been destroyed or stolen in the raids."

"Thank you, Lord Ifantor," Aelfed said, "We are grateful and will repay you. You expect the hoo-mans to attack again tomorrow?"

"Yes, soon after dawn. We try to drive them off but really, they can do as they like."

"But they don't stay?" I said, "They return to their own camp."

Ifantor shrugged. "They kill a few of my people, set fire to a hut or two, steal what they can find and then leave us."

"They are playing with you," Tenplessium said,

circling above our heads, "They are a small force sent to test your ability to fight back. When the hoo-man army starts to move they will leave none of you alive and no hut standing."

"That is what we fear," Ifantor said, sadness dripping from his voice.

I had to do something to cheer the fellow. "We'll think of something, Lord Ifantor. Prepare your people for the attack."

"Thank you," he said and left us. Major Mouse dived on the food closely followed by Hugo.

"What can we do to fight the hoo-mans?" I said.

"I have my sword," said Tenplessium brandishing her tiny blade as she soared over our heads.

"I have my dragonflies and the little electrum knife. Hugo can bang heads together, but between us we can hardly defeat a band of experienced and fearless fighters."

"What weapons do you have in your holdall, witch?" Aelfed asked.

"None," Carmine replied, "I don't get my power from wielding swords and knives or fiery dragonflies. Magic is my tool."

"Hmm," The hum thrummed through Bones nasal passages. "Perhaps we don't have to think about fighting the hoo-mans, when it is obvious that we cannot."

"What do you mean, Bones," I said, somewhat confused.

Bones continued to muse, "The elves are primitive and their weapons are simple spears and stone axes, but the hoo-mans are only slightly more advanced even if they do have metals that make their arrows more deadly. They probably have bladed weapons too, but that is all."

Tenplessium hovered in front of Bones. "You mean they do not have explosives?"

Bones nodded, "And neither do they have magic. Remember the humans we met – when we were human too – didn't have magic. Electrum did not exist in their world. Perhaps the same is true of their ancestors here."

I had become excited. "You mean we can fight the hoo-mans with explosives and magic."

"Hold on," Aelfed said. "We don't have explosives either. I can't manufacture any in one night."

"We don't need to," Bones went on, "We can use magic to pretend we have explosives. That will frighten the hoo-mans and drive them away, at least temporarily."

"Who can magic up explosions," I said, not thinking straight.

"I can of course, you fool," the sorceress said, "Making bangs and noises and shooting lights is easy. Far easier than killing big, angry hoo-mans."

We all looked at the witch.

"Would you do it?" asked Bones.

"If it is the only way of avoiding getting killed by these raiders, then of course I would do it," Carmine said.

Aelfed shook her head. "No, if we let her have the electrum to make her magic, she'll overpower us."

"No, my darling elf," said the sorceress in a soothing voice, "If at least one of you wears your electrum cloaks, as the gnome is now, and if he holds my pendant while I cast the spell, you can be sure I won't make you my slaves."

I looked at each of my companions. "Can we trust her?"

"You have to," the witch said, "This place is uncomfortable and primitive; not a place I want to stay, but I agree we are in danger. So, I will help us all stay alive until we can look for a way out of here."

"I think we have to accept her word," Bones said.

"Good, I'm glad that's decided," The witch said, "Now let's eat and get some rest. I can't do magic without sleep."

Chapter 18

In which we take on the hoo-mans

I didn't sleep well with just a thin layer of grass between me and the hard ground. It didn't take Aelfed long to rouse me when it was my turn to keep watch. We had decided to take it in turns to make sure that the witch did not change her mind and attempt to escape from us – or more likely, turn the table on us. It was still dark when I decided it was time that we start preparing for the hoo-mans. The witch though was in deep sleep and it took a lot of nudging to get her awake.

"There isn't much time if they attack at dawn," I said. The witch yawned but did not stir. The others by this time were stretching and nervously busying themselves.

"Plenty of time," the sorceress said, still not moving.

Bones spoke to Tenplessium, "Why don't you take a look? See if the hoo-mans are on the move."

The fairy agreed and flew from the hut. Major Mouse was practising some cuts and thrusts with his sword.

"I met a number of mice around the village yesterday. I'll see if they can help make things difficult for the hoo-mans."

"You do that, Major. Now Magus what do you want us to do."

At last, the witch roused herself and stood up. "Take me to the centre of the village so I can see where the raiders are coming from."

We escorted the sorceress from the hut. The elves were already active, hurrying hither and thither with their spears and wooden buckets filled with water. The sky was just beginning to lighten in the east as the Sun in his chariot prepared to start his daily journey.

We met Lord Ifantor in the centre of the village with the wizard Modrib at his side.

The elf lord greeted us rather anxiously, "Good morning, though how it is good I do not know. Do you have a plan to help us?"

"We do," I said with a confidence I did not feel. "From which direction do the hoo-mans attack?" With the narrow, wooded valley to the south and the lake to the east there was not much choice.

"From the north," the elf replied, "They usually drive straight through the village. We can do little to stop them."

"I have cast a spell to reinforce our fighting spirit," the wizard said.

"I'm sure that will help your people," I said not believing a word of it.

A ray of light from the sky showed the return of Tenplessium. "They are coming!" she cried, "They will be here in a hundred heart beats."

Bones faced the witch, "What do we do?"

The sorceress pulled herself up to her full height. She was taller than all of us except Bones and Modrib. "Fairy, patrol the edge of the village. When the hoo-mans start their attack you can harry them."

"Harry them?" Tenplessium asked.

"Yes, you know. Dive at them, slash at them with your sword. Distract them."

"Oh, right. Got it." She flew off and became just another star in the sky hovering over the border of the village.

The witch turned to me. "Release your dragonflies and send them to join the fairy."

I had been expecting that instruction, so I reached under the cloak and lifted my cap. The dragonflies flew out, their wings buzzing furiously. They circled my head until I told them what to do. Then they flew off and disappeared from sight.

The witch went on. "Ogre, when the hoo-mans appear in the village, stand in their way." Hugo grunted in agreement. "Elf, protect my holdall at all costs. Bones. I need you to watch over me. I will be concentrating on the spells, so I depend on you to warn us of any hoo-mans getting close enough to threaten us."

Aelfed took a firm grip with both hands on the holdall and crouched down over it. Bones stood statue-like beside the witch.

"And, finally, gnome," the sorceress, "since you will not give me my pendant back, hold it firmly and press it to the back of my neck. Only when electrum is against my skin can I perform my spells." I nodded and moved behind the witch. With the pendant in my hand, I reached under my cloak and pressed it to the nape of her neck below the mass of red curls. She sighed deeply. She was drinking in the metal's power.

A beam of sunlight appeared above the hills to the east of the lake. At that moment there came an elven cry from the north side of the village.

"They come," Lord Ifantor muttered. Modrib thrust out his staff, the tiny bead of electrum gleaming. He chanted spells which meant nothing to me.

The Magus Carmine lifted up her arms and spread the fingers of both hands. She said nothing, but her body trembled. I could feel the power emanating from her.

Over the huts at the northern edge of the village, the star that was Tenplessium became a thousand. In formation the swarm of pin-point fires dived to repel the attackers, weaving this way and that, soaring and then diving again. It was easy to believe that it was a huge force of fairies attacking the hoo-mans, not just one with a thousand copies.

Similarly, my dragonflies joined in the defence. With fiery breath they flew into the fray. They were not increased in number like the fairies, but the witch's magic made them grow in size. They appeared as immense dragons roaring their defiance. The sky was filled with their flame and each broad, quadruple set of wings beat the air. I wanted to leap and cheer but I restrained myself and kept the pendant pressed to the witch's neck.

A great noise came from the edge of the village, the cries of the elves and the bellows of the hoo-mans. Those hoo-man sounds seemed more like surprise and anguish than belligerence.

Then it seemed as if the ground was shifting as if in an earthquake. The dust boiled and became waves of mice racing to the fight. I thought I had a glimpse of Major Mouse at the front, blade raised for the attack.

Hugo marched after the mice. The further he moved from us the larger he seemed to become until he towered over the huts of the elves. He roared and beat his chest, urging the hoo-mans to attack him. None did.

From the witch's fingers came shafts of light that rose into the dawn sky, exploding into starbursts of coloured light. The lights fell illuminating the huts and the melee that was occurring at the edge of the village. A few arrows went up into the air but fell well short of where we stood. Then the cries of the elves turned into cheers and the roars of the hoo-mans became more distant.

It was over before the complete disc of the Sun had cleared the hills. Elves returned laughing and slapping each other's backs in celebration. There was no sound from the hoo-mans at all.

The sorceress lowered her arms. "You can take the pendant away now, gnome," she said in a tired voice. She dropped into my arms. I staggered back and only just managed to lower her gently to the ground. Bones stooped to tend to her.

"You did well, Madam. It seems the hoo-mans have been repelled."

"I have never felt like this," the sorceress said.

"What? You've never been exhausted?" I said.

"Not that. Doing magic is always tiring. No, I meant this feeling I have of…of…."

Bones completed her sentence, "Satisfaction having done something to help another being?"

"Er, is that what it is?" she sighed and relaxed into my arms.

The elf lord ran to us, laughing and waving his arms pointing to the north. "They've gone, they've run away back to where they came from. You saved us, you saved us all."

Hugo, back to his normal size, returned with Major Mouse on his shoulder whooping and waving his sword about. Tenplessium soared down and hovered amongst us. Everyone was talking excitedly about what had happened.

"All the hoo-mans have run away?" I asked still feeling a little nervous. I dropped the witch's pendant into a pocket.

The fairy replied, "All but for two or three that were so dazzled and confused that the elves caught and despatched them with their spears.

My dragonflies flew to me, also returned to their true size. I gathered them in my hands and tucked them back safely into my cap.

"We've seen the last of them," Lord Ifantor said. He looked very satisfied with the morning's work.

Bones addressed him, "I wouldn't say that if I were you."

The elf glared at the skeleton. "But you've helped us defeat them. They've gone."

"Yes, they've gone back to their camp and I daresay they're somewhat chastened by this morning's experience. We've won a skirmish, but I doubt that we have won the battle let alone the war."

"War?" The elf lord looked mystified.

"There is a huge army of hoo-mans preparing," Bones went on. "When they are ready, they won't be put off by a few flashes in the sky or scary visions of giants or dragons or myriads of fighting fairies and mice. Soon they will realise that their only losses were due to the spears wielded by your elves. They will be back, but I think we have bought you some time."

Ifantor was worried now. "Time for what? Will you stay and defend us again?"

"I'm not sure that display will work again," Bones added.

"Well, what then?"

"Time to evacuate, move all your people back to the mountains. Join up with others of your sort, and with gnomes and fairies."

Aelfed had wandered off but now returned carrying a handful of the Hoo-mans arrows.

"You can take these with you to show others. I can explain to you how to make the iron that was made into the arrowheads, and I can show you how to make other things of metal."

Modrib had been listening disinterestedly but now approached Aelfed eagerly. He took an arrow from her and examine the tip. "Does it use magic?"

"Not really," Aelfed said. "It doesn't take a mage to make iron. Any elf or gnome can do it given the knowledge and a good fire."

"I can make fire," Modrib said, pointing to the speck of electrum in his staff.

"That's good," Aelfed said, "Your help will be invaluable."

The wizard seemed happy with that promise.

"I will send you my cleverest elves to learn from you," Ifantor said, "Now though, we should eat and then start preparations for our journey if it is necessary."

"Breakfast! Wonderful!" squeaked Major Mouse scampering down the ogre's coarse tunic.

"Yes, that will be appreciated," I added, "but we have to think about what we do next.

Aelfed began explaining to the wide-eyed elves the basic ideas of metalwork while the rest of us sat around the fire in our hut, content after a simple but filling meal. The sorceress was asleep at my side."Do we have to stay with these elves much longer?" I asked.

"I do not think so," Bones replied. "They can set off very soon and the further they travel south, the safer they will be, for now, at least."

"We should deal with the hoo-mans. They must be defeated for good," Tenplessium said.

"But how?" I said, "We cannot take on a vast army ourselves."

The fairy's erratic flight showed that she was unhappy with that conclusion but could offer no alternative.

Bones spoke quietly and slowly, "If we are to help your ancestors, by that I mean elves, gnomes, fairies, ogres and other intelligent beings of this world then we must first of all find the full extent of the hoo-mans' invasion and warn the people of their coming."

"But that means travelling across the whole continent," Tenplessium said, "That would take days, even for a fairy flying the whole distance."

"I know and it's only the first part of our task," Bones said.

"What is the second part?" I asked.

"Preventing the hoo-mans from eliminating all your peoples."

"What?" I cried "Do you think that is really their intent?"

"I can see no other reason for their actions. Their vast army is obviously set on occupying the continent and their actions towards the elves here show that they do not intend being kind neighbours."

"But how can we stop them? Not even the sorceress can be everywhere at once to oppose all the hoo-mans."

Bones bowed his head, "I do not have an answer."

We fell silent as each of us struggled with the impossibility of the task we had accepted responsibility for. Lord Ifantor had more food brought to us and told us of the progress of preparations for the evacuation. The elves would move out next day and begin the long trek to safer elven settlements beyond the hills and the plain, amongst the mountains. We spent the afternoon helping the elves dismantle their huts. They didn't want to leave them for the hoo-mans to use or destroy, whichever was their intention. It was a simple job to pull the rushes from the roofs and dismantle the walls of twigs and branches. Only the main wooden posts provided much strength. How long would it be before the elves learned to build the towers that made up Elfholm, and their other cities?

Having seen the way the primitive elves lived I wondered about how my ancestors survived under the mountains. More and more I felt that we had to warn our peoples of the coming of the hoo-mans.

Aelfed returned to us in the evening, exhausted after a day of teaching the elves about metals. They had been quick learners and she was confident that once they reached their fellows the basic principles of metal extraction and manipulation would quickly spread.

"So, what are we doing when the elves leave tomorrow," she said. The rest of us shrugged but didn't answer. "We have to warn peoples across the continent of the threat of the hoo-mans."

"We do," Bones agreed, "But how do we travel so far, quickly enough."

"We've travelled in various ways on our journey," Aelfed said.

"Yes," I replied, "by train, car, helicopter and spaceship. None of which we have here."

Bones nodded and added, "As well as carriage, pigeon, on the back of the Knight of the Night's horse and carried by fairies."

"None of those are fast enough or give us the view of the hoo-mans that we need," I concluded.

"There is another way," the sorceress said. We all looked at her in surprise – she had been uncharacteristically quiet since the morning's battle. Tired, I supposed. "I shall have to speak to the Sun," she continued, "but he is at rest now."

She wouldn't reveal any more, but urged us to arise at dawn in the morning when she would organise our travel.

It seemed we would have to wait for the rising of the Sun to continue our journey.

Chapter 19

We travel with the Sun

It was still dark when we left, Aelfed carrying the holdall and me still draped in the electrum cloak. The elves were already making the last preparations for their journey. They quickly dismantled our hut. Scouts had reported there were no signs of hoo-mans approaching; it appeared that our display yesterday had put off the marauders, at least for now.

"I need my electrum on my skin," Magus Carmine said.

"I will do the same as yesterday then, shall I," I said.

"If you must."

We did not consider it safe to put electrum into the witch's hand. I doubted that we would ever trust her. I took the pendant from my purse and stood behind her as she faced east. I pressed the tiny bead of electrum against her neck.

The sky was overcast but the first glow of dawn was spreading above the eastern hills. The sorceress muttered something unintelligibly. It sounded like a conversation of which we only heard one side. She conversed for a few minutes, sometimes getting agitated, at other times speaking soothingly. At last, the exchange came to an end and she turned her head to speak to us.

"Mister Sun has agreed to convey us."

"Mister Sun?" I asked,

"Of course, the driver of the chariot of the Sun. Watch now."

In the east the clouds parted. A shaft of sunlight pierced the morning gloom, forming a pool of light on the dusty ground in front of us.

"Stand in the sunlight," the witch ordered. "Hold my hand gnome. The rest of you hold on to him."

The sorceress stepped into the circle of sunlight. I followed and grabbed her hand. Major Mouse scampered up my trouser leg and Tenplessium landed on my shoulder. Aelfed took my other hand. Bones grasped my arm in his long bony hand. The ogre's large, fleshy palm landed on my shoulder, luckily the one not occupied by the fairy.

For a moment we stood, the whole group of us bathed in the glow of the sunlight. Then we moved.

I gasped.

It seemed as if I had left my stomach on the ground, but I swallowed and that seemed to settle me. Aelfed let out a cry but the others were speechless when, as a group, we rose into the sky.

The ground receded at an incredible rate, and the panorama made visible by our increasing height broadened quickly. In a moment I could see over the hills to the north to where the hoo-mans' army waited. The land was filled with their encampments with smoke rising into the air across the whole vista.

Though fascinated with the sight below, I tore my eyes away to see where we were heading. There ahead of us was the bright orb of the Sun rising above the horizon. It was growing steadily and becoming brighter and brighter. I would have shielded my eyes if I had a hand spare, but I did not. I had to squint and peer though my eyelashes to avoid being completely dazzled by the light.

"We will be burned by the sun," Aelfed cried, her voice almost lost in the rush of the air passing us.

"Have no fear," the Magus said, "I have ensured that Mr Sun will shield us from his heat."

I was not certain that the sorceress' words made me feel secure but there was nothing else to be done and no way of stopping our inexorable rise.

As the Sun grew in my eyes, I began to see a hint of its shape and structure. Though from the ground it looks like a simple ball of fire, that is of course because of its brightness. Now that the Sun was filling more and more of my view, and by looking to its edges rather than straight at it, I could confirm that it was indeed carried on a chariot. Well, not so much a chariot, more like a sleigh, made of red-hot spars and rods. It was drawn by a dozen fiery geese, each feather a flame. Grasping the reins was the naked, red skinned figure of the driver. He was a pot-bellied, bald-headed male with short fat legs and fleshy arms. He controlled the geese with one hand while cracking a whip of flame with his other.

As we approached on the sunbeam, he hailed us. "Good day, Magus Carmine. What a pleasure to make your acquaintance. Come aboard." Mister Sun was a lot more welcoming and jollier by nature than I had expected.

Though a great heat was given off by the sleigh and its cargo, it seemed to do us no great harm. We stepped onto the footplate beside Mr Sun. Ahead of us were the six pairs of geese, their broad wings flapping powerfully, drawing us at great speed through the air.

We crowded together beside the driver, still holding on to each other for security. With the great bulk of the incandescent sphere behind us I was able to open my eyes and look ahead and down. The overcast had cleared and though there were still a few puffs of white cloud, I could see all the way to the ground, a long way down. My vision was clear for a huge distance in every direction but the features of the landscape, even hills and forests were so small that it was impossible to pick out details such as elvish settlements and camps of the hoo-mans' army.

"We are travelling very fast," I said, "But at this great height, I cannot see anything on the ground."

"I expected that problem," Carmine replied. "Look in my holdall, elf. You will find two eyes."

"Eyes?" Aelfed said.

"Yes, you know what eyes are, spherical objects."

Rather tentatively, Aelfed released her grip on me, opened the holdall and inserted her hand. She spent less than two breaths feeling around before her expression changed to one of surprise and relief. She pulled out her hand and opened it up to reveal two solid, white porcelain balls, both complete with iris and pupil.

"Who can see using these?" Aelfed asked.

"Who do you think, elf," scoffed the sorceress, "Who lacks eyes?"

"I think she is referring to me," Bones said. He held out his hand and Aelfed handed them over. The glassy balls clattered against his bones. Bones raised them to his skull and slotted the eyes into his sockets. They fitted perfectly.

"Oh, yes!" Bones said with enthusiasm, "This is a lot better than seeing with my mind's eye." He scanned us. It was strange seeing those white orbs staring out of Bones' face. I had grown used to looking at his vacant sockets.

"Look down," Carmine commanded, "What do you see?"

Bones leaned over the side of the sleigh and stared vertically down.

"My, that is tremendous," he said, "I can focus on the smallest object no matter how far away it is. I can see voles hiding in tufts of grass, and birds on their nests in the trees."

"We want to know where the hoo-mans are, their formations," Tenplessium said, "and how close they are to elf, fairy, gnome and ogre settlements."

"Yes, alright," Bones replied. "I can do that. I was just testing the range of these eyes. They are quite wonderful. Why didn't you give them to me earlier, Madam Sorcerer?"

Carmine shrugged. "Oh, I forgot I had them, and anyway, you didn't deserve them."

Bones snorted but continued to peer downwards while passing his observations to Tenplessium who had moved to perch on his skull.

I turned to watch Mr Sun controlling the path of the sleigh across the sky. Major Mouse scrambled up onto my shoulder and with the passing air fluffing up his fur he let out a joyful squeak.

We hadn't yet had any conversation with the fiery driver. "Thank you for providing us with transport," I said as politely as I could.

He glanced at me with a broad smile on his red face. "It's my pleasure," he replied, "I don't get to meet many people up here. When I was contacted by your charming witch who said she was accompanied by such a variety of beings, I couldn't resist the opportunity to meet you all."

Charming witch! I supposed that the sorceress *was* able to turn on the 'charm' when she wished. However, it was obvious that Mr Sun had not met the Magus Carmine before this time. I decided to continue in conversation.

"It must get monotonous for you, doing the same trip day after day."

Mr Sun chuckled, "Oh no, every day is different. You see, I follow a different track every day. In the summer I venture northwards and make the journey last a good two thirds of the day. In winter I track much further south and fly from east to west in half the time."

"Oh, I see, and that is how the length of days varies with the seasons," I said, revealing knowledge many gnomes – spending their whole lives below ground – do not have.

"That is correct, gnome! So, you see, I have to ensure that that the duration of the days corresponds to the time of the year. That keeps me busy and interested in my work."

"I congratulate you on your dedication," I said, "Do you watch what is happening on the ground over which you pass?"

The fiery driver shrugged, "I follow the passage of the seasons, the changing colour of the forests and appearance of snow on the mountains, but I am not acquainted with the activities of the beings that live down there."

I was concerned that Mr Sun was not aware of what was occurring down below. "You have not seen the growing numbers of hoo-mans spreading from the north?"

"Who are these hoo-mans to which you refer? I can barely tell elves, gnomes and ogres apart."

"Hoo-mans are big, muscular beings. There are a great

many of them and they are threatening to overrun all the other peoples that occupy the continent."

"That is not right, gnome. No being has the right to deprive another of its land and livelihood!"

"Hence why we are taking this journey, Mr Sun. It is kind of you to carry us so that we can gain knowledge about the hoo-mans."

"As, I said gnome, it is my pleasure."

As I looked down, I could see that we were passing over the central plain of the continent. I wondered if there was in this time a settlement on the site where we all met before we ventured into the Parting. I couldn't see, but perhaps Bones could.

"What are you seeing, Bones?"

The skeleton didn't move. His new eyes remained fixed on the ground, but he spoke with immense sadness. "They are everywhere. The north is full of hoo-mans, their army camps, their settlements and industrial sites. I couldn't count their number. Everywhere they are preparing to move south. I have seen dozens of elf towns, ogre settlements, fairy forts, within a few days' march of the hoo-man forces. I don't see how they can possibly stop the hoo-man invasion."

We continued to travel across the sky throughout the day. We talked to Mr Sun about our various lives though we did not mention that the reason for our journey was chasing the sorceress. She remained charming to Mr Sun, praising him for his life of service. The fiery driver was delighted to hear our stories of the various land-bound beings. He was equally upset to hear of the threat from the hoo-mans, but what could he do while he completed his daily journey – nothing. Bones maintained his observations, though to be truthful little changed and we became gloomier and gloomier about the prospect for all our peoples.

As the day stretched into the late afternoon, Mr Sun spoke, "I will have to set you down somewhere soon. Before long I will be beyond the west and in the land where none of you can be."

"How do you return to the east?" Aelfed asked. A very reasonable question, I thought.

"It is difficult to explain," Mr Sun said, "Once I am beyond the west I pass between and am once again in the east and ready to bring dawn to a new day."

"You mean there is nothing between the west and the east?"

"Outside of your world, no there is not, no space, no time."

We all looked at the big flaming man wondering what he meant.

Bones straightened up, his joints creaking. "I think we should go to a fairy fortress. The fairies are likely to be most informed of the advance of the hoo-mans."

We all agreed.

"You can give me the eyes back now," the witch said, holding out her hand.

"May I not keep them?" Bones said.

"Definitely not. They are for special purposes. So, pop them out."

I was surprised that Bones acquiesced so quickly. He held one hand in front of his face and tapped the back of his skull with the other. The china eyes fell from the sockets. He held his hand out to the sorceress.

"Put them back in the bag, elf," she said.

Aelfed took the two balls and dropped them into the holdall. She gave Bones a wink.

"If you would like to step onto the sunbeam. I'll deliver you to your destination," Mr Sun said. A ray of sunlight appeared, brighter than all the rest alongside the sleigh.

"Everyone, hold on," Carmine said.

We each made a grab for the other and together stepped off the sleigh. Having made the journey up to Sun I suppose we were prepared. Nevertheless, leaving the reassuring solidity of the sleigh and stepping into the air, albeit illuminated by the sunbeam, required a degree of shared faith. We fell, not vertically but at an angle to the ground while the Sun was pulled on by the geese heading ever further into the west.

Our beam of sunlight took us quickly towards the ground. Here in the western edge of the continent, the land was more mountainous, with deep valleys. Very quickly I could see where our beam was shining. It was a white structure that clung to the side of a mountain. A river poured over a waterfall into a lake beside the fairy castle. As we got closer I had a better idea of scale. Of course, it was a fairy castle, so it was fairy sized.

We landed on the meadow beside the lake which was actually a mere pond. The castle walls and towers were arrayed in front of me. They rose to about my height.

We had hardly got used to having our feet on solid earth again when a great buzzing sound came from the fortress. A swarm of pin-point lights, fairies, rose from the battlements and flew towards us.

Chapter 20

The fairies circled each of us, separating us with a screen of flickering wings. Some fluttered close to my face and I got a brief sight of them. Although they looked like Tenplessium, their dress was simpler and instead of swords or bow and arrows they carried spears about as long as their bodies, in other words, about as big as my thumb. At the tip of each spear was the tiniest point of glowing, blue electrum.

While we stood still, their agitation diminished until they hovered around us in a ring. From one of the swarm came a small, thin voice.

"Who are you? What brings you to Fort Falengin."

Tenplessium flew from her perch on Bones and took up a position between us and the speaker.

"As you can see, I too am a fairy and my companions are an elf, a gnome, an ogre, a mouse, a mage and a skeleton. We have come to warn you of the approach of a huge force of hoo-mans."

"We know of the hoo-mans. We do not need to be informed by your varied bunch of companions."

"Oh, I think you do because we have seen an army of hoo-mans just a few days march from here. When they arrive, they will destroy your fort."

"Nonsense. We are fairies, we fight."

"With those spears?"

"They are tipped with electrum. They will kill any being they penetrate."

Tenplessium flittered closer to the speaker. "They won't come close to penetrating the skin of the hoo-mans. Those we have seen are clothed in textiles and the skins of animals, thicker than your spears. Also, the hoo-mans

211

bear weapons that can destroy your fortifications from a distance."

The speaker separated from the swarm and flew towards Tenplessium, halting just a finger's width from her. "How do you know such things?"

"Who am I addressing?" Tenplessium asked calmly.

"I am Captain of the Guard, Ningolion."

"Well, we have just travelled the length of the continent from east to west with the Sun. We have observed the hoo-mans throughout our journey. There are a great many of them, right across the north and they are prepared for war. They will fight fairy, elf, gnome, mage and ogre until they have control over the whole land. We bring you this knowledge to spread to other peoples, so that they might prepare."

Captain Ningolion seemed to sag. He dropped lower. "How can we prepare if, as you say, these hoo-mans are equipped to overwhelm us."

I wondered how Tenplessium would reply since I had no answer to the fairy's lament. Nevertheless, answer she did.

"We are fairies. We do not give in. We will find a way to overcome the hoo-mans."

The captain was apparently fortified by Templessium's words. He recovered and flew back up to her.

"You must tell us more of what you have seen. Join us in Fort Falengin. Of course, your companions will remain outside."

"Of course," Tenplessium said, "I will accompany you."

The fairies flew away with Tenplessium at their centre. The swarm climbed over the battlements and disappeared inside the castle.

"I shall take a look to see what I can see." Major Mouse squeaked in my ear. He scampered down my clothing, across the ground and disappeared around the side of the castle.

Bones folded his joints to lower himself to the ground. "While we wait for the fairy to return, I am going to take the opportunity to rest my limbs."

"A good idea," Aelfed replied, "I too am weary after that long flight."

We all settled onto the soft grass of the meadow. It was a very peaceful setting only spoiled by the thought of the approaching hoo-mans and what they would make of the fairy castle.

As I looked around, taking in the pleasant views of the pond and waterfall and mountains, I noticed some figures approaching. They were coming down the valley where the peaks crowded together. As they drew closer, I realised that they were gnomes. There were three males and two females, all with shaggy beards and unkempt hair around their bald pates which were unprotected by a cap. Their clothes barely covered their bodies and consisted of bits of the skins of dead animals. They were not the sort of people who I would seek out for company, but I realised that they were my ancestors and probably deserved my respect. Four of them carried stone clubs while the last held a bowl roughly carved from a piece of rock.

When they drew close, I got to my feet and greeted them. "Hello, my fellow gnomes."

One of the males replied gruffly. "Who are you? What are you doing at the gates of Fort Falengin?"

"We have brought news to the fairies," I replied.

The gnome did not look any happier. "What news?"

"It concerns the immense gathering of hoo-mans in the north."

"Hoo-mans do not concern us."

"Why not?" I was astonished at the gnome's lack of concern.

"We live under the mountains where no hoo-man will trouble us."

The gnome's confidence was misplaced I felt. "But here you are out in the open. What brings you from your refuge?"

The leading gnome looked surprised as if he had not thought about it. He looked at his companions and then answered. "We visit the fairies to trade our electrum."

I noticed the sorceress stir from her position lying on

the grass. She had been somewhat quiet and listless since we left the Sun. I had wondered if she was planning something and not sharing it with us.

"Electrum? Did you say, electrum?" She got to her feet and approached the gnomes. She looked down into the pot held by the gnome. Her eyes opened wide in delight, and her fingers moved as if in preparation for grabbing the precious metal.

I could just see the blue glow from the bowl. "May I see it too?" I asked.

The gnome looked at me uncertainly but stretched her arms to hold out the bowl. I saw inside a few tiny grains of electrum.

"Where did you find this electrum?" the sorceress asked.

The leading gnome replied, "We collect it from streams that flow under the mountain. The fairies have a use for it, so we exchange it for honey. They give us a lot more honey than the electrum we have."

"I should hope so," I said wondering if these gnomes had any idea of the value of electrum.

"Is this all that you have found?" the witch said.

"It is what we have collected in recent weeks," the gnome replied, "We come to Fort Fallengin every month."

The mage continued to look at the electrum, paltry sample though it was, with avaricious eyes. I tugged on her arm.

"Come, sorceress. Let us leave these gnomes to complete their transaction with the fairies."

She resisted me, "But… electrum. I must – "

"No, it is not for you." I pulled harder and drew her away from the gnomes. They looked at us with some confusion but moved on up to the castle walls. A fairy appeared on the battlements. His thin voice carried to us.

"Ah, gnomes. You have brought us electrum." Some more fairies appeared fluttering in a circle above the castle and holding between them a sheet of fine cloth. They floated down to where the gnomes stood. The gnome carrying the pot tipped its contents into the sheet. Despite being smaller than my palm, the pieces of electrum seemed almost lost in it, only their faint glow indicating their presence.

"Thank you, kind gnomes. Your electrum is much appreciated. The agreed quantity of honey will be provided."

A door at the base of the castle wall opened and a host of fairies appeared rolling out a barrel. While many times the size of a single fairy it was no bigger in height or diameter than the length of my hand. The gnome bent down and lifted it up with ease. The smile on all the gnomes' faces showed that they were fully satisfied with the exchange. They turned and started to walk alongside the stream back towards the mountains.

"My friends," I cried, running to their side, "do you trade in other goods?"

They stopped and looked at me with surprise. "Other goods?" The leader obviously had no understanding of my question.

I could think of many things but wondered what they would understand. "Er, copper, iron, or their ores, ochre, cinnabar, or diamonds perhaps."

They looked at me blankly then shook their heads. "What are those words you speak?" the spokes-gnome said.

They knew nothing of the substances I mentioned. It could not be because they did not understand the names I used, as the sorceress' spell that enabled us to speak their language would surely have translated my words into those of their language. Gnomes at this time obviously had a lot to learn about the riches of their home under the mountains. How long would it be before gnomes became the famed purveyors of such goods?

"Oh, it doesn't matter," I said, "I hope you have a good journey back to your home. But please take heed of our warning about the hoo-mans. They are a great threat."

"Hoo-mans will not find us," the gnome said and turned away from me to resume his walk.

I watched them until they were out of sight around a bend in the stream.

"We should go after them," the sorceress said.

"Why?"

"There is obviously a sizeable electrum lode in that mountain. I could make them mine it."

I looked at her. There was that special madness in her eyes which had seemed to go out the last day; the desire for electrum and the power it provided.

"No doubt you could subjugate the gnomes if we let you, but the hoo-mans are our concern – not letting you get hold of electrum."

Bones, Aelfed, Hugo joined me to encircle the witch, just in case she decided to run after the gnomes.

She sagged. "…I suppose you are correct."

Aelfed had not said a word while we had our visitation but now she spoke to me. "Your ancestors are as primitive as mine."

"It shows how far in our past we are," Bones added. Hugo grunted in agreement.

"They have little knowledge of the power of the electrum that they collect and trade for such a small quantity of honey," Aelfed added.

"They did not even recognise that I was wearing an electrum cloak," I said.

"But the Fairies must have an abundance of electrum," Carmine said, recovering her spirit.

"Perhaps they do, madam," Bones replied, "But that is no business of ours. Stealing fairy electrum is how we came to be in this predicament."

There was movement over the castle again. Tenplessium flew back to us. She was buzzing with fury.

"Those fairies have no idea. They think their spears with their tips of electrum can stop the hoo-mans. They have no understanding of the number of the invaders or how they are equipped."

Bones spoke, "But they will inform other fairy fortresses and settlements of elves, gnomes and ogres?"

Tenplessium shrugged. "They did agree to spread the

news to other fairies and elvish towns nearby, but they won't go under the mountains to visit gnomes and they won't attempt to speak to ogres."

Aelfed had a worried look, "Even if all the peoples of the continent are warned, that will not stop the hoo-mans' invasion."

We all nodded in agreement but had nothing to add. Finally, the sorceress spoke, "Perhaps we're looking at this somewhat pessimistically."

I was confused. "What do you mean>"

The witch looked at each of us in turn as if choosing what to say. "We are agreed that this is our own world?"

It was what I felt but I wanted to be certain, "How do we know that?"

"Look at us," the witch said spreading her arms. "You are yourselves. You are not human replicas like you were when you chased me into the world of humans."

We each shook our heads. Having checked our response, the witch went on.

"Neither are you living your dreams with an extra set of life-long memories."

Those memories of being King of the Gnomes along with my life as a human in my little cottage remained in my head, but I knew them to be false. We all nodded again.

"That all suggests that this is where we were born, where we grew up, where we belong," she concluded.

"But – " Aelfed said.

"Yes, I know, this isn't quite our home. We are in the past, a long way in the past. Am I correct?"

We all muttered agreement.

"But in our time, there are no hoo-mans living in our world. Our peoples live, if not happily then without threat of attack by invaders. Is that true?"

Yes, yes, we all said enthusiastically.

"So, what does that mean?" She looked at each of us intently.

"Um," I began but found I had nothing to say.

Bones raised a bony hand. "I think I see where you are

going, Madam. The hoo-man invasion and elimination of all our ancestors cannot have happened."

The sorceress clapped her hands. "Yes, you have it. Something or someone stopped the hoo-mans before they could put their plans into action. That something also eliminated them from our world."

"But, who?" I started again but my voice faded.

Magus Carmine spread her arms to encompass the six of us, her eyes wide encouraging an answer.

"Us?" I said.

"It must be. There is no one else," she said.

"But we cannot think of a solution," Aelfed said. "Unless..."

"What is it, elf?" Bones said.

Aelfed stared at the sorceress. "Perhaps if you used the spell that you cast in the dream world, when you sought to overthrow all the governments of the fairies, elves, gnomes and so on."

The witch shook her head. "No, that spell was not selective. It was a threat to every sentient being. You were supposed to give in to my demands, not die."

I felt anger building in me. "Instead, it killed many sea-people as well as dolphins and whales."

The sorceress hung her head. "I'm sorry about that. My dream of domination was... very powerful. I regret that spell."

"You regret that it wasn't successful," I spat at her.

She shrugged, "We all know that that world wasn't real."

"It was real enough while we were there. It was real to me when I was King of the Gnomes."

"And I was happily resting in peace," Bones said, "But that world has gone. This is our real world and as Madam says, her destructive spell would not be appropriate here. Is there another way?"

"Perhaps," the sorceress said, "There is one other difference between our world in this time and that of the future."

I swallowed the nasty taste in my mouth from arguing

with the sorceress and answered, "The elves and fairies and gnomes now are more primitive and have no knowledge of metals and other materials."

"Apart from that," Carmine replied.

Aelfed jumped up and down. "I have it," she cried.

"So, what is it?" the sorceress said.

"There is no Parting here!" Aelfed glowed with satisfaction.

It was so obvious. We had flown across the whole continent with the Sun and none of us had commented on the lack of the Parting.

Tenplessium was flying in figures of eight. "Why is the lack of the Parting important now?"

The sorceress looked sad as if she was teaching dunderheads. "What does the Parting do in our time? It is a barrier cutting off the north from us. Nothing can come through the barrier into our world. Yet when we crossed the Parting, we found ourselves in a world of humans, civilised Hoo-mans if you like."

Bones nodded. "The Parting prevents Hoo-mans or Humans from entering our world."

The witch sighed, "At last, they see the truth."

I felt a weight lift off me and I shouted, "That's the answer. We have to make the Parting."

The Magus nodded knowingly.

Chapter 21

Our plan takes shape

A tremendous outcry erupted from the fairy fort. We all looked towards it. Scampering toward us across the meadow was Major Mouse, followed by a swarm of angry fairies. The Mouse reached me, climbed my trouser leg and crawled into my pocket. The fairies whirled around me, their wings beating furiously. I waved my arms, swatting at the fairies as they thrust out their tiny blue pointed spears at my face. I was afraid they were going to pierce my skin and I trembled at the effect of the electrum on my wellbeing.

Bones careered around with his long arm bones rotating like a windmill. He would have batted the fairies out of the way if he had been able to make contact with any.

"Stop, stop," cried Tenplessium in her thin, high voice. She landed on the peak of my hat. Whatever she was doing must have got the attention of the fairies, because they calmed and came to rest hovering around me.

"What are you doing?" Tenplessium asked.

"The mouse was attempting to steal our electrum," one of the fairies announced. I guessed it was Captain Ningolion.

A muffled squeak came from my pocket. "No, I wasn't."

"He was sneaking around our treasury," the fairy said.

"Well, yes, I had found where they keep their electrum," Major Mouse said.

"Major Mouse," I said, "Come out and explain to the fairies what you were doing," I held my hand at my pocket for the Major to crawl onto. "I'll keep you safe from the fairies."

Whiskers, then a quivering nose, appeared from my

pocket, then a pair of eyes and ears. Major Mouse crawled onto my hand curled into a ball.

"The mouse intended no harm," I said to the assembled fairies. "He was just making sure that Tenplessium was safe and able to report to us."

"Then why was he in our treasury?" Ningolion demanded.

"I got lost," Major Mouse said, although I cannot imagine him ever being unaware of his location. "I had to crawl in through your drainage tunnels and found myself in the cellar. I was surprised to see you have a sizeable store of electrum."

"They do, do they?" the sorceress said, her eyes gleaming.

"We have not come to steal your electrum," I said. "We just wanted to warn you all of the coming of the hoo-mans."

"We will join with other fairies to destroy the hoo-mans," the Captain of the Fairies said.

Bones replied, " No you won't. They are far too powerful. Rather than fighting them you must alert all the peoples, so that they can prepare."

"Prepare for what?" Ningolion said, "If, as you insist, we can't defeat the hoo-mans, what can we do?"

Tenplessium rose into the air and with a firm voice replied. "Get your people away from the battle that will come. Harry the hoo-mans to slow their advance. Give us time to erect a defence."

"*You* can defend us." The fairy's response was incredulous.

"Yes," Tenplessium said. The rest of us looked at each other blankly. The fairy was being presumptuous. How could we create the Parting?

The sorceress pulled herself up to her full height. "The fairy is right. We will defend you all. We need to prepare, so bring us food and drink and make shelter for us."

The fairies buzzed and fluttered in agitation. After a few moments of discussion, the Captain responded. "You cannot expect us to provide sustenance for you large creatures. Your demands are far greater than we can provide."

The sorceress shrugged, "We need shelter and provisions while we prepare your defence. If you cannot look after us then – "

"Perhaps you can find others who can," Bones interrupted, "People like those gnomes with whom you just traded honey for electrum."

Tenplessium joined in, "There are elves nearby. You told me so. I am sure they can provide food and drink."

The Captain fluttered in agitation. "Well, yes, there are other peoples. We are not accustomed to negotiating with them."

"It's about time you started," Aelfed said, stamping her foot.

My eyes were drawn to the air above me. Something had caught my attention. Something up there was falling. Drops of rain? Leaves from the trees? No, it was a flash of silver, a flicker of gossamer wings. Fairies were dropping from the sky.

The Falengin fairies saw them a moment after I did, they soared up two or three to each falling fairy, catching them in their arms, supporting them, lowering them gently to the meadow.

I crouched down to examine them. Major Mouse leapt from my hand and went to each in turn. The arrivals were exhausted, their wings torn, their silver clothing dulled by soot, some even showed wounds oozing violet blood.

"What has happened? Where are they from?" I asked.

Captain Ningolion paused in flying from one injured fairy to the another. "They are not part of my complement."

One of the strange fairies lifted herself from where she had fallen on the grass. Her voice was thin and weak.

"We are from Fort Camorpholgin. We bring terrible news." She coughed and sank back on to the meadow.

"Camorpholgin," repeated Nongolion. "That is north of here, half a day's flight. What has happened."

Another of the fallen fairies stirred. "Our castle was

attacked by hoo-mans. It is destroyed, our comrades killed."

"Did you not fight the hoo-mans?" the Captain asked, his voice angry and pained.

"How can you fight when, from afar, they throw burning tar into our fortress and consume it in fire."

"But you have electrum tipped spears. One thrust would kill any being that threatened you."

"Only if you can pierce their flesh. The hoo-mans wore clothes of leather, some even wore metal over their heads and faces. Our spears rarely reached their skin. They swept us up in nets of silk and pounded us with clubs. We could not defeat them."

The Captain did not reply for a number of breaths, then quietly, he said. "Take these heroic fairies into our fort. Tend their wounds and see to their needs." The Falengin fairies quickly responded to the orders.

Ningolion flew to the Magus and hovered in front of her. "Work on your defence against the hoo-mans. We will provide whatever you need."

Carmine smiled graciously, "Thank you, Captain. I'm glad you have learned wisdom."

The fairies returned to the castle with their wounded and exhausted guests. I sat myself on the grass and was quickly joined by the others.

"That was convenient," Bones said.

"The hoo-mans were going to attack a fairy fortress sometime," Tenplessium replied.

"It's persuaded these fairies that our help is necessary," Aelfed said.

"Exactly," I said, "but what can we do? How do we construct the Parting?"

"I need to think," the sorceress said. She wandered towards a grove of oak trees beside the river.

Aelfed followed her, "It's getting dark. We'll need a fire. Hugo, help me find firewood." The ogre lumbered after her.

I looked around. Night was indeed upon us. I had forgotten that the day was approaching its end when we left the Sun. I picked up the witch's holdall and, with Bones, joined the others under the shelter of the trees.

Aelfed soon had a sizeable heap of twigs and branches. I released my dragonflies from my cap and they soon got the bonfire burning with their fiery breath. We sat around it, warming ourselves in silent thought. Only the sorceress sat apart. She leaned against a tree trunk, her legs crossed, eyes open but unseeing.

"She is in a magical trance," Bones informed us, "No doubt designing a spell that could create the Parting."

"I hope so," I replied, "We have very little time before the hoo-mans overrun more settlements and head south. It will be too late then."

We would have continued to talk but then our small copse was filled with the sparkling light of fairies. There were small groups of them, each group carrying a leaf. The laden leaves were laid beside each of us. Major Mouse immediately started sniffing at one. His whiskers quivered with excitement.

"I smell honey," he said, "first class fairy honey."

One of the Fairies spoke. "We bring you food. Honey-cakes. All that we have that is suitable for beings of your type. We have sent word to the elf village to ask for their assistance in feeding you."

Bones nodded his head graciously. "Thank you. This is very kind. How are your comrades from Camorpholgin?"

"They are weak and injured but will recover. However, they are but a few survivors of the fairies who occupied that castle."

The fairies departed leaving us to the cakes. They were tiny and there were just two or three each. I popped one in my mouth. The exquisite honey flavour seemed to fill my head. The cakes were quickly gone but they seemed to satisfy hunger more than their size promised. The sorceress remained in her trace, her three tiny cakes untouched beside her.

Perhaps it was the honey cakes or maybe it was the day's activity, but I soon found my eyes closing. I lay beside the fire and pulled my jacket tight around me. Major Mouse crawled into a pocket to keep himself warm.

I was woken by sunlight filtering through the leaves of the trees, and by unfamiliar sounds. I opened my eyes and looked around. I was surprised to see craft crossing the river towards us. The sound was water slapping against the sides of the rough-hewn logs serving as boats and the cries of the elves poling across the shallow, slow-moving stretch of the river.

Aelfed had stirred and was on her feet on the riverbank hailing her fellows. They soon made the shore and pulled their craft onto the bank. They were laden with bundles wrapped in the leaves of trailing vines. The elves unloaded the bundles and brought them to us.

"You are the ones who will protect us from the hoomans?" the leading elf asked. He was somewhat cleaner and better dressed than the others

"We hope so," Aelfed replied.

"The fairies told us you needed food, so we have brought supplies from our home, Elvenham." Some of the elves opened the bundles to reveal loaves of bread, fruit and nuts.

Aelfed said. "Who should we thank for this generous offering?"

"I am Melchior, Lord of Elvenham."

"Thank you, Lord Melchior." Aelfed bowed to the elf lord. The rest of us added our thanks and tucked into the food. Carmine, too, joined us having stirred from her trance. The elves also sat by the river and ate.

"Have you prepared a spell?" I asked through a mouthful of bread and walnuts.

"I have the beginning of an outline of an idea," she said. "The spell will need electrum; a lot of it. We will have to lay a line of electrum across the continent from west to east."

"Along the line of the Parting?" I asked.

The sorceress nodded. "It must be done soon."

Aelfed had been listening "What form must the electrum be in?"

"A powder, that can be poured in a continuous line."

"I have my tools," Aelfed tapped the satchel that she wore at her waist. "But grinding electrum will be hard work."

"Yet it must be done," the sorceress said. "First we must collect all the electrum stored by the fairies of Falengin and other fairy castles, and that collected by elves such as these and the gnomes that seek it under the mountains."

Tenplessium had also been fluttering amongst us. "I will instruct Ningolion. He can send messengers to every settlement of fairy, elf and gnome."

"Do that," Carmine said. The fairy flew off at speed.

"Electrum is easier to work if heated," Aelfed said, "I will ask Melchior if he has suitable furnaces in Elvenham, though, like the elves at Elvenwick, it does not appear that they have metals." She left us to speak to the elf lord.

I turned to the witch. "You know that we don't have to wait to get electrum from all these peoples. We have your, or rather The Fairy Queen's, hoard in the holdall."

"You don't have to remind me, gnome. I am fully aware of how much electrum is stored in my holdall. We will need it all. A spell of the power required will take every particle of electrum that we can find." Her face was almost as red as her hair as she struggled to hold in her temper. She took herself back to her tree and composed herself to return to her trance.

"Are we going to be able to do it in time?" I asked Bones.

His shoulders rose and fell in a sad shrug. "We must. Perhaps to gain time we should organise the fairies and others to disrupt the hoo-mans preparations and put off the day when they flood south."

"Hmm, yes." I was not a fighting gnome, but my experience as King gave me a little insight into military planning. "Perhaps some retaliation is called for – an attack on a hoo-man camp to destroy their supplies. It won't hold them for long, but might delay them. Far better than trying to meet them in battle when they attack villages and forts. We must do some planning, Bones."

"Indeed we must."

We were all occupied. Tenplessium we did not see again. Aelfed went off with some of the elves to Elvenham, taking the holdall with her. The sorceress sat beneath her tree. Bones and I engaged in discussion with Lord Melchior. At first, the thought of a raid on the hoo-mans was not to his liking. Direct action was never the method that elf lords employed if they could have a choice, but the hoo-mans would not submit to negotiation and deals. It was when Melchior mentioned that a group of ogres lived nearby that we started to convince him that a raid was possible. Ogres and elves together might just be able to take the fight to the hoo-mans. We explained slowly to Hugo what was required and then an elf took him to meet his fellows. Meanwhile, Major Mouse was sent back into Fort Falengin to request that the fairies reconnoitre a hoo-mans' camp that would be a suitable target for the raid. This time the mouse was accepted without fuss, and was able to carry our message successfully. It wasn't long before a group of fairies returned to us with their observations.

By lunchtime, the plan was made. By then, also, Ningolion had delivered the Falengin electrum. It wasn't as much as I expected. The total hoard was a heap of dust no bigger than my thumb.

Soon a group of armed elves arrived from the other side of the river and Hugo returned with four ogres who were bigger and rougher looking than he was. Each carried a large wooden club. We were also joined by a trio of fairies from the castle. Our little expeditionary force was ready to set out and create our diversion. First however the witch stirred from her trance.

"I can give you a spell to assist you," she said, and moved from one Elf to another gently touching the speck of electrum at the end of their spears. "Now everything that your spears touch will burst into flame. Take care."

Our raiding party embarked in three of the elvish boats with elves assigned to pole us down the river. We set off with some banter for those remaining behind. The jollity, I think, hid some apprehension about our task ahead. Ogres like nothing more than bashing heads together, the armed elves were experienced spearmen and fairies are ferocious fighters when roused, I had my false memories of battles, but none of us had set out to war before. I had expected Major Mouse to be eager to join us as he was always declaring his love of a good fight, but he disappeared shortly before we assembled by the boats.

The first part of our journey was quite idyllic and relaxing. We floated downstream, the river meandering around rocky outcrops as it found a path out of the mountains. In our own time this part of the continent was mainly fairy country, with castles in many strategic sites. There were gnomes in the mountains, but I had rarely visited them. In this period, the land was quiet, and habitations few and far between.

As Mr Sun completed another day's journey across the sky, the river left the mountains behind and flowed into the great inland sea that bordered the central plain. Our pilots brought our boats to the shore, and we disembarked. We took up our packs. They were small, just enough provisions for one night's journey. We said farewell to the boatmen. They would wait a day for our return, if return we did.

Our target was a night's march away across the plain. It was an easy passage by the light of the stars, but our hope was that we would take the hoo-mans by surprise at dawn.

We walked in silence across the dusty grassland, each with our own thoughts. I have said often enough that I am no fighter. I have relied on my luck to get me out of awkward situations, and I hoped that would be true again this night. I still wore the gossamer thin electrum cloak. Although all but invisible to an observer it would, the sorceress assured me, provide protection against hoo-man weapons such as their iron-tipped arrows. I hoped she was not giving me a false sense of safety, but even with that reassurance I was scared of the battle that was coming.

Apart from a brief halt to consume our rations, we walked through the night, across the grass covered plain. It was still dark when we drew close to the hoo-man encampment. Their fires illuminated the plain ahead of us, and the smell of the wood smoke and fat from the flesh that they cooked to eat drifted to my nostrils. We lay down on the grass and peered ahead at our objective. One of the fairies that accompanied us rose into the air and flew forward. Soon she was indistinguishable from the stars in the heavens and I hoped she was as invisible to any hoo-mans that were awake.

We waited patiently till she returned. She landed on my hand resting on the ground.

"It is as we observed earlier," she said in quiet voice. "There are many hoo-mans lodged here. Most are lying beside the fires and appear asleep. There are also large stocks of provisions and equipment and workshops for manufacturing their weapons."

"Thank you," I whispered, "We will continue with our plan then, avoid the hoo-mans as much as possible, but attack their stores and create as much destruction as we can manage."

The elves nodded and the ogres gave a low rumble of approval. In the east the sky showed a hint of a glow.

"Let us go then," I said, "Before we lose the darkness. Take care all, but let's give the hoo-mans something to think about."

We each got up into a crouch and slunk forward using the occasional shrubs as cover. We spread out and, as we approached the camp, selected our targets, avoiding the fires where the hoo-mans slept.

The elves were the first to act. They approached a heap of stores. I don't know what it was, food, clothing, fuel. Whatever it was, when the elves thrust their spears into it, there was an eruption of flame, just as the sorceress had promised. Smoke rose into the dawn air, coloured orange by the fire raging below.

The conflagration lit the encampment and I could clearly see its layout. There was no pattern or organisation in it, the heaps of stores were scattered amongst the resting places of the hoo-mans. We would have to be quick to set more fires before the hoo-mans were roused. The elves were already heading for their next targets, accompanied by ogres swinging their clubs.

It was time for me to do something. I lifted my cap and my dragonflies flew out, eager for a bit of freedom. They knew what was required and swooped over the camp releasing gouts of flame.

Now there were blazes starting all over the campsite. Some ignited like bonfires and were presumably fuelled by wood and leather and foodstuffs. They produced a sweet smell. Others roared and spat gouts of flame and produced thick acrid smoke. They must have been the tar that the hoo-mans had used to attack the fairy castle.

The attack, of course, awoke the hoo-mans. They arose and ran hither and thither looking for the cause of the flames. Now the ogres' clubs found their marks, felling the surprised hoo-mans. The elves jabbed with their spears and the hoo-mans burst into flame like torches. Their screams spread across the camp. I was pleased to see the chaos we had created, but it was becoming difficult to keep track of my companions.

It couldn't last of course. Some hoo-mans began to take control. They shouted orders to calm their fellows, to organise putting out the fires and to attack my force. In the melee that ensued I could not tell what my elves, fairies and ogres were doing, but still new fires broke out and the cries of the hoo-mans grew. My dragonflies continued to soar and dive, flames flaring from their throats.

Watching was almost my undoing. I did not see the hoo-man approaching me at a run until the last moment. Luckily, he tripped over a clod of earth just as he was about to launch himself at me. His cry alerted me. At least I was prepared; I had my tiny electrum blade in my hand. As the Hoo-man fell on me, I side-stepped and jabbed at him. He fell to the ground with a thud and my blade nicked his calf. His scream was quite unnerving, and I was appalled to see his flesh pucker and tear. The result of the little cut made by my blade was to rip his body into two. The stench of his corrupted flesh assailed me and I was almost sick.

I turned and ran, not wanting to see the result of my action. Most of the encampment seemed to be ablaze now, but the hoo-mans were fighting back. I saw a dozen surround an elf. I'm glad I did not see how the poor fellow met his end, but when the hoo-mans moved away there was nothing to see of him.

I decided we had done enough. I whistled and my dragonflies rose into the sky forming a circle of fire visible to all. That was the signal for our attack to break off. I began to back away from the camp searching for signs that my sign had been acknowledged.

Only a few dozen heartbeats had passed during the whole action and the Sun was still just rising in the east. It was still dark away from the camp but gradually I counted one, two, and more elves and ogres moving in the same direction as me. The three fairies appeared over my head.

"Bring everyone to me," I said, "we must get away." They flew off and I turned from the camp and started to trot. Running is not an activity I am fond of; soon I was breathless and reduced to a walk. I was joined by elves and ogres and we continued our escape. However, there was a growing noise of a pursuit. The hoo-mans roared their anger and followed us at a charge. There was no chance of us outrunning them; they were larger, longer-legged creatures than any of us.

This was always expected to be the most dangerous part of our mission. We hoped to get far enough away from the hoo-mans to be able to hide from them. That hope was becoming less and less likely. Most of the shrubs that might have provided shelter had been torn up, presumably to be used on the hoo-man campfires. The plain was almost bare and offered no hiding places.

Then I heard a sound, one that I had not heard for some time. It was a deep but loud "coo". Out of the darkness in the southwest came three great shadowy shapes. Vast wings flapping lazily but noisily as three giant pigeons came into land.

"Quick, jump on," Major Mouse cried from the head of the pigeon closest to me.

"Wonders of wonders, Major Mouse," I answered. Turning, I looked back and saw the silhouettes of the rampaging hoo-mans approaching from the burning camp. "Come on elves and ogres. Get on the pigeons. Let's get away."

I counted them as they appeared in the dawning light, elves and ogres. They clambered onto the backs of the pigeons. Then there were no more. We were two elves and an ogre short.

"Come on, gnome," Major Mouse, "The hoo-mans will be upon us in a breath."

Two of the pigeons beat their wings and rose. I took one last look towards the camp. The hoo-mans were indeed close and there was no sign of our missing fellows. I flung my arms around the pigeon's feathered leg and it lifted off at once.

The first of the hoo-mans arrived beneath us roaring with fury. We rose higher and I clung on with all my strength. Arrows fizzed through the air around us, but luckily none found a target. Then the hoo-mans and the burning camp were falling away from me and their cries became fainter.

I clung onto the pigeon's leg for some time as we put distance between us and the camp. My arms soon became tired. I had to call out. "Please can we go down. I can't hold on much longer."

The pigeon responded immediately, descending in large circles until we touched the ground. Hugo, sitting on the pigeon's neck reached down and hauled me up to sit astride, behind Major Mouse.

"Is that better?" the Mouse asked.

"Much," I replied.

"Then on!"

We took off again. The sky was lightening now and ahead I could see the two other pigeons flying towards the sea and the mountains.

"So, this is why you didn't join us in the fight," I shouted at Major Mouse as the air rushed past us.

"Yes. A means of escape is an important part of any plan," he replied, "and you didn't seem to have one."

"We couldn't think of one." I wondered if we had given much thought at all to what would happen after our attack on the hoo-mans.

"That's what I thought," Major Mouse said. "I hadn't seen any pigeons, but I thought they must be in the world somewhere and I wondered if they would respond to my call."

"Seems that they did."

"Yes, shows that the relationship between mice and pigeons goes back a long way."

"Hmm, I wonder why that is."

The pigeon had begun to descend again. Ahead was the shore where the elves and their boats were waiting for us. We landed just after the other two pigeons. Elves and ogres dismounted, stiff-legged but grateful for our rescue.

The elvish boatmen were delighted, if surprised by our arrival and were rather wary of the three huge pigeons who pecked at the ground beside the sea.

I went from elf to ogre thanking and congratulating them while the fairies flew over our heads. They were all exhausted, filthy from soot and smoke but unhurt. All were delighted that they had survived and pleased that we had succeeded. However, we missed our comrades that hadn't returned with us. I was worried that we had deserted them but the others reported that they had seen the other elf and the ogre fall under the hoo-man weapons. Reluctantly we had to admit that they were gone and there was nothing more we could do.

It was time to head back to Fort Falengin and report.

The elves and ogres got on board the boats to commence the slow upstream punt. I wanted to return more quickly. I asked Major Mouse if the pigeon would convey us. A quick negotiation of squeaks and coos fulfilled that request. So, while two pigeons took off and headed east, the mouse, Hugo and I clambered onto the neck of our mount.

We rose into the air as the boats set off from the shore of the sea. Our pigeon circled over them then headed towards the mountains.

It was still afternoon when our pigeon landed on the meadow, and we were greeted by some fairies. There was no one else beside the river other than the sorceress sitting by her tree. She aroused from her trance as we dismounted.

"I see you have found faster transport than the elves' boats."

"Yes, thanks to the Major," I replied.

"And your venture was successful?"

"I think we destroyed a lot of the hoo-mans' supplies," I replied feeling proud of our action.

"Let us hope it delays their attack for a day or two. Of course, that was but one camp among many."

"Yes, I know that."

The witch seemed to think that our raid was of little importance, which I suppose was true, but it made me feel that I was doing something to hold back the hoo-mans.

She sniffed as if that was the end of the discussion. "That is alright then, because we have to proceed with the important business. I have completed the composition of the spell."

"Oh, good." I could see what was happening. Magus Carmine could not avoid taking control, even when it was for the good of everyone and not just herself.

"What do we have to do?"

"It is already organised," she replied.

"Oh good," I repeated. It seemed that things had been happening during my absence.

"We are laying a trail of electrum dust across the continent from west to east. The fairies are doing that. They are conveying quantities of electrum to the fairy castles near to the line of the Parting. The elves of Elvenham are making the dust from all the electrum that has been collected. I will have to go to the mid-point of the trail in order to initiate the spell. Everything should be ready by tomorrow."

"Oh, very good. What can I do?"

"What you always do, gnome. Follow along behind me."

I swallowed the bile that rose in my gullet at the witch's comment. She was working for the good of the inhabitants of the world, so I had to suppress the anger at my wounded pride.

"Where is everyone?" I asked.

"Oh, they have gone to Elvenham to assist in the distribution of the electrum."

It seemed that the witch had got everyone working for her.

"If you wish," she continued in a disinterested manner. "Your tame pigeon will be of use to convey me to the place where I will recite the spell. I was thinking I might have to organise another means of transport. I suppose that Bones and the elf will want to come as well."

"I will go and fetch them then," I said.

The sorceress shrugged to signal she couldn't care less what I did and returned to her place beneath the tree.

I told Hugo to stay and keep watch on the witch. She may be fully behind our mission, but I couldn't help thinking that there were always plans within plans in Carmine's thoughts. Major Mouse and I climbed onto our pigeon and we ascended for the short flight over the mountain to the elven village of Elvenham.

As we descended, I could see that the village was in an unusual bustle of activity. There was far more smoke rising than at Elvenwick. There were elves and gnomes and ogres hurrying hither and thither, carrying containers of various sizes and bundles of wood. Fairies also were landing and taking off in huge numbers. There were even a couple of tall, dark-robed mages acting as if they were helping.

We landed outside the village and the pigeon cheerfully began pecking the ground.

"Come on Major. Let's see what is happening," I said. The mouse scampered up my trousers and sat in my jacket pocket with his head just visible, ears and whiskers twitching.

Hardly anyone noticed our arrival in the village, each seeming intent on their errand. In the centre we found Bones directing the activity, pointing this way and that with his long finger bones.

"Ah, gnome, you have returned." He greeted us with some warmth. "Your mission was successful?"

"We achieved our objectives," I replied, not really wanting to go over our adventure again, "though the sorceress did not seem impressed."

"Little impresses her. Fairies report some withdrawal of hoo-mans in the direction of the camp you attacked," Bones said, "So I think you can be happy with your result. It has taken some threat away from the elves here and the fairies of Falengin."

I looked around trying to make sense of all the activity taking place in the village.

"But this is where the real business is happening," I said.

Bones nodded, "The sorceress has given her instructions and we, or rather Aelfed, has brought them to fruition."

"What is happening?" I asked.

"Come let me show you." The skeleton led me towards one of the elvish round houses. I expected it to be dark inside or perhaps illuminated by a fire but instead it was filled with the bright blue light of electrum.

On the floor in the centre of the hut was a heap of the metal larger than I had ever seen. It was a pile of nuggets and bars of electrum that came up to my knees and would have covered my feet.

"What a huge treasure," I said with amazement.

Bones sighed. "It is all we have left. Fairies have brought it from across the continent from elves, gnomes and other fairy castles where it has been hoarded."

"All that you have left? What about the rest?"

"Follow me," Bones said. We left the hut as a group of elves arrived to collect a portion of the remaining electrum, crossing the centre of the village to another hut from which a large plume of smoke was emerging. Inside the heat was tremendous, and the glow of electrum mixed with the yellow tinge of fires.

Aelfed was there, clothing covered in soot, red of face and hair dripping with sweat. Other elves stoked the furnaces with charcoal and logs while yet more were putting electrum into the fires on stone platters.

Aelfed saw us and welcomed me with a broad smile and hug which left smuts on my cheek and jacket. The heat made me feel that I was about to melt, and the smoke caused me to cough and splutter.

I was astounded by the activity. "I didn't know the elves had the knowledge to refine metals." I said wiping spittle from my beard.

Aelfed shook her head. "They didn't. I have adapted the ovens they used for the baking of bread. A much higher temperature is needed to smelt metals and we can't achieve that, but they have charcoal that can heat the electrum sufficiently to make it easier to work."

"So, this isn't the final stage of the process," I said, noting that Elves were leaving the hut carrying trays of electrum that gave off such heat as to make the air shift and distort my vision.

"No, there is another. I'll show you." We followed Aelfed from the hut. I was relieved to leave the intense heat. We went to a neighbouring hut from which a huge noise emanated. It was the sound of thunder, of mountains crashing together, which was almost what it was. I was familiar with the noise but was surprised at the scale of what I saw. Inside the hut were great wheels of stone being turned atop other disks of stone by almost naked ogres. Electrum from the furnaces was being fed into the centre of the millstones and the still hot dust collected from the rims. As well as the noise there was the heat from the electrum and the friction of the grinding stones. The ogres worked tirelessly but sweat ran down their broad backs. Elves took away the heaps of electrum dust on stone plates.

"So here you convert the hot lumps of electrum to dust," I said shouting over the noise of electrum being crushed between the mighty millstones.

"That's right," Aelfed said. "The sorceress demanded it be as fine as possible so that a continuous trail can be laid. The gnomes brought these stones from their mines. It took dozens of them to roll them here. Luckily it was but a few thousand paces, and done in a short time. To cross the continent, we need a tremendous amount of the electrum dust even if it is laid in a very narrow, thin line."

"Do you have enough?"

"Barely. We have used every last nugget that the fairies and elves possessed, even the specks in their spears."

"And all the electrum in the sorceress's holdall?"

"That was where we began. The Fairy Queen's hoard is no more, and neither is the dream world electrum that the sorceress acquired. That is all except your cloak."

"You need it?"

Aelfed nodded. "Every last piece."

I lifted the cloak over my head. It was so light and fine I had almost forgotten I was wearing it. I handed it to Aelfed.

"We no longer need it to protect us from the sorceress?"

"She appears committed to completing this great work," Aelfed replied, "The construction of the Parting will make her the saviour of the world."

"That may be enough to satisfy her." I acknowledged. "Oh, you might as well take this too." I took the tiny stiletto from my purse and handed it to Aelfed. Having seen what it did to the hoo-man I did not want it any longer.

She wrapped the tiny blade in the cloak and gave it to a passing elf.

"Come and see the final stage of our plan," Aelfed said to me. We left the hut and walked to the edge of the village. A swarm of fairies filled the air but as I watched I saw that they were actually formed into a spiral. There were thousands and thousands of them. Each in turn descended to the ground to be handed a leaf bearing a tiny pile of electrum powder. Having received their burden, each then flew off to the north-east and north-west. Tiny specks of light flying in from all directions joined the spiralling pyramid of fairies.

"So many Fairies," I said, staring up into the twilight. While we'd been in the village, Mr Sun had completed his journey across the sky for the day.

"They come from fairy castles across the continent," Aelfed said. "They are forming the line of electrum that will divide the north of the continent from the rest."

"It will when the sorceress casts her spell," I replied. "Until then it is a glowing blue line in the dust. Surely the hoo-mans will notice it."

Aelfed looked at me and I saw anxiety in her eyes. "That is what we are afraid of. Creating the trail may provoke the hoo-mans into starting their attack, but we're not ready yet."

"When will it be complete?"

"Late tomorrow afternoon, is the plan."

"Hmm. It could give the hoo-mans time to start their invasion."

"We must just hope. . ."

The remaining light in the sky disappeared as if a torch had been extinguished. The stars were obscured and only the light of the fairies and the electrum they carried remained.

Only one thing in my experience was capable of creating such darkness. My recollection was confirmed when a great gust of wind brought a whiff of horse. A shadow on shadow of huge extended wings descended in front of us. With a great clanking of armour, the Knight of the Night dismounted and towered over us. I felt his presence although my eyes could not pick out his figure, huge though it must be against the darkness of his mount and the night sky.

I summoned the courage to speak, "Good evening, Sir Night, what cause have you to disturb your nightly ride across the heavens?"

"A disturbance indeed." The deep rumble of the Knight's voice made my whole body tremble. "Something strange is happening across the continent and you are the origin."

"Um, something strange?" I asked.

"A line of electrum is being laid. Its glow defies my darkness. To what purpose are you engaged in this project?"

I was wondering how to explain when Bones, standing beside me, spoke. "It is our answer to the threat of the hoo-mans, Knight of the Night."

"Hmm, the hoo-mans?"

"You must have noticed them, Sir," Bones continued, "their campfires burn all night long across the north."

"Yes, I have noticed them increasing in number."

"They are amassing a force for an invasion of the rest of the continent."

"An invasion?"

"Yes, Sir. Already they have attacked settlements of fairies and elves and they threaten all sentient creatures."

"That would meet with my disapproval."

"We're sure it would, Sir Night, so that is why we are planning to separate the hoo-mans from all other peoples."

"The line of electrum is part of this?"

"It is." I said.

"There must be magic involved."

"There is," I added, "We have a powerful sorceress who has devised a spell that will protect all the peoples."

"All the peoples? The hoo-mans as well?"

It was Aelfed's turn to speak up, "Yes, Knight of the Night. No-one will be harmed if we are allowed to complete the plan without hindrance."

"I detect some agitation amongst the hoo-mans. There is movement around their campfires."

"That is what we're afraid of," Aelfed said. "The hoo-mans must not cross the line before the spell is cast."

"Hmm. Perhaps I can be of assistance."

We waited for a few heart beats without any further words from the Knight. Finally, I decided to speak.

"What could you do, Knight of the Night?"

"I was thinking," the Knight growled. "If I were to hang around a bit in the north so it remained dark over the hoo-mans they would be unable to find their way to your border line."

"Um, yes, that might work," I replied.

There was a clanking as the Knight re-mounted his horse.

"When might you be ready?" The Knight's voice came from above us.

"This time tomorrow," Alfed answered.

"Very well. I will speak to Mr Sun and get him to delay his next flight until you are ready. When you see the dawn that will be when you should cast your spell."

Aelfed replied, uncertain but grateful, "Right, er, thank you Sir Night."

Although it remained dark it was as if a heavy black blanket was lifted off us. The Knight had departed. The stars re-appeared, in the south at least.

We looked at one another, each somewhat mystified.

"So, the Knight is going to help us by keeping it dark for a whole day," I said.

"By delaying the rising of the Sun," Aelfed added.

"And keeping the hoo-mans in the dark," Bones concluded.

"Sorted!" Major Mouse squeaked, "You'd better get on and complete the plan."

Chapter 22

The sorceress casts her spell

The elves, the gnomes, the ogres and the fairies, especially the fairies, worked throughout the night and the night that replaced the day. I watched them all working without rest. The heap of electrum disappeared gradually; the furnaces roared until the last piece was heated; millstone turned on millstone until the last fragment was turned into powder; the fairies flew in and collected their leaf of electrum dust until it was all gone, or almost.

While there were still a few fairies waiting to pick up their final consignment, Bones turned to me and said, "The long night will soon be over. We should collect the sorceress and take her to the centre of the line."

The night had gone on so long and I had become so mesmerised by watching all the workers repeating their tasks over and over again that what was to follow had slipped from my mind.

"You're right, Bones, as always. We must move. Major, call the pigeon."

"On your command, gnome," Major Mouse said from my pocket. He sent out a high-pitched squeak. Very soon the undignified flapping and cooing signified the arrival of the pigeon in the darkness. I, Bones and Aelfed, holdall in hand, clambered onto the pigeon's back.

"To Fort Falengin," I cried. The pigeon launched itself with a great beating of wings and we flew the short distance to the fairy castle.

The sorceress was seated outside the fort, accompanied by Hugo and Captain Ningolion.

"About time," she said, "I have been awaiting you throughout this over-long night."

"You heard about the Knight of the Night?" I asked.

"Yes. The fairies have kept me informed of progress and the Knight's intervention. Timely, one might say."

Bones spoke, "The Knight seems to have done what he promised and kept the hoo-mans in their camps. Now, madam, the electrum trail is ready for you to pronounce your spell."

"Well, get me there as soon as you can." She stood up and strode to the pigeon. The bird lowered its head to the ground and the sorceress stepped astride without effort. The rest of us scrambled to take our places. The captain and a few of his fairy guard flew up above us.

"Can you fly with all of us aboard?" I asked the pigeon

The great bird assured us that she could manage though we were indeed a heavy load. She lurched across the meadow, flapping wings determinedly until we were airborne. Then she caught a current of air blowing down from the mountains and soared up into the sky.

We flew north-east until the line of electrum came into sight. While as thin as a hair, its strong blue glow made it clearly visible in the night. It crossed the northern plain from the western horizon to the east. The pigeon banked and we flew eastwards and low just south of the line.

Hundreds of heart beats passed until I was feeling stiff and cold as the interminable night went on. My eyes grew heavy, but fear of falling from my seat kept me awake and gripping the sorceress in front of me. Though almost insensible I noticed tiny sparkles of light ahead of us.

"Those must be fairies," I shouted above the noise of the rushing air.

The sorceress turned her head to answer me over her shoulder. "They are carrying the final portions of electrum to complete the line. We have caught up."

Like the fairies, we descended, and the pigeon came to a skidding halt on the sandy ground. We dismounted and hurried to where the blue line crossed the plain. The straight line travelled west and east. In the latter the sky was at last turning from black to red.

Bones gazed into the distance. "Ah, the day begins at last."

A fear gripped me. "With the light, the hoo-mans may well begin their advance. We do not know how much time we have."

The sorceress ignored me. She had gone right up to the line and was kneeling at the gap between the western and eastern thread. One by one Fairies flew in, deposited their tiny portions of electrum and then flew off.

Captain Ningolion circled over my head. "I will go and see what the hoo-mans are doing."

"Take care," Bones said, "Do not spend too long north of the line. If the sorceress casts her spell while you are gone, you will be trapped."

"I will not be long," the fairy said, "I shall view the invaders from a distance." He climbed into the air and was soon lost from sight.

Aelfed was beside the sorceress, supervising the remaining fairies. The very last flew in and dropped her sprinkle of dust, then flew to me and Bones. It was Tenplessium.

"The task is complete," she said.

"Well done," I replied, "The fairies have done a wonderful job."

"As indeed have elves, gnomes and ogres," Tenplessium replied. "Now it is up to the mage to prove she can halt the hoo-mans."

The witch was kneeling, motionless, behind the line. I was about to approach her when the fairy captain soared towards us, halting in a fluttering of wings.

"They're coming," his thin voice cried. "They have left their camps and are advancing as far as I could see east and west."

"How much time do we have?" I asked.

"The sun will barely be in the sky before they arrive here," Ningolion replied.

I knelt beside the witch. "Did you hear that? The hoo-mans are coming."

She turned to face me. She looked calm and confident. "I heard, gnome. Do not fear. My spell will halt their advance. However, you have something of mine that I need."

"I do?"

"My pendant."

I had forgotten the pendant with its core of electrum. If I had remembered it, I may have handed it to Aelfed for conversion to dust.

"Of course," I said. I pushed my hand into my wallet and pulled out the pendant on its gold chain. I handed it to the sorceress. She grabbed it from me.

"Now go. Move away from the line and leave me be."

I wasn't going to argue. I stepped back and rejoined the others standing in a line. We all looked to the north.

The sorceress bent over the line, pressing the pendant to the join between the two continent spanning strands. She began chanting words that I did not understand. Nothing happened. A beam of sunlight cleared the peaks of the eastern mountains and illuminated the plain in front of us.

"They're coming," cried Tenplessium from above my head.

"You can see the hoo-mans?" I called up to her.

"Yes, they're a long way off but, oh, so many. The ground is black with them."

I glanced at the sorceress still bent over the thin line of electrum, still mumbling untranslatable words. Surely the spell would work; surely our effort was not in vain, surely the world would not fall to the hoo-mans. A ball of doubt was in my stomach and I worried that our plan would not succeed.

"I can see them too," Bones called. He was a good head and chest taller than me so could see further. I peered into the distance but for me the plain to the northern horizon was still empty.

The sorceress hadn't moved but was still chanting in a monotonous tone. Did the line of electrum look brighter? The sunlight was stronger, the day brightening and yet the thin blue ribbon was glowing more intensely, in fact it was whiter than it had been.

Major Mouse crawled out of my pocket, climbed up my chest on to my shoulders then he scrambled up my conical cap.

"Higher, gnome. Tip toes."

I stretched up.

"Yes! There they are. I see them." The mouse was excited, as if he had forgotten what the coming of the hoo-mans meant.

My heart pounded in my chest. I squinted into the distance. Yes, there they were. A black line rippling along the horizon, growing thicker by the breath. I couldn't watch. I dropped back on to the soles of my feet, looked down at the witch. She was singing more loudly now with a simple tune, the same gibberish that meant nothing to me.

But something was happening. Wisps of grey mist rose from the line of electrum. The blue-white light shone through so it looked a little like flames dancing on the ground. To my left and right all along the thread of electrum, the same filaments of vapour rose. Now they were growing thicker and reaching higher, up to knee height, before dispersing in the air.

I glanced to the north. The band of charging hoo-mans was thicker. I fancied I could also hear their cries. How far away were they? Three or four furlongs? It was getting less every heartbeat.

Now the mist was up to my waist and climbing into the air faster. It was growing thicker too, obscuring the glow of the electrum. To the west and the east it looked like a fast growing hedge of constantly waving and changing grey branches.

"Will it stop them?" Aelfed cried, "I see them. It cannot be long before they reach us."

Now I could make out individuals. Thousands of them formed the line that was approaching. They brandished weapons – spears, clubs, bows and arrows. Dreadful oaths came from their wild-haired, bearded faces, and still they charged towards us.

But the mist was rising, becoming denser. It was too thick to see through now and I was just able to peer over it. My view was partly obscured by the wisps rising from the thickening wall of fog.

The sorceress had risen to her feet and stretched her hands up to the sky but she had not ceased the continuous song of her spell. She sang aloud a tune that rose and fell with a strange but compelling rhythm.

My last sight of the hoo-mans was when they were a few hundred paces away. They must be exhausted by their charge yet still they came. Their cries were louder and a few arrows flew through the air, over our heads, landing in the ground behind us. Then my view was obscured by the barrier. Still I heard their shouts, but as the fog thickened and rose so they became muffled.

On the sorceress went, singing her hymn to the fog. Faster and faster it rose into the sky. Soon even Tenplessium and Ningolion, flying high above us must have lost sight of the land beyond the Parting.

The Sun had risen above the mountains and we were bathed in warm morning light when the sorceress stopped. She lowered her arms and sank to the ground. Bones ran, legs and feet clattering, and cradled her.

"She's exhausted," he said, "Does anyone have water."

Aelfed, ever prepared, unslung a leather bottle from her shoulder and passed it to the skeleton. He held it to the witch's lips.

Ningolion flew down and hovered in front of me.

"The hoo-mans must have reached the barrier by now. Surely, they could pass through. It's only mist."

I shook my head. There was no sound from beyond the fog, no sign of anyone or anything coming through and I did not expect there to be. I pointed up. As high as we could see, higher still, higher than Mr Sun's track, as high as the heavens, the barrier rose.

"Nothing's coming through, not even a bird."

We looked as far west and as far east as we could peer, and it was the same. Ever moving, seething, swirling, the Parting was unchanging, a permanent barrier.

Bones helped the sorceress to her feet and escorted her to us, away from the fog.

"You did it," I said, "You created the Parting."

Carmine favoured me with a half-smile. "I said I would."

Ningolion fluttered anxiously. "What if the hoo-mans find a way to break through? Will it last? What has *happened* to the hoo-mans?"

The sorceress glared at the fairy. "They won't and it will last forever. The hoo-mans are not trapped in the north, they will not be able to imagine passing through."

The fairy continue to circle. "I do not understand," he said.

"You see," said the Magus Carmine with a proud sparkle in her eyes, "It's not just a barrier, it's more than that. It had to be. What I have created is a rift between our world here on this side and the hoo-mans' world to the north, except it's not the north anymore. It is somewhere different. What I have created is a parting between two very different worlds. In the other world, the hoo-mans' world, there is no sign of the rift. They see no wall of fog so they cannot think of finding a way through it. They can continue their own belligerent and messy lives while all of us remain safe here in our own world. Nothing can come through from the other side of the Parting. It only has one side – this side."

"But can we go through it?" the Captain asked.

"You can enter the Parting," the sorceress replied, "but nothing and no-one can return. No doubt in the future, fairies, elves, gnomes, mages, perhaps even ogres will wonder what will happen to them if they cross the Parting. They will disappear from this world and find themselves in the hoo-mans' world, but they cannot return."

"I see," the fairy said, although I'm not sure he fully understood that the Parting would become a feature of the world for all of the future.

"Now, Captain," the witch said, "I suggest you and your guard go and take the news to all your peoples. The

Parting is the northern boundary of your world for evermore."

"Yes, yes, I will. Farewell." The fairy and his companions spiralled up into the air and headed south towards the hills and the fairy castles, the villages of elves, the mines of gnomes and the settlements of ogres.

We were left, the seven of us – the sorceress, Bones, Aelfed, Hugo, Tenplessium, Major Mouse and me. We stood in a circle looking from one to another wondering what to say next.

A thought came to me. "Actually, Magus, you're wrong. Something has returned having crossed the Parting."

She frowned. "What has?"

"Us."

"Us?"

"Yes. We're back where we started in our world, on the south side of the Parting."

"So we are," chuckled Bones, "A somewhat... roundabout route we have taken."

"And we can't exactly say we're home can we," Aelfed added, "Our homes and families are a few thousand years in the future."

"Hmm, that is true," I said, "I *would* like to go home."

The others nodded agreement but I for one had no thought of how my wish could be achieved. After a few moments silence, however, the sorceress spoke. "There may be a way."

"How?" Aelfed asked.

The witch pointed to the holdall that Aelfed kept at her side. "Put your hand inside."

The elf knelt, undid the buckle, pulled the opening wide and slipped her hand inside. "What am I looking for."

"You'll know when you touch it."

"Ah, yes, I feel something." She withdrew her arm and her hand emerged from the holdall grasping a golden ball with lines etched around it at various angles.

"That's...that's," I spluttered.

"Yes, I know," Carmine said, "It's the ball that held the black hole. Which also is a time travel machine."

"You kept it," Bones said.

The sorceress shrugged. "Well, I just dropped it in the holdall when we arrived in the time of the fungus. I'd forgotten it really."

Aelfed held up the ball. The morning sunlight glinted off it so that it looked like a miniature sun.

"You said the fungus made it," the Elf said.

"That's right. I asked the fungus to build a machine to take me back to human civilisation. It needed a black hole, or electrum from our world, to fold the fabric of space and time. I used the Fairy Queen's electrum."

Aelfed examined the golden sphere closely. "Do you think it could take us to our own time in this world?"

The sorceress sucked in her cheeks. "I don't know. The structure of our world is different to the human world, but we're connected by the rift. My spell that created the Parting contains the code for the human world. So perhaps it could be used. It needs electrum though."

"You have your pendant," I said. Was there really a chance to get back to my normal life.

Did I even want that?

She nodded. "That is so. I will have to study the ball carefully."

Aelfed was tracing lines on the surface of the ball with a finger. "There are markings that may be a way of setting the machine."

"Yes, but they apply to the human world. I will have to work out how to translate them to our own. Let me have it."

Aelfed reached out her hand. The witch grabbed the ball and turned away. She crouched down shielding the ball with her body. Her neck was bent so that her eyes almost touched the surface.

Bones sighed and folded his bones into a sitting position on the dusty ground. "We could have some time to wait, if she manages it at all."

I sat too. "We didn't really think about what we would do after the Parting was created, did we."

Major Mouse jumped off my hat onto the ground. "There are easy pickings in the settlements here. With our knowledge we could easily set ourselves up as the bosses. You could even be King of the Gnomes again."

I thought about it. Did I really want the worry of running a kingdom especially if there were other gnomes who wanted my throne? And I thought of the other things that the people of this period lacked such as smart clothes, hot water from a tap, and ambrosian gin.

"If I was stuck here, I think I'd spend all my time teaching them how to use metals," Aelfed, "Perhaps it will be better if they find out for themselves."

"If Fort Falengin is typical then I don't want to stay here," Tenplessium said. "A dark, dirty, primitive place it is. No, give me the comfort of the Fairy Queen's Castle."

"I think we're all agreed," Bones said, "We want our own time. Apart from you Major Mouse."

"No, no, it was just an idea. I desire to see my old comrades again and share our story. It's just if we *were* actually to be stuck here…"

"Well, let's see what the sorceress can come up with," I said. "I don't know about you lot, but I'm pretty tired after a night three nights long." I lay out flat, pulled my cap over my eyes and thought about going to sleep.

"Wake up, wake up, I have it!" The sorceress' cry stirred me from my sleep. I opened my eyes and pushed myself up on my elbow. Mr Sun was past the zenith of his day's journey and the air was warm. Aelfed was sitting with the holdall, but the others looked as though they too had been asleep, even Tenplessium, who was resting on Bones' breast bone.

Moving made me conscious that my stomach was empty. "I'm hungry," I said.

"Me too," Aelfed replied.

The witch came and stood over us. "Why didn't you look in the holdall?"

"What for?" I said.

The sorceress tutted. "There's always a picnic in the

holdall. You don't think I went without food on my travels, do you?"

I might have replied that she could have told us earlier, but she went on urging us to move before I had a chance to open my mouth.

"There's no time now. I've worked out how to use the machine."

That got us to our feet. We crowded around the sorceress expecting to be shown how it worked. She pushed us away.

"Out of my way! I need to explain."

I thought we were in for another lecture about how clever she was but instead of looking proud she had a grave expression.

"The fungus warned me of the dangers of time travel," She fixed each of us with a glare. "Nature abhors a paradox."

"A paradox?" Aelfed asked.

"Yes, you know, travelling back in time and killing yourself, so that you could not have lived to travel back in time to kill yourself."

My head spun, but I think I got the idea.

"It turns out," the witch went on, "that you can't have two versions of yourself in any time. The world won't allow it. That was why the fungus never attempted time travel as it had existed in one form or another throughout the history of the world, well, from the origin of life."

Aelfed frowned. "But you said you travelled back and forth between the times of the humans and the fungus, on many occasions."

"Yes, of course I did, because it wasn't my world. I had had no previous presence in it, so as long as I hopped between different times, I could do what I wanted. Here, it is different. We all have a presence in the future we want to go to. That and adjusting the controls for the structure of space and time in our world means I am not sure of our chances, but I am quite confident I can take us to our time."

Bones drew himself up straight and declared, "Well,

I'm prepared to give it a go. It seems as good a way as any of ending a life."

We were all in agreement that we wanted to take the chance to get back to familiar surroundings and end this odyssey at long last.

"Alright. In that case, reach out and touch the ball. It's set and I just have to press 'go'."

Fleshless finger bones, a furry elf hand, stubby ogre fingers and my hand reached out to join the sorceress' palm on the ball. Major Mouse ran down my arm and reached out a paw to touch the gold. Tenplessium landed on the ball itself and crouched down.

With a look of manic satisfaction, the sorceress stabbed the ball with her forefinger. "To the future!"

I know I'd felt hungry, but now my stomach seemed to shrink into itself and absorb all my flesh. My eyes spun in their sockets and the world turned inside out.

Chapter 23

We find time goes on

The woman who sat in the corner of the railway carriage with her eyes shut was attracting a good deal of attention. A band of armoured outlaw mice scrabbled at the catch of her capacious handbag with their steel tipped claws. The skeleton sitting beside her swatted at the creatures with its brittle white fingers with no obvious result.

I watched what was going on thinking, this scene was familiar. The railway carriage rocked. I grabbed the door frame. My arm seemed to have a ghostly shadow as if there were two of me occupying the same space. The same shadowy duplication affected the woman and the skeleton. The ghost of the woman leaned forward and twisted a golden ball.

Bright sunshine, dusty earth. I staggered, my brain still revolving in my skull. I fell and hit the ground with a painful thud. I blinked a few times, shook my head and looked around. The roiling fog of the Parting was a few paces away. My companions were sprawled on the ground, as disorientated as me.

"Where are we," I muttered.

"Back in the past where we started from," the sorceress said, clambering to her feet. She still had the golden ball in her hands.

"What happened to us?" Bones said.

"For a moment I was flying with my squadron," Tenplessium said.

"I was in our workshop with my father," Aelfed added.

"We were almost trapped in a time-loop," the mage said.

"A time-loop?" I repeated.

"The setting was a little inaccurate," the witch said, "We arrived too soon and were about to integrate with our previous selves. I just had time to reverse the transfer and spring us back to now."

"How long were we there?" I asked.

"Just a heart-beat," the witch replied, "any longer and the time-loop would have fixed."

Aelfed had her questioning frown again. "What would have happened to us?"

"We would have been one with our older selves and relived all that has taken place in our lives between then and now."

I was appalled by the thought. "Over and over again?"

The sorceress nodded. "Of course, you wouldn't be aware of the repetitions, but they would continue for eternity."

We looked at each other, each of us thinking how horrific that outcome would be.

"So, shall we give it another go?" Carmine said, with a jollity that I didn't feel.

Aelfed asked the question we all wanted answered. "Can you be sure we won't get caught in another time-loop?"

"I think I have the time machine calibrated now. It should take us to a time after we all passed through the Parting so we will not have any presence in our world."

Did we trust the witch? She sounded confident and she was in as much danger as us, I thought. We all thrust out our hands to touch the ball again.

I can't say I was prepared for the gut-wrenching, mind-bending effect of the time jump the second time but it passed in a breath. When the dizziness passed, I saw that we were sitting in the dirt beside the Parting.

Had we moved through time? It seemed not until I looked more closely at our surroundings – the vegetation looked thicker, the ground not as dusty. I stood up and looked into the distance, to the south and saw a line of people. They were elves and ogres. A squadron of fairies sparkled in the sky between us. I started walking towards them.

"I think we've made it," Bones said, getting up and standing beside me. "We've arrived not long after we entered the Parting."

I recalled it was early morning when we began our journey and the Sun now was just above the eastern horizon.

"How can you be sure it is the same day?" I asked.

Bones pointed to the crowd ahead of us. "They are still there watching us depart."

"Come on," I said, "let us go and meet them." I picked up the witch's holdall that Aelfed had dropped. I set off to meet the party that had seen us off and now would welcome our return. Bones was at my side

"They'll think we have turned back and haven't entered the Parting at all," Aelfed wailed. "They'll make us turn round and enter the Parting again." She ran to catch us up.

"Fear not," came the faint voice of Tenplessium who had climbed into the air above us. "My squadron observed us walk into the fog. They will have seen us disappear and return from nothing."

Fairies have good eyesight but Aelfed's concerns had infected me. I didn't want to have to go through the Parting again. It would hardly be better than getting stuck in a time-loop.

"They will believe us," said Bones in a confident manner. "We have brought something for them."

"What?" I said.

"The sorceress."

"Of course," I turned around expecting the witch to be with us. She wasn't. She had stayed where we arrived, back ten or twenty paces. She was twisting the golden ball between her hands, pressing it with her fingers. "No...!" I cried and ran towards her.

She looked up at me. "I am not staying to be interrogated by a bunch of fools," she cried.

There was a burst of violet light that engulfed her, before it shrank as if imploding. When it reached the size of a poppy seed it disappeared with a noise a lizard makes when it sucks up a fly. The sorceress was gone.

We were surrounded by fairies, swords drawn, whirling and soaring around us in a quite unsettling fashion. Then elven guards arrived with pikes levelled corralling us together.

The fairy commander addressed us. "You will be escorted to the camp and interrogated to discover if the mission was a success."

Success? How do you gauge success? On the one hand we had survived our adventures; we returned, having passed through the Parting. On the other, we had not brought back the Fairy Queen's electrum, and we had lost the sorceress.

The days in the camp passed with short sessions of anxiety and longer periods of boredom. We were looked after, first of all in the rough camp that had been established before we left. Then we were accommodated in the new buildings that quickly sprang up at the campsite, given a comfortable bed to sleep in and good food to eat. Sometimes we were together, but more often we were kept apart.

It wasn't that we were suspected of dodging our assignment. Fairies had seen us disappear into the fog of the Parting, but our almost immediate return in a flash of blue light had them and the others questioning what we had done, and where we had been. We each told, many times, the story of our journeys through the different worlds, of our various other lives and how the Parting had been constructed to keep out the hoo-mans. We each told fundamentally the same story which stood up under repeated telling and questioning.

Gradually the fairies and the elves and the gnomes who had joined the convocation, came to believe our extraordinary tale. They were impressed by the cooperation shown by the ancient peoples in preparing for the erection of the Parting. As a result, the Fairy Queen's representatives, the Parliament of Elven Lords and the High Council of the Federation of Gnomes set up the Union for the Investigation of the Parting and other Artefacts. It began as a temporary camp on the site of the ogre settlement, but soon the fairies had grown a small but effective castle and the elves had erected sumptuous pavilions for the lords and liveable tepees for their workers. The gnomes had dug out caverns in the rock of the plain. Even the ogres had stirred themselves to rebuild their ramshackle houses in a sturdier fashion.

The principal question that was asked, and we asked ourselves of course, was to where – or rather, to when – had the sorceress gone. The Union sent out messages across the continent for reports of sightings of her, but none were received. Perhaps she had jumped into the future and we had not arrived in her time yet. Or, I wondered, if she had travelled back and integrated with a past version of herself, perhaps in the time before she stole the Fairy Queen's electrum. In that case she was condemned to repeat our expedition time after time.

At last, after many days of interrogation we were taken to the smart new headquarters of the Union, a joint venture of elves, gnomes, fairies and even mages. It was built of stone quarried and carved by gnomes, metal and glass refined and worked by elves with silk hangings and wooden furnishings provided by Fairies and protected by the spells of the mages. We were shown into a room where the three joint leaders of the Union were waiting for us. They didn't offer us a seat, so we stood in a line facing them. Major Mouse climbed up my leg so that he could see, and Tenplessium settled on the top of Bones' skull.

"We thank you for your presence today, and for your testimony of your mission beyond the Parting," said Lord Rismagodril, the leader of the elf delegation. He didn't make it sound that they were that grateful.

"Your report has brought a new understanding of the Parting and the worlds beyond it," added Marshall Solgilessant, the fairy representative, although what that understanding was, she didn't make clear.

"It has provided a fresh spirit of cooperation to the

peoples of our continent," concluded Albertus Taranto, a gnome from my own mountain, though I barely knew him. The various peoples had certainly put aside their current disputes and had entered into the union with an enthusiasm which had lasted longer than any previous attempt to foster friendship.

Bones was the first of us to respond. "We are pleased that you have found our experiences illuminating."

Taranto snorted, "Yes, well, now you are free to go. All of you."

"Is that it?" I asked. It seemed that they were just getting rid of us. "A thank you and good-bye?"

The Marshall flapped her wings. "Your testimony, Philobrach Hohenheim, was informative, but the task entrusted to you as leader of the fellowship was to return with the Queen's electrum. This you failed to do and neither did you hang on to the sorceress. Therefore, there can be no reward for your return. However, we welcome back Squadron Captain Tenplessium into the Queen's Forces."

Tenplessium fluttered, "Oh, I've been promoted! Perhaps my memories of the dream world are useful after all."

The elf lord addressed Aelfed, "Lord Pelladil awaits your return to his service in the position of Chief Electrum-smith."

I didn't see the young elf at my side leaping with glee at that announcement. She whispered in my ear. "I will get back to my father's workshop, I suppose – perhaps we will find a way of bringing him back to health and I will be allowed to sculpt metal in whatever forms I like."

"Such as the likeness you made of me as King?" I said, chuckling.

"Maybe." She gave me a warm smile.

"You may leave now," the gnome Taranto said and waved us away.

Outside, on the square between the new buildings we said our farewells. Tenplessium flew to each of us in turn, expressed her joy at having shared our experiences and then soared away to join her comrades. Aelfed hugged us all and said goodbye with tears on her smooth cheeks.

"Please visit me in Elfholm if you are passing through. Oh, this may be useful to you." She put a hand into the purse on her belt and drew something out. She held it up for me to see. It was a small gleaming metal egg with a cord attached.

"What is it?" I asked.

"A metal diviner," Aelfed answered. "This was my father's but he has no use for it lying senseless. I have my own. It will help you find valuable metals and test their purity."

"How?" I was quite confused.

"I think I can explain its use to you," Bones said.

I took the instrument from Aelfed's hand. Gratitude competed with sadness within me.

"I'm sorry that we did not meet your father in happier circumstances, but this will remind me of him and of you. Thank you."

Aelfed smiled and then with a wave she departed towards the elven pavilion. I placed the diviner carefully into a pocket. The band of renegade mice appeared from nowhere, surrounding Major Mouse, slapping his back and shaking his paws.

"What are you going to do, Major?" I said.

"Oh, look for more adventures," he replied.

"Adventures?"

"Well, sources of gold, and perhaps a little electrum." He scampered off with his cronies.

"That leaves just you and me, Philobrach," Bones said.

"And Hugo," I said noting that the ogre was hanging around apparently unwilling to return to his settlement, only a few paces outside the Union compound.

"What will you do?" the skeleton asked.

"Oh, I don't know," I replied. In truth I felt a sadness at the breakup of our ad hoc band, but I had given little thought to my future. "I suppose I'll look in on my family under our mountain but, to tell you the truth, I prefer to see where my luck takes me. In fact, I'd quite like to see the south coast. I've never been there, and I wonder if it is anything like how it was in our dreamworld. Perhaps I'll meet the sea-people."

Hugo made a series of grunts which sounded as if my words had excited him.

"Do you want to come too?" I asked him. His big round head nodded and a smile spread across his broad face.

"Perhaps he thinks he'll meet his merman and sail the southern seas," Bones said.

"You never know," I replied. "What about you, Bones? Are you going to find a nice, peaceful grave and lie in it?"

Bones shrugged his shoulder blades. "That certainly has appeal, but you know, since being released from the sorceress' service, I have started to enjoy life a little. Well, perhaps *enjoy* is an exaggeration. Nevertheless, being in your company, Philobrach Hohenheim, has been... what can I say, amusing?"

I laughed, "Amusing! Well, let us three set off together. Where shall we go?"

"I don't know," Bones said, "but you have been hanging onto that holdall. Why not look inside for an idea."

I had indeed been holding the witch's bag. It had been with me ever since we arrived back in our time. Our investigators presumed it was mine and contained my belongings, and none of us ever let on that it belonged to the sorceress.

"I wonder what *is* in there," I said. I lifted the bag and tugged it open.

"The witch said it was precious, did she not," Bones said.

The three of us peered into the black void that was inside the bag.

"I can't see anything," I said. Hugo grunted agreement.

"Put your hand in," Bones said. "You may feel something even if it is just a packet of sandwiches."

I thrust my arm into the bag up to my elbow and felt around the vast space. There was an object. It felt hard.

"I have something," I said.

"Let us see it," Bones said with an edge of impatience on his voice.

I drew out the object. It was a large golden key. There were marks along the shaft and around the bow which was in the shape of a figure eight on its side. The marks may have been writing, but they were indecipherable to me.

"Well, that is something," Bones said, "It will be an adventure finding out what door or container that key opens."

I stared at the key, wondering what the sorceress would do if she discovered she needed it.

"Come on, Philobrach. Let's go," Bones urged, "With your luck there will be a train about to leave and we can make a start on our new quest."

. . . .

Acknowledgements

An Extraordinary Tale began as a one-off task for my weekly writing group. My friends in the group loved it and encouraged me to keep writing episodes. When it was finished, a number of them read the whole thing and gave me useful comments and criticism. So, my first thanks go to all my dear friends and fellow members of Ross-on-Wye Writing Group.

I am delighted that Elsewhen took on publication of the novel so that once more I can thank Sofia, for her detailed and considerate editing of the manuscript; Alison, for her cover which exactly matches my vision; and Peter for all the other necessary tasks that go into publishing a novel.

To any reader who has got this far having read the novel, thank you for picking it out from the hundreds of thousands published every year.

Finally, this novel, like all my works, is dedicated to Lou, my wife. She has my thanks for all her support, for giving me the opportunity to spend my time writing, and for letting me be me.

Preview of

The Mage Returns:
The Further Adventures of a Gnome

#1

I settled into the deckchair and contemplated the dazzling white sand of the bay. From my home beneath the mountains, I had visited the forests of the fairies, the towering cities of the elves and the broad northern plains; but sitting on a beach was a new experience for me, Philobrach Hohenheim, adventuring gnome. I had sailed the seas in another reality, the memories of which jostled with other lives in my mind becoming more confused and vague as time passed. Watching seagulls circling over the distant sea while enjoying the rest and the warmth was a fresh pleasure.

Actually, it was getting rather hot. Here on the southern edge of the world-spanning continent, the Sun was close. The Sun's chariot was approaching the zenith of its daily journey across the dome of the heavens and heat was radiating down from the cloudless sky. I had already removed my conical woollen hat and replaced it with a handkerchief knotted at each corner to save my bald head from sunburn. I was considering loosening the buttons of my waistcoat.

One of the specks above the sea appeared to be growing larger. It was approaching. In fact, it was coming straight towards me. With its wings tucked to its side it swooped down. Its dark red eyes focussed on me and me alone. I grabbed hold of the hankie to protect my head from the seagull's bill and talons. The bird grew huge in my sight. A thought passed through my head, a very brief thought. The bird couldn't be attacking me, could it? Not even the largest seagull could lift a slightly more than averagely rotund gnome.

At the last possible moment, the bird spreads its wings and pulled out of its dive. It soared over my head. Something white dropped into my lap. I looked down in disgust but saw a ball of screwed up paper lying there.

The seagull climbed into the air and disappeared over the dunes surrounding the bay. I picked at the paper to loosen and spread it out. When it was almost flat, writing was revealed.

I jumped from the deckchair as if catapulted and took a kick at the mound of sand twice my height in length beside me. Sand sprayed in all directions, but my foot connected with something solid. A pale white bone was revealed, a femur. The whole heap of sand shivered and flowed.

The skeleton sat up, sand pouring from its rib cage.

"What now, gnome?" Bones said sounding somewhat irritated. "Just when I'm looking forward to resting in peace, you disturb me. When does a body get to enjoy their death round here?"

"I've had a message," I said.

"What? A flash of divine inspiration or has the heat of the sun caused you hallucinations?"

I waved the sheet of crumpled paper. "No. A seagull dropped this on me."

"Let me see." The skeleton extended a thin, fleshless arm. He grasped the sheet of paper and held it to his vacant eye sockets. "It says, 'she's back'."

"You know who 'she' is," I said with some trepidation.

Bones snorted. "It's signed by Major Montgomery Mouse of the Grand Order of Renegade Mice. The Major does like his title doesn't he. Anyway, it can only mean one thing, the sorceress has returned."

"Your boss."

"My ex-boss. I feel no remnant of connection to her."

"Nothing? Not even a hint of a feeling that she might be somewhere in this world."

"Not an iota. She is lost to me." The skeleton rose to his feet shaking the sand from his bones and joints. "But if she really is back amongst us, I daresay she has plans and those plans will no doubt affect us all."

I nodded agreement. "That is why the Major has informed us."

"He suggests a meeting." The skeleton tilted his head to read the smaller writing on the note. "It says we will find him in The Purple Porpoise, Seaville, this evening. We must journey there."

"We had better call Hugo then," I said. Having dug the skeleton's grave and helped to bury him, the Ogre had moved fifty paces along the beach and begun to build a sandcastle. Ogres are not renowned for their architectural skills. He had only succeeded in digging a huge hole while heaping the sand into a high bank on the seaward side.

Bones let out a piercing whistle. How he does that while lacking lips and lungs I don't know, but it attracted Hugo's attention. He emerged from his hole and loped towards us, his shovel grasped in his stubby hands.

"Seaville is a great distance from here," I said, "How are we going to get there in time for the Major's meeting?"

Bones pointed at the deckchair. "With that, of course. The elf that sold it to me assured me that it was capable of bending space to allow us to transport."

"That might explain why I had such difficulty in setting it up to sit on," I said. I gave the back of the deckchair a light shove and it collapsed into pile of struts and cloth.

"I'm sure it's quite simple to operate," Bones said. He bent down, lifted the tangled contraption and gave it a shake. Miraculously, the wooden rods fell into place to form a self-supporting structure as tall as me. Bones placed it gently on the sand. The cloth that filled the frame shimmered as if it was not really there.

"How does it transport us?" I asked.

"I believe we merely step through it and the contraption will sense where we want to go," Bones replied. He sounded authoritative but I wondered if he was just guessing.

"Magic, then." I said.

"Of course. Off you go. The Purple Porpoise, Seaville."

I picked up the holdall that had lain on the sand beside me and stretched out a hand to the surface of the deckchair. My hand went through with just the merest tingle. I followed it, raising my foot and taking a step.

#2

My foot came down on hard gravel. I felt a mild shock as one gets when one rubs a piece of amber but then I was through and standing in twilight with buildings around me, clutching the holdall to my side. There was a huff and a puff and Hugo emerged from the portal, squeezing his bulk sideways. I took his arm to tug him through the deckchair. Then Bones' skull appeared. He was bent almost double to fit his tall frame through.

At last, we three stood together on the road. Bones grasped the portal and gave it a brisk shake. It reconfigured back to a deckchair which Bones passed to Hugo.

"Carry this please Hugo, we may need it again soon and I don't want Philobrach losing it in that holdall."

Hugo tucked the deckchair under his long arms.

Bones added, "Now where is this place, The Purple Porpoise."

I looked around. At least three signs hung from the stone buildings close to where we stood but light shone in the windows of just one. The sign showed a leaping sea creature that I took to be a porpoise.

I pointed. "That must be the place the Major meant."

"Indeed, it seems so," Bones said. "He has brought us far enough. By the position of the Sun I'd say we are a long way from our pleasant, sandy beach. Somewhere to the far east of the continent I would say. If this inn's sign and the name of the town is anything to go by, we are still, however, near the ocean."

I nodded and strode towards the tavern. The heavy wooden door opened easily when I pushed on it. We entered a warm saloon filled with the odours of a burning fire, cooking food and ale. All so welcoming. Then I saw the mice.

They covered every table and bench. They scampered across the tiled floor and perched on the rafters. There were brown mice, black mice, even a few white mice. Some wore armour, others leather jerkins. Some had swords at their sides, others were, apparently, unarmed.

I stepped up to the bar, avoiding stepping on the scurrying creatures. The landlord was a gnome. I was about to greet my fellow but he spoke first in a bad tempered voice.

"Have you come to get rid of the mice?"

"Er, I'm not sure," I muttered in reply.

"We have come to meet a mouse," Bones said, "Major Montgomery Mouse."

"Ah, you've arrived at last!" The squeaky voice came from a table to the side of the bar. There indeed was Major Mouse, sitting on the rim of an earthenware tankard with a long straw dipping into the vessel which presumably contained ale. "Come and join me. Landlord, bring more malt beer."

The gnome made an irritated mutter but nevertheless set to providing us with drink. Major Mouse shooed his companions away from the benches beside his table and bade us to sit down.

We were soon sitting in relative comfort with jugs of foaming malt beer in front of us. Hugo downed his in one gulp, I took a mouthful and savoured the flavour while Bones ignored his completely. With no stomach or other parts of a digestive system, drink is of no interest to him.

Wiping the froth from my lips, I looked around at the mouse-infested bar. "Are these all members of your Renegade band?"

The Major found my words hilarious and almost fell into his tankard. "Oh, dear me no, Philobrach. We have joined forces with several other orders of fighting mice. There's the Grand Army of Fieldmice lead by Fieldmarshall Frederick Fieldmouse." A chorus of cheers sounded from the adjacent table. "And of course there are the Old Invincibles commanded by my old friend, General Marmaduke Mouse, and…"

"We get the idea, Major," Bones said, "What are they all doing here and what was the point of your message?"

"Surely you understood it," the Major squeaked.

"She's back," I blurted, "the sorceress, the Magus Carmine."

"The very same," the mouse said, "I guessed you would want to know the news and discuss what we should do about her."

"That rather depends on her intentions," Bones said.

"Her intentions!" Major Mouse screeched, "World domination of course. What else does she ever want?"

"That is a little vague," Bones said. "What do you know of her plans?"

"Nothing," the Major replied.

"Well, then," Bones said, "What do you know? Presumably she has been seen. Where is she?"

"That's the point," The mouse said, leaping down from the tankard and hurrying across the tabletop to stand, rear legs apart, forepaws on his hips, facing the three of us. "She has been seen in lots of places across the continent many different times on successive days. She appeared in at least three cities of elves. Fairies noticed her in glades near a number of fairy fortresses. The merpeople saw her on cliffs looking out across the ocean. She was even seen in the mine tunnels of your folk, Philobrach."

"Ah, she is reconnoitring," Bones said.

"But how?" The Major spread his short forelegs in a gesture of frustration.

"It's the time orb," I said, suddenly inspired, "You know that ball that enabled us to travel from the past and the future."

Bones nodded. "You are undoubtedly correct Philobrach. She is travelling repeatedly from whenever and wherever she has made her base, and appearing to be in many places almost at once, though taking care not to overlap with herself, no doubt."

"But why?" I asked.

Bones shrugged. "To assess our state of readiness? To prepare for her next move? She will have a plan."

Major Mouse was indignant, "If she thought she could sneak back unseen she made a mistake. My fellows have been on the lookout for her ever since we returned. These multiple appearances have drawn attention to her."

"I doubt that matters to the sorceress," Bones said. "The point is that having made these appearances and perhaps gathered all the information she needs, with the time orb, as the gnome calls it, she can act whenever she desires."

I was puzzled so took another swig of beer. I looked around the tavern at the thousands of mice that covered every surface.

"Why have you all gathered here, Major?" I asked.

The mouse approached us and spoke quietly. "Because we think we have discovered a pattern in the sorceress's visits."

"Have you indeed?" Bones muttered, "What pattern?"

Major Mouse clicked his claw. A party of mice ran across the floor carrying a roll of parchment, which they dropped at my feet. I bent down to pick it up then unrolled it on the table. It was a map of the world. It showed the whole continent with The Parting marking the northern boundary and the ocean to the south. Mountains and rivers and plains were depicted as were many fortresses and cities and towns of fairies, elves, gnomes and other folk. There was also a scattering of coloured dots. Spots of the same colour formed arcs of a circle.

"Um, these coloured dots," Bones said, "what does the colour signify?"

Major Mouse jumped up and down. "Appearances on the same day are in the same colour. Red for the earliest appearances, then yellow, then blue."

I stared at the map. The pattern was obvious. There was a red arc outside a yellow arc, with the blue the innermost. The circles had the same centre. I bent close to the map to read the name of the location. It was as I suspected. A tiny dot with the name Seaville by its side.

"You see the sorceress' plan?" The Major said with a mixture of excitement and pride.

"We do," Bones replied. "The sorceress is focussing on this very location. Is that why you have assembled your forces here?"

"That's right, skeleton," Major Mouse answered, "We're ready for her when she appears here in Seaville."

"And when do you think that might happen?" Bones asked.

"Today, this evening!" Major Mouse shouted triumphantly.

Bones cried, "You fool, Major, you have brought us…"

There was whump and a huge gust of air almost blew me from my seat. The mice were blown from the tables and the rafters, dropping like warm hail to the floor. Jugs of beer were overturned; candles and oil lamps were extinguished.

In the gloom, a figure appeared. She was instantly recognisable from her long hair, tight jacket and skirt. The sorceress stepped to my side and bent to pick up the holdall. Then she was gone creating another blast of wind.

I had scarcely recovered my senses but I knew what we must do. "Quick! Everyone get out of here!"

I ran for the door. Once on the road, I ran as fast as my short legs could carry me. I had no idea in what direction I was running, although it felt that I was heading down hill. I just ran until I felt the ground under my feet become soft and shifting. I kept going, slower now, not just because my feet could not find purchase in the sand but because I was puffing and panting.

I came to a stop, my sides hurting, gasping for breath. The pale figure of Bones joined me with the vague dark blob that was Hugo alongside, sucking in air as noisily as me.

"Why did you run?" Bones asked, apparently not fatigued by the speed of our escape.

"I'll explain." I said between breaths. I looked around. In the darkness. I felt rather than saw the cliffs that were behind us. The crash of waves on rocks came from one side, to the other there were a few dim lights of Seaville.

"She took the holdall," I said, as my breathing returned almost to normal. "That's what she came for. I suppose it was hers and contained her belongings but there is probably one thing that she expects to find in it that isn't there."

Bones replied, "What is that?"

I reached into my waistcoat pocket and drew out a large gold key. "I've kept it separate since we found it," I continued. "There may be other things she wants in the holdall but I'm guessing that this key is important. When she discovers it's not there, she will come back to get it, so we had to get away. She must not know where it, I, we, are."

"I understand," Bones said. "The time orb, as we discovered, is not very precise. She can perhaps set it to a time of day but not the exact hour. All those appearances the sorceress made were not for reconnaissance but to lure us here on this evening using the mice as her unsuspecting accomplices. You acted sensibly, Philobrach, in getting us away from the tavern. Now she does not know where to find us."

"But we now have two tasks," I said.

"Which are?" Bones said.

"To keep out of her way and to discover why she needs the key." I held the key up for examination.

Elsewhen Press

delivering outstanding new talents in speculative fiction

Visit the Elsewhen Press website at elsewhen.press for the latest information on all of our titles, authors and events; to read our blog; find out where to buy our books and ebooks; or to place an order.

Sign up for the Elsewhen Press InFlight Newsletter at elsewhen.press/newsletter

Also by P.R. Ellis

Fantasy for fans of Celtic mythology from P.R. Ellis

P.R. Ellis' thrilling fantasy series, *Evil Above the Stars*, appeals to fantasy and science fiction readers of all ages, especially fans of JRR Tolkien and Stephen Donaldson. Were the ideas embodied in alchemy ever right? What realities were the basis of Celtic mythology? Visit bit.ly/EvilAbove

Volume 1: Seventh Child

September Weekes discovers a stone that takes her to *Gwlad*, where she is hailed as the one with the power to defend them against the evil known as the Malevolence. September meets the leader and bearers of metals linked to the seven 'planets' that give them special powers to resist the elemental manifestations of the Malevolence. She returns home, but a fortnight later, is drawn back to find that two years have passed and there have been more attacks. She must help defend *Gwlad* against the Malevolence.

ISBN: 9781908168702 (epub, kindle) / ISBN: 9781908168603 (256pp paperback)

Volume 2: The Power of Seven

September with the Council of *Gwlad* must plan the defence of the Land. The time of the next Conjunction will soon be at hand. The planets, the Sun and the Moon will all be together in the sky. At that point the protection of the heavenly bodies will be at its weakest and *Gwlad* will be more dependent than ever on September. But now it seems that she must defeat Malice, the guiding force behind the Malevolence, if she is to save the Land and all its people. Will she be strong enough; and, if not, to whom can she turn for help?

ISBN: 9781908168719 (epub, kindle) / ISBN: 9781908168610 (288pp paperback)

Volume 3: Unity of Seven

September is back home and it is still the night of her birthday, despite having spent over three months in *Gwlad* battling the Malevolence. Back to facing the bullies at school she worries about the people of *Gwlad*. She must discover a way to return to the universe of *Gwlad* and the answer seems to lie in her family history. The five *Cludydds* before September and her mother were her ancestors. The clues take her on a journey in time and space which reveals that while in great danger she is also the key to the survival of all the universes. September must overcome her own fears, accept an extraordinary future and, once again, face the evil above the stars.

ISBN: 9781908168917 (epub, kindle) / ISBN: 9781908168818 (256pp paperback)

And now, September Weekes returns...

Cold Fire

September thought she was getting used to transporting, but this time it was different. As far as she could tell, her appearance hadn't changed, she was still even wearing her school uniform. But in a London of 1680, others saw her as a lady of considerable social standing. She had been brought here to stop something happening that would give the Malevolence an opportunity to enter the universe. But she didn't know what. Her first stop would be a tavern, to meet Robert Hooke, and then off to see Sir Robert Boyle demonstrate to the Royal Society the results of his investigations of the phosphorus and its cold fire.

ISBN: 9781911409168 (epub, kindle) / ISBN: 9781911409069 (256pp paperback)

Existence is
Elsewhen

Twenty stories from twenty great authors
including
John Gribbin, Rhys Hughes
Christopher G. Nuttall, P.R. Ellis

The title *Existence is Elsewhen* paraphrases the last sentence of André Breton's 1924 *Manifesto of Surrealism*, perfectly summing up the intent behind this anthology of stories from a wonderful collection of authors. Different worlds... different times. It's what Elsewhen Press has been about since we launched our first title in 2011.

Here, we present twenty science fiction stories for you to enjoy. We are delighted that headlining this collection is the fantastic **John Gribbin,** with a worrying vision of medical research in the near future. Future global healthcare is the theme of **J A Christy's** story; while the ultimate in spare part surgery is where **Dave Weaver** takes us. **Edwin Hayward's** search for a renewable protein source turns out to be digital; and **Tanya Reimer's** story with characters we think we know gives us pause for thought about another food we take for granted. Evolution is examined too, with **Andy McKell's** chilling tale of what states could become if genetics are used to drive policy. Similarly, **Robin Moran's** story explores the societal impact of an undesirable evolutionary trend; while **Douglas Thompson** provides a truly surreal warning of an impending disaster that will reverse evolution, with dire consequences.

On a lighter note, we have satire from **Steve Harrison** discovering who really owns the Earth (and why); and **Ira Nayman,** who uses the surreal alternative realities of his *Transdimensional Authority* series as the setting for a detective story mash-up of Agatha Christie and Dashiel Hammett. Pursuing the crime-solving theme, **Peter Wolfe** explores life, and death, on a space station; while **Stefan Jackson** follows a police investigation into some bizarre cold-blooded murders in a cyberpunk future. Going into the past, albeit an 1831 set in the alternate Britain of his *Royal Sorceress* series, **Christopher G. Nuttall** reports on an investigation into a girl with strange powers.

Strange powers in the present-day is the theme for **Tej Turner,** who tells a poignant tale of how extra-sensory perception makes it easier for a husband to bear his dying wife's last few days. Difficult decisions are the theme of **Chloe Skye's** heart-rending story exploring personal sacrifice. Relationships aren't always so close, as **Susan Oke's** tale demonstrates, when sibling rivalry is taken to the limit. Relationships are the backdrop to **P.R. Ellis's** story where a spectacular mid-winter event on a newly- colonised distant planet involves a Madonna and Child. Coming right back to Earth and in what feels like an almost imminent future, **Siobhan McVeigh** tells a cautionary tale for anyone thinking of using technology to deflect the blame for their actions. Building on the remarkable setting of Pera from her *LiGa* series, and developing Pera's legendary *Book of Shadow*, **Sanem Ozdural** spins the creation myth of the first light tree in a lyrical and poetic song. Also exploring language, the master of fantastika and absurdism, **Rhys Hughes,** extrapolates the way in which language changes over time, with an entertaining result.

ISBN: 9781908168955 (epub, kindle) / 9781908168856 (320pp paperback)
Visit bit.ly/ExistenceIsElsewhen

The Magic Fix series by Mark Montanaro

The Magic Fix

The Known World needs a fix or things could get very ugly (even uglier than an Ogre!)

"Did we win the battle?" asked King Wyndham.

"Well it depends how you define winning," answered Longfield, one of the King's royal commanders.

In fact, the Humans are fighting a losing battle with the Trolls. Meanwhile the Ogres are up to something, which probably isn't good. Could one flying unicorn bring about peace in the Known World? No, obviously not.

But maybe a group of rebels have the answer. Or perhaps the answer lies with a young Pixie with one remarkable gift. Does the Elvish Oracle have the answer? Who knows? And, even if she did, would anyone understand her cryptic answers (we all know what Oracles are like!)

The Known World is in danger of being rent in twain, and twain-rending is never good!

Did I mention the dragon? No? Ah... well... there's also a dragon.

ISBN: 9781911409731 (epub, kindle) / 9781911409632 (240pp paperback)
Visit bit.ly/TheMagicFix

The Enchanting Tricks

The Known World is still not fixed... and things <u>have</u> got ugly

In the Goblin realm, Queen Afflech was doing remarkably well considering the circumstances. She had seen her husband die, and both her sons killed within the space of a couple of weeks. That kind of thing does tend to bring you down a bit.

Losing three kings in a few days looked rather careless. But of more concern to the Goblin warlords was whether it looked weak to their enemies. They suspected the Humans were behind one death and the Ogres behind another. The Pixies were no threat, the Trolls would probably soon be killing one another again, and the Elves were irrelevant (or, to be precise, just annoying).

Meanwhile, King Wyndham wanted to show the Goblins that Humans were not to blame (apart from the two that might be to blame). Petra, the most famous Pixie in the Known World, knew exactly who was to blame and wanted to rescue them. Lord Protector Higarth was determined to help the Goblins with their predicament, whether they wanted Ogre-help or not.

But on the plus side, the dragon's gone; and there are still plenty of unicorns... maybe they can somehow solve everything?

ISBN: 9781915304193 (epub, kindle) / 9781915304094 (270pp paperback)
Visit bit.ly/TheEnchantingTricks

Life on Mars
The Vikings are coming

Hugh Duncan

Racing against time, Jade and her friends must hide evidence of Life on Mars to stop the probes from Earth finding them

Jade is on her way to meet up with her dad, Elvis, for her sixteen-millionth birthday (tortles live a long time in spite of the harsh conditions on Mars), when she gets side-tracked by a strange object that appears to have fallen from the sky. Elvis' travelling companion Starkwood, an electrostatic plant, is hearing voices, claiming that "The Vikings Are Coming", while their football-pitch-sized flying friend Fionix confirms the rumour: the Earth has sent two craft to look for life on Mars.

It then becomes a race against time to hide any evidence of such life before Earth destroys it for good. Can Jade and her friends succeed, with help from a Lung Whale, a liquid horse, some flying cats, the Hellas Angels, the Pyrites and a couple of House Martins from the South of France? Oh, and a quantum tunnelling worm – all while avoiding Zombie Vegetables and trouble with a Gravity Artist and the Physics Police?! A gentle and lightly humorous science fantasy adventure.

Cover artwork and illustrations: Natascha Booth

ISBN: 9781915304124 (epub, kindle) / 9781915304025 (400pp paperback)

Visit https://bit.ly/LifeOnMars-Vikings

About P.R. Ellis

I was born and brought up in Cardiff and now, retired, have returned to Wales to live in Monmouth. In between, I spent my career teaching Chemistry and a bit of Physics, and writing "educational materials", in various parts of southern England.

Science Fiction has been a pleasure all my life; the variety of sub-genres and range of authors that I have read, amazingly broad. I have also been writing since I was 10. Strangely, the first novel I had published, by Elsewhen, happened to be more Fantasy than SF. *The Evil Above the Stars* trilogy contains science but it is pre-Copernican. The sequel, *Cold Fire,* is also Fantasy with a touch of C17th chemistry. I am still working on my first-contact SF novel.

Since I was in my 20s, I have felt a conflict between my masculine and feminine traits. That has been resolved by adopting a non-binary/gender-fluid identity. I have advised the police on transgender matters and write regular articles for a transgender magazine.

Lou and I have now been married for 35 years and enjoy our time together. We play tennis, go for walks and have holidays on our shared-ownership narrowboat. I have two step-children and four delightful grandchildren. Despite having passed the biblical three score years and ten, I am hoping for many more years of putting on screen and paper the ideas that come into my head.

Ingram Content Group UK Ltd.
Milton Keynes UK
UKHW011525070623
423041UK00001B/29

9 781915 304254